PHANTOM NIGHTS

by John Farris from Tom Doherty Associates

PHANTOM NIGHTS

John Farris

A TOM DOHERTY ASSOCIATES BOOK

New York

PHANTOM NIGHTS

Copyright © 2005 by John Farris

This book is printed on acid-free paper.

Book design by Mary A. Wirth

A Forge Book
Published by Tom Doherty Associates, LLC
175 Fifth Avenue
New York, NY 10010

www.tor.com

Forge® is a registered trademark of Tom Doherty Associates, LLC.

Library of Congress Cataloging-in-Publication Data

Farris, John.
    Phantom nights / John Farris.—1st ed.
        p. cm.
    "A Tom Doherty Associates book."
    ISBN 0-765-30778-2 (acid-free paper)
    EAN 978-0765-30778-1
        1. African American nurses—Crimes against—Fiction.   2. Southern States—Fiction.
    3. Teenage boys—Fiction.   4. Mute persons—Fiction.   5. Daredevils—Fiction.
    6. Friendship—Fiction.   7. Revenge—Fiction.   I. Title.

PS3556.A777P47 2005
813'.54—dc22

                                                                                2004056117

First Edition: February 2005

Printed in the United States of America

0 9 8 7 6 5 4 3 2 1

for Tom Doherty

Author's Note

The italicized part of Ramses Valjean's lament
found on page 167 is from a fellow sufferer named
Lionel Johnson in his *The Precept of Silence*.

In a dark time,
the eye begins to see.

—Theodore Roethke

ONE

When Leland Howard *got out of his car in front of* the homestead, he saw his half-brother, Saxby, and sister-in-law, Rose Heidi, on the front porch, either just arrived or about to depart; he wasn't sure which. At any rate Saxby had got there first.

Figures, Leland thought. He'd had a deal of driving to do, Sax, all the way from Elizabethton. The Tri-Cities area, where Sax had his dealerships: Chevrolets and Case farm equipment.

July 30 and not a breath of air stirring. Not much rain in West Tennessee for a month, six weeks probably. But the deep front lawn and flowerbeds behind a white wrought-iron fence looked freshly watered. Magnolia and gingko leaves glossy as wrapped Christmas candy. There were artesian wells on the six-acre property, four blocks west of the courthouse square and midway down a wide street of mostly antebellum homes, some of which stood long unclaimed in the sun, suffering stupors of dry-rot.

Leland took off a cocoa-colored panama hat and mopped his forehead while his man, Jim Giles, parked the Pontiac Eight in the shade of a monster cedar across the street. Got out and leaned against a high fender of the Pontiac. He was a lanky man, country-saturnine, simian hang to his arms, outsized hands, wearing a shiny blue suit a size too small for him. The suit spoke of a lifetime of meager gleanings, of hand-me-downs and thrift-store racks. Giles looked middling poor, but not servile.

Leland lingered on the sidewalk with a certain aplomb that had always come naturally to him, drawing everyone's attention up there on the shady porch. No hearse in sight, but one might be parked round back to spare the family's sensibilities. Doc Hogarth taking his ease in one of the chain-hung gliders, drinking lemonade, as was Rose Heidi beside him. She looked to be about seven months gone this time, setting herself down at every opportunity. They'd hauled along the children, all dressed up, so no fooling: Priest Howard's low state of health finally could be terminal, after all of the false alarms Leland often had not bothered to respond to.

The two kids around Rose Heidi were bored and acting up. A third boy, Sax's oldest, was off by himself reading a *Batman* comic book. Burnell the houseman hovered just behind the screen door and threshold he had never crossed in twenty-six years. One of those nigras every family of means had, been around so long he had a certain proud status in both of Evening Shade's communities, white and colored.

Spare me, Jesus. Leland put his hat on and walked through the open gate, up the brick walk to the three-story Classic Revival house, his boyhood home. Gold toothpick in a corner of his mouth. Seersucker suit looking a little wilted this time of day. There was a ruptured duck in the buttonhole of his right lapel. Couldn't remind the voters of Tennessee often enough that he'd served his country well, shrapnel in his back to prove it. War wounds always a good subject of conversation at the VFW.

Half-brother Saxby coming down the steps to meet him part way. Sax had four-effed it during the last great world conflict, flat feet and nearly blind in his right eye. His face in the late afternoon sun was florid, overfed. And he'd developed a wheeze.

"Didn't know how quick you could make it, Lee; said they hadn't seen you up at the farm in a while. On the stump around Union City, your campaign people told me."

"That was seven-thirty this morning. Then I stopped in Dyersburg for a Rotary lunch, drove on down to Memphis pay a courtesy call on Boss Crump. Which is where the sad news caught up to me, Sax; in the lobby of the Peabody."

Saxby offered to shake hands. Leland kept his hands hard and callused. Chopping wood was good exercise, another benefit. The farmers whose votes mattered to him as much as Boss Crump's captive wards in Memphis disliked politicians with pampered palms "slick as snot on a doorknob," a saying Leland recalled from his youth. That was what Sax's hand felt like, manicures a ritual along with his weekly hair trim.

"Boss Crump! I'll bet you snuck his endorsement right out from under Walker Wellford's nose."

"No way to carry West Tennessee without the Boss," Leland said comfortably.

"You know I been keeping my ear to the ground, but it looks too close to call in my neck of the woods without the Knoxville *Sentinel* on your bandwagon."

"Expect I'll get their endorsement next week. And I surely do appreciate how you've been busting your hump for me in the Tri-Cities."

Saxby's customary smile resembled a wince. He stared past Leland at Jim Giles, leaning against the Pontiac.

"Still having convicts drive you around?"

"Parolees. It's in my nature to forgive another man's transgressions. The preachers and the church ladies go for that."

"What's that one there paroled from?"

"Manslaughter. Twenty years, mandatory eight."

"He killed somebody?"

Leland couldn't resist. "Bare-handed. But James is a gentle soul. Just on occasion takes a deep disliking to one fella or another."

Leland looked up at the second-story windows, drapes partly drawn, of the large northwest-corner bedroom. Pyracantha hugged the wall up to the windowsills. Partly drawn? Old Doc Hogarth sitting outside right now with his raspberry lemonade the color of weak blood and a paper fan in his other hand, courtesy of Malfitano's Quality Furniture on the Square. Nothing left for Doc to do but pronounce Priest Howard dead; a job of comfortable waiting, no doubt.

"Guess I'm not too late, the look of things."

Sax glanced where Leland's attention was focused. "I thought it was all over for sure about two-thirty; then he opened his eyes and even said a couple of words. It's like he's hangin' on for your sake, Leland."

Leland's lip curled. "Same old song and dance. Hour from now he's sitting up eating a good supper."

"Catch sight of him and you won't be sayin' that. Any breath might be his last. I stayed with him for an hour and a half, just walked outside when you showed up. Had to give myself a short break, use the—" Sax allowed himself to choke up.

"Dying can be a hard business. Who's up there with him now?"

"Mally Shaw."

"For a fact? Thought Mally went off to Nashville to live with her Daddy after William blew his brains out."

"She did, and studied nursing. Came home again; it's been eight months, she said. And from what Burnell tells us Mally has been a pillar of strength for Daddy."

Saxby's youngest boy was surreptitiously torturing his sister; the little girl wailed. Sax said sharply, "Rose Heidi, do somethin' about those chirrun."

"Well, they are just awfully *hot*, Sax. They want to watch television inside. It's almost time for *Howdy Doody*."

"Not with my Daddy bein' called home this very instant. Have some sense." To Leland Sax said, "I'll just go on back up there with you. Maybe if he hasn't drifted off too far you could tell Daddy the good news about Boss Crump. Much as he's always had a deep regard for that old sumbitch."

Leland nodded. From a coat pocket he fished out the little sack of hard candies he always had with him on the campaign trail and handed some out to the kids who clamored around him. He took off his hat again to Doc Hogarth and Rose Heidi. A ceiling fan on the porch ruffled his wavy blond hair.

"So pleased to see you again," Rose Heidi said with the minimal amount of enthusiasm she thought she could get away with.

Whisking a wad of scented handkerchief through the blue-moon hollows of her dark belligerent eyes. "Hasn't it been such a long *time*, though?" She had been born accusing the world of a vague something, Leland thought; and all of the world's deeply flawed—by her lights—inhabitants.

The little girl, whose name Leland couldn't remember, sprawled half in her mother's lap, inviting another pinch in her behind from the troublemaking brother, who danced away from the glider with a smirk.

"Joe Dean, you keep it up and there will be a switchin' in your immediate future," Rose Heidi said.

Leland turned his attention elsewhere.

"Doc."

"Leland." Nod. "You're looking fit."

Leland nodded back proudly; a man whose ego was always on the lookout for a stray stroking, like a cat passing through a crowded room. He glanced at Saxby, who obviously despised what he considered to be a subtle reference to his own girth.

"Believe me," Sax said to Leland when they were walking up the curved stairway inside, "I have tried every diet known to man, and I can't lose an ounce." Wheeze. "What's your secret?" This with a sidelong glance. In spite of a forced smile his eyes, like bees in a violated hive, were busily angry.

Light passing through a stained-glass window above the front door made a rainbow splash on the gloomy brown wallpaper, illuminating the depressions in the wall on either side of Sax's boyhood room where Leland had on occasion pounded Sax's head.

"My mother," Leland said, "was trim as a willow sapling. Could have something to do with it. How much exercise do you get, Sax? I don't count fucking Rose Heidi. My guess is she does most of the work anyhow."

Silence as they walked toward their father's room.

"Trust you to come up with a trashy remark," Sax said dourly as they paused at the door.

"Sax?"

"What?"

"Just wait out here in the hall while I say my fond farewell." Sax hunched his shoulders grudgingly. Leland said with a slight smile, "Our Daddy's not going to have a deathbed change of heart and turn loose a single dime has my name on it."

Snuffle. *For God's sake,* Leland thought, the old days flashing through his brain. Sax still snuffled like a little kid.

"None of us can be sure what is in Daddy's heart at this fateful hour. You may be underestimatin' his capacity for forgiveness."

"I seriously doubt it," Leland said, his smile wise and cold. They heard a car with poor brakes outside, then voices of newcomers. "More company to grieve with us?" Leland said. "How many did you invite, Sax?"

"That would be Pastor McClure and his wife." He turned and went back along the squeaky hall to the stairs, saying "Hope you choke on that toothpick." Leland allowed Sax's mood and attitude a few moments' study, then gave an exaggerated snuffle and nose-wipe that Sax had to hear. Just to remind him who had taken charge early in their relationship and was still on top. Childish of him, but how satisfying.

Mally Shaw looked up when Leland entered his father's bedroom. She was sitting in a rocker near the old man, a Bible open in her lap. The Howard family Bible, no less. Ponderous to hold, the pages fragile as moths' wings from age. He caught a little of what she was reading aloud as he opened the door. Psalms.

"Go on, Mally," Leland said.

Instead she placed a bookmark in the Bible, closed it, glanced at Priest Howard's face elevated on pillows, and stood.

"Appears that I'm in time," Leland said.

"Praise be, Mr. Leland," Mally said, and she put the Bible on a stand near the bed, where diffused sunlight brought out what was left of the gold stamping on the leather cover, darkened by the oils from countless fingers over a century and a half.

Leland admired the profile Mally presented against that same light. She would be, he guessed, four or five years younger than he was. Even a man who had no liking for dark meat—never one of Leland's prejudices since he'd been old enough to take up the chase—couldn't fail to be attracted to such a comely woman. It was obvious that more than one white man had temporarily roosted in the family tree, going back at least a hundred years.

Leland approached his father's massive and ugly old mahogany bedstead. Initial shock at how desiccated the old man looked, this bone-sack, toothless, eyes agley, caved face the color of a harvest moon. The old enchantment ebbing, its nucleus deveined. He was taking fluids and holding at his low level on morphine. Nothing left of him to dread or despise, this relic who in his prime could change the weather with his scowl. Leland wasn't at all sure in the eclipselike pallor of the sickroom that Priest Howard was still drawing breath. Still, Leland felt uneasy. Then he saw the dying man's chest rise convulsively and fall again beneath tangled fingers, the flickering of lashless eyelids.

"Who's there?" Priest Howard said, voice phlegmy but surprisingly strong.

"It's Leland, Daddy. How you feeling today?"

"I've seen . . . the Light."

"How's that, Daddy?"

"There's . . . shadows in the Light. They're . . . waitin' on me."

Leland, perplexed, looked across the bed at Mally, who was smiling sympathetically down at the old man.

"Hasn't said that much in two days."

There were bad odors in the room, among them human flesh on its way to the grave; and something good, refreshing, the mild appealing scent Mally wore.

"What light does he mean?" Leland said with a slight, unexpected shudder.

"I don't know. First time he's spoken of it, Mr. Leland." Her face calm, but her lower lip folding between white teeth.

Priest Howard's veiny eyelids trembled again. His head moved fractionally on the pillows.

"Come closer . . . Lee. See you."

Leland took the toothpick from his mouth and popped in a piece of candy to suck on before he approached the bed. There were a few chick-feather remnants of hair clinging to his father's long, runneled skull. No further movement. Leland bent over the old man, growing tense, thinking he'd heard that telltale death rattle in the throat. Eyes flicking to Mally, who was frowning as if she'd heard it too. Then his father breathed again.

"Mally. Oxygen."

There was a tank beside the bed. Mally placed the mask over Priest Howard's mouth and nose, opened a valve on the tank. Leland liked the compassion he saw in her eyes. Totally absorbed, the ministering angel. She had fingertips on the pulse in one of the old man's thin wrists.

Half a minute passed; she removed the mask.

"Can't give him all he wants," Mally explained. "Enough so his lungs stop reaching, hard on his heart." She picked up a moist sponge and gently wiped it across the dying man's forehead.

Leland motioned her back and leaned over his father, who apparently had been restored to the point of being able to keep his eyes open. Pale, pale blue beneath an overgrowth of wilderness eyebrows.

"Do you want to say something to me, Daddy?"

". . . Can't win."

"What's that? Can't win what, Daddy, the Democratic primary?"

"See to it . . . myself."

Leland drew back, a burning sensation behind his breastbone. He bit down hard on the piece of cherry-flavored candy.

"Hard news for you, Daddy. I'm stronger than Wellford everywhere. Come November when the flowers have all withered in your crypt, I'll be the incoming junior senator from Tennessee."

"Mr. Leland—" Mally said, small-voiced.

"Don't be shocked, Mally. We've always carried on like this, haven't we, old man? Hammer and tongs all my life." He put his face closer to his father's, forgetting in his anger to hold his breath, not caring to hold his tongue. "Still rankles, doesn't it? Couldn't forge me to your likeness. Now understand this before you go off to Jesus or the devil. Leland Howard is the winner in this family, and you have lost again—you miserable sumbitch."

He wasn't prepared for the hand that shot up, the strength of the long fingers at his throat. The almost merry look in eyes that had been so dim and distant moments ago.

"No. You . . . lose. *Thief.*"

Priest Howard's brown lips curved just a little, tendons standing out in his neck. He rolled his eyes toward the evening's light and the figure of Mally Shaw between himself and the light as Leland brushed away his clutching hand, outraged and demeaned. And, it occurred to Leland as the burn worked deeper into his heart, possibly outmaneuvered in a last gesture of contempt and hatred by a long-time spiteful and hating man.

Leland felt Mally's eyes on him as he straightened and backed off from the bed. His father's eyes were closed again. That rattle of oncoming death in his frail throat. Unmistakable. Someone knocking at the door. Sax. Leland looked at Mally, his mood baleful. Instantly her gaze went down. She used the sponge again on Priest Howard's forehead, as if her protective tenderness were the proper response to Leland's outburst. Goddamn if it didn't look to him like the old man was still smiling. The door opened, Sax sticking his sweaty balding head inside.

"Leland? I've got Pastor McClure with me."

"Yeah, bring him on; I'm finished here." Not caring, soon as he spoke, for the taste of the words in his mouth.

Mally Shaw was listening close for another breath, fingers on the old man's pulse again. But she looked up momentarily. Something about Leland's tone. Their eyes meeting. Something in his eyes too, that she'd spent her life resenting, the white man's calculated appraisal of her. But other concerns claimed her attention.

"Would someone ask Dr. Hogarth to come up, please? I'm needing him now."

When it was all over and Mally could take her leave from the old man's house, which was oppressively filling up with relations and everyone of importance in Evening Shade come to pay their respects, she drove in her '41 Dodge sedan to her favorite getaway place at Cole's Crossing, on the main line of the Southern Railway outside of town. The railroad spanned the south fork of the Yella Dog River there on a low trestle. The Yella Dog was hardly worthy of the name "river," only a few feet deep most of the time, but it swelled to cover a floodplain in the wooded bottomland when the heavy rains fell. Other times it was a fine place for picnics on the gravel bars shaded by high hickory and osage orange trees.

Sun burning red half the length of the horizon in a drought-shroud of atmospheric dust; in the bird-flecked waning light she parked just off the narrow gravel road a hundred yards south of the track. On the side of the road opposite the river loop were the remains of an old railroaders' hotel with breached walls and the roof fallen in, and a still-active Negro church that had a bell rusted soundless in its squat belfry. Behind the country church lay a cared-for burial ground where Mally's late husband, William, and a host of kinfolk on both sides were interred.

Hoping to catch a breeze, she left the car door open on the driver's side, cracked window glass aglow with the light of the vanishing day and enjoyed a Chesterfield while she thought about her future. Now that she would no longer be caring for Priest Howard, Jesus cherish his lonely soul. Mally was a registered nurse, but there wasn't much call for her services locally. The physician running the county's clinic for indigent Negroes—which was pretty much of a redundancy in one of the poorest counties in the forty-eight states—could use her. But the pay was a pitiful fifteen hundred a year; aside from near-starvation wages, she considered the doctor in charge to be incompetent, and she wasn't in a crusading frame of mind. John Gaston Hospital in Memphis paid better, but it was either find a place to live in Memphis or drive a hundred miles round trip six days a week. Mally had her doubts that the old Dodge could survive many such trips. Balding tires, a front-end shimmy whenever she drove faster than thirty-two miles an hour. Repair bills would eat her alive.

The thought of teaching at Evening Shade Community High School depressed her. She could teach physics or math, but the school didn't offer either basic math or science courses. A total disgrace in Mally's opinion; not the least of the consequences to the school's graduates was that they could not meet admission requirements for Tennessee's state universities, even if they had the money for higher education. The school's roof leaked shamefully; there were rats; the library was one shelf in a dank room, the spines falling off old textbooks stored inside.

Hoot owls in the live oaks, radiator hiss as it cooled down. She sat sideways on the seat with her sandaled feet on the running board. Feeling used up, all in. And obscurely guilty, as if somehow she had failed Priest Howard. Then that ugliness with his son Leland in his last hour . . . Couldn't he have been spared the indignity of that visit? Although surely he'd seemed to want it, to insist on his estranged golden boy being at his side before he gave up the ghost. Simply to have the pleasure of calling Leland—what? *Thief.*

She had no notion of what might have been unsettled in their bellicose kinship to account for that. But whatever had weighed so heavy on the old man's mind, he hadn't confided it to Mally during his last lucid weeks.

Spite of what Mr. Leland might be thinking right about now, that look he'd given her.

High-power white man with a leching eye—they always spelled

trouble. Gold toothpick and two-toned shoes, thought he had *style*. But Mally had some experience in telling the wrong ones, those men with a history of default in the romance game.

Mally tugged at a bra strap that was too tight under her dress. Finished her cigarette and dropped the butt in the gravel, squirmed uneasily. She looked at the sky, dusky blue now, the sun gone. The air seemed to be cooling but wasn't moving, still felt thick as wet paint on her maple-toned skin.

She calculated there was light enough left to walk across the road and around behind the church, pay a visit to William. Wrong of her to be almost there and not go to the graveyard. Because she was not a blaming person. Her anger long gone, sadness still around and always would be, but at a distance, no longer a torment. Still, a lot of sorrow to deal with in one day . . . She had to go.

Mally heard a dog howl not too far off as she stepped out of the car. The sound made her quiver. A fright from childhood, lore of the easily haunted. And then, a couple of years after The War—that business in Korea, couldn't think of it as a *war* after what they'd been through only six years ago—there had been an actual dog pack roaming Evening Shade and the next county over. At least thirty wild dogs. Killing livestock and unwary domestic animals. An elderly white woman had been dragged, her apron full of snapbeans, off a rickety screened porch and mauled in her dooryard, bitten through and through, the wild dogs lapping her gore from the hardpan ground. Sharpshooters from the sheriff's department had exterminated that pack, but talk was lately that a new pack of stray dogs had formed and been spotted near a horse farm off the Worthington Pike. A foal had been torn apart in the paddock.

Which was, Mally calculated as she walked around the unpainted frame church, some whitewash from a bygone year still clinging stubborn as lichen to the woodgrain, about three miles as crows flew on up the road from Cole's Crossing.

She heard a rattling and hard slither in the gravel of the road behind her and turned to catch a glimpse of a towhead boy crouched over the handlebars of his bicycle, pumping hard, unbuttoned shirt flapping palely as he swerved around the car door she hadn't closed. A wavering light on the fender of the bike. His sudden appearance gave Mally a moment's cold spell, hair frizzing on the back of her neck, but he didn't stop for a look around. Had somewhere to get to, in a hurry. She listened hard, thinking there might be others behind him. Wishing she had brought the flashlight from the glove compartment. Steel barrel, a weapon of sorts.

But so far just one white boy, on up the road toward the railroad tracks and out of her line of sight now, not several to be acting big for one another if they spotted her there all alone.

Smart for her to remember that even one teenage boy could be too many, depending on his size, in these circumstances.

Hurry on up then, Mally told herself. *Make your visit, and go.*

The *Washington, D.C.,*–bound *Dixie Traveler,* out of the Memphis Union Station promptly at eight-thirty every night, was due at Cole's Crossing at four minutes past nine, give or take a few seconds. Mally had been parked there many a night collecting her wits after a trying day attending to Priest Howard when the streamliner whipped past the unguarded crossing at seventy-two miles an hour. Mally seeing flashes of faces in the diners and club cars, sometimes wistfully imagining herself aboard in one of the coloreds-only coaches, all settled down with a sandwich from the buffet car and magazines to read, a new life waiting at the other end of the line—but her imagination never made it that far. Stepping down in Washington or Philly or even New York, not knowing a living soul up there, fifty dollars in her purse. What next, Mally? She hated the blankness this question afforded, the fear in her bones. Why couldn't she find the gumption to leave this hard-luck and heartbreak place? The standard poesy, but of course hearts didn't "break": no, they withered to the roots from longing while blood turned pale as mercury, filling the chasms of memory and regret. Her eyes felt heavy with unshed tears.

As she kissed William's stone and rose from beside his grave, which could have done with some weeding, Mally heard the scream of the *Dixie Traveler,* that distant and important voice, knew that the *Traveler* was two miles down the line at Watkins' Junction. Later on, well past Evening Shade's modest depot, the *Traveler* would stop for a minute and a half in Jackson, not again until it reached Nashville. She walked quickly back to her car, glancing up the road where steel rails, if you put your ear to one of them, would be singing with the energy of the oncoming train.

The sky was slate now; big trees stood out in sharp silhouette against the three-quarter moon beginning to command the sky and a few stars. Not much light by which to make out the boy nearly a hundred yards from her, standing on a rise at the edge of the railroad right-of-way, his bike laid down next to the road behind him. His back was to Mally as she reached her car and slipped inside under the steering wheel. The boy didn't turn when the door thunked shut. He continued to stand close to the northbound tracks, hands at his sides. White shirt like a drooping flag on his slender body, its pallor tinged by the green highball light on the signal bridge in front of the trestle.

Now, why hadn't he gone on across? Mally wondered. Or had he pedaled hard this far just to be there for the passage of the *Dixie Traveler,* an imaginative train-watcher like herself?

But to her mind he was dangerously close to the track, and in his stillness—she put on the car's headlights to see him a little more clearly in spite of the distance—in his stillness seeming ready to give himself up to something, to the enormous power of a diesel engine.

Mally didn't turn the key in the ignition. There was a disagreeable rumble in her stomach, reminding her that she hadn't eaten since early morning. And a small disturbance, a premonition in her heart as she studied the blond boy in his cut-off jeans. No sign from him, no uneasy movement to indicate he might be aware that he was being observed.

What was this? Mally thought, a little annoyed with herself. Too soon released from the inevitable end of Priest Howard, death still on her mind and in her nostrils, gloomily trying to make something ominous of a farm boy just waiting for a train to go by, nothing more . . .

Mally started the engine, which coughed itself to life and gave her a shaking in the process. But her attention was still on the boy on the railroad grade. He had turned his head west and was looking down the line as the *Dixie Traveler* rounded the long bend at Half Mile, its powerful cyclops headlamp ghosting the telegraph wires alongside the tracks, giving shine to a water tank and a no-longer-used coal tipple leaning on rusted legs. The boy's face also lighting up. Too far for Mally to accurately judge what he looked like, but guessing at his age she thought maybe fourteen, and close to six feet tall with that gangly, just-growed look about him.

She put in the clutch and let off the handbrake, shifted into reverse to back up and turn around. The boy had to know she was there, but paid no attention. He was entirely focused on the onrushing streamliner, as—

—he stepped up on the end of a railroad tie, then stepped across the outside rail and laid himself face down in the *Dixie Traveler's* path with arms outstretched suppliantly, as if to a raging deity.

Mally ground the gears getting out of reverse and into low, the old Dodge spinning its all-but-shot tires in gravel and clay ruts then lurching forward as she stood on the accelerator. A hundred yards to cover, and she could see the green-and-white diesel engine of the varnish, as old-time railroaders called the deluxe passenger trains, out of the corner of her eye, moving, oh Lord, too fast to stop in time even if the engineer or the fireman in the high cab saw the boy lying there.

She pounded on the horn, which was feeble, and screamed, which no one could hear, as she raced the *Dixie Traveler* for the crossing and the prone boy about to give up his life. Memory of her Uncle Cletus, who had worked on the L&N and been mangled after a fall from a crummy one icy night, memory of him being fed his meals all stumped up on pillows at the table during family get-togethers and oh Christ Savior, who was this young boy craving to be mangled or die in such a terrible way, what had life done to him already that he hated it so bad?

Mally hit the brakes at the crossing and piled out of the sedan with the howling of an airhorn and the four-thousand-horsepower thunder of doom in her ears, partly blinded by the looming light. And knew she could not hope to reach in time the motionless boy lying fifty feet from her on his face, top of his head barely visible, laid down tight enough between the rails to be eating ballast.

She turned away from the furious blast of wind in her face and pounded a fist against the long hood of her car, then buried sobs in her cupped palms as she hunched over the fender, grit exploding against her bare arms, dust everywhere. . . .

The train passed, and she slowly raised her eyes to it, to the dwindle of red lights atop the rounded end of the club car as a lumbery clatter from the weight of the *Traveler* on the long trestle carried back to her.

She couldn't look down at the roadbed, bring herself to cast about for scattered remains near where the boy had laid himself down, presumably to be destroyed.

Tears to wash some of the grit from her reddened eyes. A draining force, exhaustion so compelling she could have slumped down beside her car and fallen asleep there in an instant.

Instead Mally wiped her eyes and took a breath, holding it grimly as she walked around the front of her Dodge to make certain. She had stopped the car askew in the road, and in the sullen yellow of headlights, insects whizzing through the beams, she saw the boy rise up on one knee from the track.

Mally's heart kicked up in her throat, as if a dreadful night had suddenly acquired lightning.

His arms and his shirt were streaked with black. He was bleeding from his mouth and nose, but only trickles. When he tried to stand, he wobbled and wheeled a little and his eyes slid up in his head. Then he pitched forward across the outside rail, only half-conscious but, as far as Mally could tell, in one piece.

Mally *always had a first aid kit handy.* The one in the Dodge contained smelling salts. When she brought the kit the boy was on his hands and knees. She held him up in a sitting position on the rock ballast and passed the little bottle of ammonium carbonate under his nose. She felt strength returning to his body and he jerked his head sharply aside, wincing. Mally had a strong grip; also she was angry with him and not about to let him go until he came up with some kind of explanation for what she now considered to be a terrifying, crazy stunt. Her own heartbeat had just begun to settle down.

She'd had a look at the place where the boy had stretched out and flattened himself between the rails to await the train, more or less tucked himself in, and she had seen that a sharp tool of some kind, probably an adze, had been used recently to gouge a couple of inches from three of the six-inch-square creosote-dipped ties. A dangerous, deranged thing to do, because if the weakened ties broke under the weight of the train a rail could come loose, sending the dozen cars of the *Dixie Traveler* slewing off the right-of-way and into the Yella Dog. With, count on it, tragic loss of life.

"Look at me," Mally said, putting the cap on the bottle of smelling salts. The haze was nearly gone from the boy's green eyes.

Head drooping, breathing through his mouth, he looked up with a youthful hothead's whiplash impertinence, perhaps just realizing it was a colored woman talking to him in that tone.

Mally wasn't having any. "I don't know who you are, but I saw what you did to those railroad ties. Was you, wasn't it?" A downward shift in his gaze confirmed that. Her grip on him tightened. "God would show you no mercy if you'd wrecked that train tonight, which I suppose you never gave a thought to while you were presuming to play daredevil."

At least he hadn't been trying to kill himself, as she had first suspected. But Mally wasn't in a merciful mood either.

He brushed the dirty forefinger of his free hand against his cut lower lip. More blood welled. Chest still heaving, given to a chill, molten memory of an eyelash escape. His blond mop needed washing. His bright, sharp skin bathed in boy-sweat, smelling of diesel, of tobacco. Already a smoker; there was a mangled cigarette behind his right ear. In spite of appearances, Mally didn't think he was from a rag-tag family. He wore a gold ring with a small diamond in it—of course it might be stolen—and an ID bracelet. Those were a big fad with kids nowadays.

He tried to squirm away from Mally, run for it. But she could deal with what strength had returned to his body, which was neither childlike nor with the full breadth of maturity, more bone than muscle yet. His body hair was soft and sunburnt silver.

"Just you sit still. I'm a nurse, and you need tending to."

There had been no traffic on the road for a good fifteen minutes, but now a pickup truck came by, stopped at the grade crossing. Two overalled men in the front seat, a barking dog in the truck bed. Mally recognized one of the men who leaned out through the window space of the cab to ask if they could be of any help. He was married to a childhood friend of Mally's.

"He fell off his bike, but I think he'll be all right, Cuffy. Either of you recognize this boy? Can't seem to get his tongue working yet."

They didn't know him, and drove on. Mally said to the boy, who couldn't stop squirming, "Need to do something about that bloody nose now. Tilt your head back like this"—showing him— "pinch either side of the bridge with your thumb and forefinger 'til it stops. That's it. Lord, I never seen anyone foolish as you in my born days! Please tell me that was the first and last time you'll ever act that stupid."

He looked at her with one eye, pinching his nose, quiet while Mally poured a little alcohol onto a cotton ball and began to clean around his nostrils and upper lip. Before she was half done he got antsy again and tried to get to his feet. He was looking at his bike, which he had seen was half under the front end of Mally's car. She hadn't noticed in time where the bike was in her anxiety to reach him before the *Traveler* got there first. Lost that race, and the bicycle probably was damaged. Nonetheless she yanked him down again on his butt.

"Give me any more aggravation and I will flat turn you over to the sheriff! I'm tired, and if you'd like to know, I had a pitiful day, not to mention the scare you handed me. My name is Mally Shaw if I didn't say so before, and if there's any courtesy in you, you'll be telling me who *you* are."

She waited. He was mum. With a stillness that conveyed a hint of grievance. Mally sighed.

"Be that way. I can find out if I want to, and I've a mind. Got to let the railroad know what happened here, 'less their trackwalkers don't come across those damaged ties in time to prevent an accident."

That warning seemed to bother him more than being run over by a passenger train.

Mally looked over the ring, which struck her as an odd thing for a boy his age to be wearing, and the steel-link identification bracelet. "And I was serious about the sheriff."

Maybe she ought to have been more cautious, invited the two men in the truck to stick around until she was through with her ministrations. But she didn't believe this boy was bad and a threat to her. He was just reckless and a danger to himself. Nothing about him suggested a violent disposition. Mally was confident of her instinct there. And he did have nice looks beneath the grime.

She changed her grip on him to his left wrist and turned it so she could read the engraving on the bar of the ID bracelet in the lights of the old Dodge.

"So you're Alex. Too much trouble just to open your mouth and tell me that?"

His lips compressed; he shook his head, and a couple of drops of blood from his nose spattered her.

"Look out now, look at what you did!" She let go of him. "You don't want my help anymore, fine with me."

Mally turned away to close her first-aid box and was startled when he put a hand on her. But he released her quickly, and there was a look of pleading in his eyes. Pleading what? It was then she realized maybe he wasn't being plain stubborn not talking to her. Could be he had no power of speech, couldn't answer for or explain himself. If he was a mute, what a hard thing that could be for an adolescent boy.

Looking down at him, Mally nodded.

"*Can't* talk?"

Alex nodding too.

"Always been that way?"

This time he shook his head.

"Been to school though; you can write?" *Yes.* "Something you want to tell me, then, write it down for me?" *Yes.* "I'll be right back, Alex."

Mally noticed how feeble the car headlights were, battery running down, must have stalled the engine when she skidded to a stop. On her way to start it up again and keep the battery charged, she looked under the bumper to see how much damage there was to his bike. Looked like an almost-new blue-and-white Schwinn, run over by the right-side tire. A pedal pushed up, chain off, and the front fender bent out of shape. He wouldn't be riding it anywhere else tonight.

She took a pocket spiral notebook from her purse on the front seat and went back to where Alex was sitting, arms around his knees, nose elevated again. His lower lip was swelling, bitten, she supposed, during his fifteen seconds of extreme terror beneath the *Dixie Traveler.* A wonder he hadn't loaded up his jean shorts too.

Mally handed him the pad and pencil.

"Write down anything you want me to know. Where you live, who your folks are."

He took the pad, hesitated, then slashed two words across the page and thrust pad and pencil back to Mally. Licked his cut lip, hunched himself tighter in a mime of misery.

THEYRE DEAD!!!

Mally stared at the words he had scrawled, then stared at him, her perspective forever changed.

"But that's no reason for you to throw your life away, is it?" she said to Alex. "What is it you need to be provin' to yourself?"

TWO

"The Situation"
Wyatt Sexton and Silver Ghost
Unconfessed Demons

Bobby Gambier arrived *home a little past ten p.m.* from Memphis, where he studied law three nights a week at Memphis State College. Cecily was still up and so was ten-month-old Brendan, fretful from feverish gums where a couple of teeth were erupting in front. Cecily walked him up and down the front porch in her robe and pajamas, crooning a made-up song in Brendan's ear.

Bobby dumped his law books on a wicker table, batted away a hardshell beetle winging too close to his face, kissed his humid wife and took the sleepy irritable baby from her. He looked in Brendan's mouth by porchlight, then gave Brendan his little finger to teeth on.

"Should wash your hands first," Cecily reminded him. "You had anything to eat?"

"Mars bar."

"Bobby."

"Let's get Brendan quieted down first, then I'll eat some eggs. Where did we hide the brandy Uncle Pete gave us last Christmas?"

"Bottom drawer of our dresser. But you're not thinking?"

"Works like a charm, doesn't it?"

"We'll be raising ourselves a little alcoholic," Cecily said, smoothing the fine golden hair of their child across the crown of his head. She opened the screen door and Bobby carried Brendan inside.

"I'll get the brandy," Cecily said, "but easy does it or he'll be sporting a pip of a hangover." She paused on the stairs going up. "Bobby?"

"Yeah, hon?"

"Alex has been gone since I guess middle of the day, and doesn't

37

he have a curfew after he was caught going through other people's mailboxes?"

"He thought his *Boy's Life* might have been misdelivered but, yeah, he has a curfew."

"We need to talk," Cecily said, that little lump of muscle showing at the corner of her jaw; it looked as if she were double-jointed there.

"Couldn't we—"

"No, tonight. Let's get this settled about Alex, once and for all."

"Cecily, I'm dog-tired and I've got studying to do."

She shook her head tautly, and he saw a shine of tears in her eyes just before she went on upstairs to their bedroom to fetch what had become an illicit object in their household. Cecily's mom had been married to a convivial guy—not Cecily's dad, but Bernice's third husband—who had turned heavy social drinking into a string of lost weekends before kicking off with a liver hard as a meteorite. Bernice subsequently became wrathful in the cause of temperance, particularly in Robert G. and Cicely's house, where she was a frequent drop-in presence. *Snoop* said it better, Bobby thought. Cecily was her only child, and Bernice, like a lot of women getting along in age and with nothing in particular to occupy their time, had an overprotective streak. Bobby liked his beer after his shift with the Evening Shade Sheriff's Department, something harder on occasion when his hours caught up with him and he needed a stiff snort to put himself to sleep. But that was just how *it* got started, Bernice, the expert on alcoholic husbands, told Cecily at every opportunity, drumming her theme home with a marching-band tempo.

And, Bobby knew, Bernice was relentless in her condemnation of what she called "The Situation"—not Bobby's fondness for Budweiser but his obligation to his little brother Alex, whom "Bernie" had no regard for and mistrusted and constantly had Cecily on the ropes about, to the point where she might be imagining things . . .

He walked Brendan back to the kitchen, little finger still in the baby's mouth, as always a little awed by the snug bundle against his shoulder, not minding the crankiness and poop diapers, feeling a quiet kind of joy about the whole business of fatherhood when, only a year ago, the tumulus of Cece's glazed belly and popped navel like a skin balloon had unnerved him badly. So that he found himself unable, in her last months, to provide her with a decent hard-on although Cecily, too shy during the first couple of years of their marriage, had developed a real liking and lusty facility for oral sex.

Cecily came down the back stairs with the brandy bottle and a change of diapers from the nursery. She silently cleaned up and changed Brendan on the kitchen table while Bobby poured a thimbleful of brandy into a saucer.

"How about a couple of biscuits with your eggs, and I think there's sawmill gravy from last night I could heat up." She hesitated. "Honey, would you like a beer? Out of Bud, but there's Blue Ribbon left over from our barbecue Sunday."

"Okay," Bobby said, stopping and making a show of looking under the checkerboard oilcloth on the kitchen table, pretending to see if Bernice was hiding there, putting another check after his name in her Day of Reckoning book, the one she kept for the Lord's benefit in case He overlooked something. Cecily caught Bobby's drift and retaliated by booting him in the rear with a slippered foot.

Bobby grinned and took Brendan from her, moistened a fingertip in the brandy and rubbed where the baby's gums were fiery, touching the merest edge of a tooth about to come through. It made him feel happy. Brendan suckled, his eyes on Bobby's face. He could pull himself erect now using a sofa or a wall for support, stand for half a minute without wavering, looking around. The schedule he was keeping, Bobby thought, eighty hours or more a week away from the house, probably he would miss Brendan's first steps. That troubled him, so much time apart from the two loves who gradually had separated him from the ongoing despair of his loss. Occasionally Bobby's mother still sang in his dreams: she'd had one of those true and glorious voices that are the beauty part of humaness. Always he awoke in tears.

Cecily levered the cap off a sweaty-cold bottle of Blue Ribbon and set it on the table, smiling a little at the two of them, and Bobby knew she was thinking *Wouldn't it be perfect if . . .*

Bobby glanced at the clock on the wall, then at the cork message board where Alex was supposed to post his intended whereabouts day or night. But he seldom knew where he was going when he left on his bike. Like many friendless kids, he was a wanderer.

Cecily put the omelette pan on a low flame to warm and cracked three eggs, whisked them in a stainless-steel bowl.

"When was the last time you saw Alex?" Bobby asked her, figuring just to get it over with so he could eat in peace and not have heartburn to keep him awake at three a.m.

"I told you already; middle of the day, which is when . . . I caught him upstairs in Brendan's room just after Brendan went down for his nap!"

"Doing what?"

"Sitting on the window seat, staring at the crib." Whatever resolve Cecily had to keep bitter feelings from pouring out vanished when her voice broke. She turned to Bobby. "But he was *told*. Wasn't he? Never to go near Brendan again! If he wants to go on staying with us."

"I'll take care of it, Cecily."

"How many times have you said, 'Oh, I'll take care of it,' and Alex goes right on doing just what he pleases! He pays no attention to any of us, Rhoda included, and Bobby—I'm s-sorry, but your brother has me in such a state—"

Brendan's eyes were closing, the brandy drawing fever from his gums, numbing them. Bobby said, "I've almost got him asleep. I'll put him upstairs now. Then, okay, we'll talk."

"Thank you," she said with a wan show of grace, took a deep breath, and whipped eggs furiously before pouring them into the heated skillet. "That's all I'm asking. I know you have your hands full with this situation, Bobby."

The Situation. Well, he couldn't lie to himself, that's what it came down to.

When Bobby returned to the kitchen, Cecily had served him and was sitting at the table buttering a biscuit from that morning's breakfast.

"Sound asleep," Bobby said, sitting opposite her. "Did you get in some tennis today?"

"Marcy couldn't play. And it was hot as the hinges from nine o'clock on. Bobby, Priest Howard died."

He nodded. "Calls for a big funeral. Saturday, I'd say. I'll have to work." He dug into his omelette, took a bite of the biscuit she extended to him. "Cecily, he's not, talking about Alex now, he doesn't mean Brendan any harm."

She sat back abruptly in her ladder-back chair as if an attack had been signaled.

"I don't understand how you can say that! You know he was crazy jealous when Brendan was born, sulking around here all the time . . . Then when he took Brendan from his playpen when I was out shopping and Rhoda had her back turned a minute and we didn't know where either of them were for *three hours*—what do you think was on his mind that day if he didn't intend to, I don't know, maybe what Mom says, drown Brendan in Fulkerson's pond?"

"Jesus Jumping Christ, Cecily, that is so like your mother; she's been doing it to you all your life—"

Cecily dodged the accusation with a side twist of her head.

"Doing *what* to me?"

"Sabotaging your relationships. Your best friend and roommate at Sweet Briar. Bernice takes a dislike; she spreads dirt like a nigger gravedigger. Then, when we started going together—"

"We won't get into it about my mother; this is about Alex."

"Not to say Alex didn't show poor judgment, but he only wanted to show Brendan those huge goldfish that have been in Fulkerson's since I was a kid."

"Which you know for sure because you can read his mind."

"Alex can't defend himself very well against ridiculous accusations. The way he is."

"Bringing that up again. Bobby, don't lawyer me, please."

"Try to imagine what it must be like. Hearing 'dummy' most all his life. If kids aren't acting mean, they're being malicious."

"Not my Brendan. He won't ever act like that."

"So Alex withdraws, doesn't have, what do you call it, social skills, and you interpret his reaction to the shit he has to put up with as hostile behavior."

"He is hostile, and I'm not imagining. Please don't curse in our house, as I've reminded you a thousand times. Ugly words create an atmosphere; they bring trouble."

"Just make an effort, why don't you? Show Alex a little affection like when you first met him. Where'd that go to?"

"And when did you start saying 'nigger' again? I hate that in you."

"You were raised in Wisconsin. Only black you ever saw was dairy cows. This is the South. Down here they are what they are. Show him some honest affection again, Cecily, instead of that grim look you put on whenever he's around. Alex is probably out late tonight because he knows Wednesdays I don't get back from Memphis 'til after ten."

"Bobby." Near tears. "All I want is to have a happy home, a *normal* home, is that asking too much of you?"

Bobby laid his fork down, already feeling hot twinges in his esophagus. He picked up the bottle of Blue Ribbon and had a couple of swallows. They made an okay beer up there in Milwaukee, but nothing compared to Budweiser.

"What does that mean?"

"I don't want Alex in my house anymore! I'm afraid of him and what he might do. Can I make it any plainer?"

"I made a promise. To my dying mother."

"It was okay when we were first married," Cecily said, hoping to ignore what she knew they were about to get into. Sometimes talking to Bobby was like knocking down a hornets' nest. "Alex was younger then. But now we've got Brendan, and Alex is big. Going on fourteen. And he—"

"Burnt over seventy per cent of her body. Daddy never even made it out of the house." Army Transport Command had flown Bobby back from Heidelberg, where he was stationed, a military policeman. He was granted a hardship discharge a year early to look after Alex, who had been spending the night in a cousin's treehouse three blocks away. But he ran home in time to witness the worst of it, his house a glowing pyre collapsing into the cellar. "Fuckin' faulty space heater," Bobby said, a burning reflected in his own eyes.

Cecily overlooked his profanity this time. Better for him to get it out now, or he'd be grinding his teeth in his sleep. She hadn't been acquainted with his parents. They had met nearly two years after the house on Old Durham Trace was destroyed. The property was now a vacant lot, worked over by a bulldozer so that no sign of the tragedy remained except for a bronze memorial plaque on a flowering quince tree Bobby had had transplanted on that plot of ground, which would never be for sale while he had anything to say about it.

Getting back to Alex. "Another thing he's been doing. He masturbates."

Bobby was going to say *Don't we all* but thought better of it. Cecily had been in fragile shape emotionally for the months since Brendan's birth, which had not gone smoothly, and the truth was she still couldn't handle much stress. Since puberty she had suffered from monthly migraines: they blanched her in a way that tore his heart.

"How do you know?" he asked in a reasonable tone. "Catch him at it?"

"Rhoda does Alex's laundry too."

"Fact is Alex is having what I've heard called 'nocturnal emissions.' I can vouch for those, my pajama pants used to get—"

"Not talking about pajama pants, Bobby. And there's nothing nocturnal about it. Does it in his handkerchiefs, then leaves them wadded up under his bed." Cecily shuddered at the thought.

Bobby let out a slow breath and looked at his wife, not knowing what to say anymore. That bulge of muscle had reappeared in Cecily's small jaw, and the hollows of her eyes were moist. Usually hers was a lively, humorous face, streaked blond hair brushed back from her brow in a neat arrowhead, emeralds in her earlobes the exact shade of lazy-looking eyes that always seemed to be on low simmer. Humor had largely been missing lately, the hijinks in her smile.

"There is an answer, Bobby. I was talking to Dr. Leathers about it yester—"

"No. Promises are sacred to me, Cecily."

"What about your wedding vows? It isn't like you wouldn't be taking care of Alex anymore! You would be doing exactly what needs to be done for him if he's going to grow up and amount to something instead of climbing radio towers and getting into fights."

"You know those schools cost a ton of money we don't happen to have."

But as soon as he spoke he realized what was up.

"Mom said she would loan us whatever is needed to do the right thing for Alex."

"Out of the goodness of her heart," Bobby said slowly, stalling, trying to think how he was going to get out of this. An opportunity had been presented to his mother-in-law, and obviously she had pounced on it. Bernie, as her friends called her, had realized a profit of nearly forty thousand dollars when she sold her late husband's printing business. She was sixty-two and still looked good when she was dolled up. But arthritis was evident in both her hands: Prospects for another husband, given what was available in Evening Shade, looked dim. Cagey as always, she had to be thinking ahead to a safe haven in which to spend her declining years. What could be more appealing than to ensure Alex Gambier's absence and move into the roomy house Bobby had bought Cecily as a wedding present with the insurance money? Spend the rest of her life with her two most precious possessions, Cecily and Brendan, while Bobby found himself slowly relegated to the status of odd man out in his own household?

He had wryly observed the same thing happening to other married men; it was like being squeezed to extinction by one of those big South American snakes.

Bobby smiled at Cecily as if he'd been enlightened instead of outmaneuvered, then put the brakes on.

"It's worth thinking about," he said.

"Seriously, Bobby?"

"Sure I'm serious."

"Because you know—when it was just the two of you, Alex and Bobby, you had all the time in the world for him, and it was what he needed after the trauma. But now it isn't true anymore. You don't have the time to play baseball and fix cars together and take fishing trips. I think that's what he resents so deeply and has him doing reckless things to try to get your attention back." Bobby nodded, knowing the truth when he heard it, quick flush of guilt in his face, which encouraged Cecily all the more. "And resents Brendan and me for—we've taken you away from him, probably is how he sees it. That's why I think Alex needs a complete change of scene, a school with other kids who have handicaps. Kids he can relate to, not some of the bullies around town. But of course his hostile attitude. I think Alex *wants* to get into fights."

"Just give me a little time with this, Cece."

She took a breath, relief in her eyes, getting ready to wind it down. "Mutism isn't such a terrible burden, after all. What about polio, or— I know it's a big decision, but you'll see there isn't a better one you can make. Aren't you having any more to eat, Bobby? There's tapioca Rhoda made."

"Raisins in it?"

"A few; you can separate them out."

"I believe I've already had my fill."

"I'm feeling awfully tired," Cecily said with a small yawn. "You wouldn't care if I went upstairs now?"

"I'd call it a night myself, but I've got at least an hour's reading. Tort law."

"You know how proud I am of you," she said, getting up to put dishes in the sink. "Working so hard and going to night school besides. *My* husband's going to practice law!" She caressed Bobby, her hand lingering on the side of his face. "Couldn't you read in bed tonight, Perry Mason? Because I want you next to me while I go to sleep." She lowered her eyes in that sharpie way of hers that indicated she wanted sex to happen. Although she was too shy to directly say so.

Bobby was tired too, but he never got so tired to resist being drawn, weightlessly, into the spell of her glisten.

"Let me call Dispatch, and I'll follow you on up. Wherever Alex is, poolroom or just riding circles around the courthouse, I want Tuff or Terry Ray see that he gets his butt home pronto."

They *called my husband William 'Highpockets,'"* Mally said to Alex. "'Cause that's what he was, all arms and 'specially legs."

She tapped a forefinger on one of a wall of framed photos: the team picture of the 1939 Memphis Red Sox.

"William played short and batted cleanup for the Red Sox. That was before the war. Marty Marion—are you a St. Louie fan?—saw William play a couple times. He said William had the range and arm to be a big-leaguer. But that was years before Jackie Robinson, Campanella, and that boy Doby plays for Cleveland now."

They were in the front room of the small house that William and his brother Cal had built fifty yards deep into the hollow behind the rib shack on Highway 19 that William had tried to make a go of the last two and a half years of his life. Playing days over with; he'd come back from the Pacific with only two and a half fingers and a thumb stub left on his throwing hand.

Mally explained that to Alex, who was sitting on the bamboo sofa Mally had paid eight dollars for at a yard sale and made over with bright slipcovers. His hair was nearly dry after his meager bath; both wash water and flush water were getting scarce at her house, so she'd had him do his business in the seldom-used privy out back and handed him a bucket of water to use in her own bathtub. He had put on the pants and shirt Mally had pulled from a trunk of things she would never part with—William's letters home from the Pacific, his baseball spikes and dowdy old fielder's glove that enclosed a baseball with frayed stitching autographed by Satchel Paige. The alternative was to have an unfamiliar white boy sitting in her parlor in a too-small towel because he couldn't put filthy clothes back on after a washing–up. Mally had no neighbors to tell malicious stories, but still it would have been an uncomfortable thing.

Highpockets' plaid shirt hung to Alex's knees, and the boy had rolled up half a foot of cotton trousers on each skinny, tanned leg. He was drinking from a tall bottle of Nehi orange pop, sugar a hypo to his store of nervous energy, foot tapping the floor.

Mally had learned that even though he couldn't speak, he did a good deal of talking with his eyes and head motions when he wanted to be understood. Now he was looking at the centerpiece photo of William so handsome and dashingly proud in his Navy dress whites.

"Were you too little to know what was going on in the war?" Mally asked, fingers trailing along a series of photos on the image wall, stopping at a picture of a Navy destroyer. Alex shrugged. "Well, this was William's ship, the USS *Taneycomo*. William was one of the first colored ensigns commissioned by the Navy. At the battle for Okinawa, what I believe was the last big battle of the Pacific war, the *Taneycomo* took a direct hit from a Japanese *kamikaze*. That was their name for suicide pilots. When the magazines blew up all at once, the *Taneycomo* was sheared in half. Went down real fast. William and maybe two dozen of his shipmates found themselves in the flaming sea. Blood in the water, Lord, and sharks everywhere. William hurt bad and just clinging to some flotsam. Hours, it must've been, before he was rescued. Terrible things going on around him. Burned men screaming."

Alex flinched, trembled. He looked down.

She'd told it too strong, Mally thought; he was just a kid, after all.

"But William did come back from Okinawa. Spent some months

in the Navy hospital in California, being treated because he couldn't get out of his mind, like a lot of them who suffered in the war, all he'd seen and heard. William tried his best, and I—I tried hard for him too, but in the end he just couldn't shake it."

Her next thought came with barely a pause: her half-mad, will-o'-the-wisp mother and her betrayed, emotionally benumbed father; she might have been speaking to herself.

"Sometimes I think it's my fate to suffer for haunted men."

Alex put his soda bottle down, more or less bolted from the sofa and went outside on the porch, where he stood looking at the stars through the tall pine trees. When she followed and touched his shoulder he looked back at her with sore-looking saddened eyes.

"Didn't mean to upset you. I don't get to talk about William to anybody much anymore, but it's good for me not to keep him shut up inside my mind. Was there somebody close in your family didn't make it home from the war?"

Alex shook his head.

"Then what is it has you in such a state, flapping around on your bike after dark, jumping under trains?"

After a few moments, Alex put his head down again. Like an ol' lop-ear mule, Mally thought. Suddenly she felt very tired and aching in spirit and wanted this day over with.

"You want to write down where I'm supposed to take you, then we best get started; it's going on ten-thirty already."

A s soon as she saw the house on West Hatchie Road they were going to, Mally knew immediately a lot more about Alex and understood his reaction to her tale of the ill-fated USS *Taneycomo*. Her aunt, Rhoda Jenks, worked days there as housekeeper; afflicted with the dooms of their subjugated race, Rhoda moved through her daily chores like a bus in heavy traffic, humming moodily to herself.

So the Alex she had in the backseat of her car had to be Bobby Gambier's brother, called "Twig" when he was little. Bobby was undersheriff to Sheriff Luther Tebbetts, and Bobby's own father had been high sheriff of Evening Shade for better than twenty years before Luther, until the Gambier house burned down with Robert Senior unable to escape in time.

Mally had hoped to leave Alex and his damaged bicycle off without having to offer an explanation of what they were doing together this time of night, but no such luck. Porch lights were on and Bobby Gambier was outside having a smoke, wearing only pajama bottoms, chest hair like finely shaved copper. Not tall but put together just fine, wide shoulders making him look shorter than he actually was.

When she pulled into the drive next to the brick house and he saw that it was a woman driving, one he knew on sight, he had the courtesy to go inside and put on a robe.

"Aren't you Mally Shaw?"

"Yes, sir."

"Reckon I know who that is with you," he said with a vexed grin.

"Yes, I've brought your brother home," Mally said, employing the fine art of speaking to a white man she barely knew without looking him directly in the face but also not appearing to avoid his gaze.

Bobby's grin got bigger, and he seemed truly amused when he saw Alex climb out of the backseat in clothing way too big for him.

"What did you do, ride your bike into the Yella Dog?"

Alex looked at Mally, who said, "He had a little accident, Mr. Gambier. Gone too fast, I reckon. Messed up his bike some. It's there in the trunk of my car."

"Where'd those clothes come from, church barrel?"

"No, sir. They were some things of my late husband William's I had around the house. Your brother's clothes was too dirty for him to wear, so I put them in with my wash."

"Where did he have this accident, out by your place? That's way out, isn't it, Highway 19?" Alex standing right there at the bottom of the porch steps, but Bobby, aside from a couple of quick glances, paid his attention to Mally. Alex watched her too, with uneasy eyes, probably afraid of all she could tell although she'd made it plain, to put him at ease on the ride home, that she wouldn't let on about the *Dixie Traveler.*

"Yes, sir. It wasn't far down the road where I am, and I just happen to come along about then."

"So you weren't anywhere near him—in your car—when he had this accident?"

"I didn't run into him, if that's what you're asking, Mr. Gambier." Alex was shaking his head vehemently. Bobby looked from one to the other and made up his mind he was hearing at least some of the truth.

"See you got some scrapes and bruises," he said to Alex and made a rotating, over-and-under motion with his fists. *Over the handlebars?* Alex nodded, looking sheepish.

"I put some iodine on the worst of those scrapes after he had his bath," Mally said.

"That's right, you're a nurse. At your place?"

"It was close by. Like I said, Mr. Gambier, I'm washing his clothes, and I'll have them ironed and ready to leave off in the morning, if that's all right."

"Real kind of you, Mally. And thanks for taking care. Alex, help me get that bike out of Mally's car. Then you can go on in. But keep it quiet: Everybody's asleep. Mally, if you'd stay around just another minute?"

It wasn't exactly a request, but Mally wasn't bothered. What she knew about Bobby Gambier as a lawman was, he didn't go out of his way to make trouble for her people. That had been his daddy's philosophy as well. Luther Tebbetts, he was a different sort.

While she stood by admiring some trellised morning glories and climbing roses, no expression, but a headache beginning like wasp buzz behind her eyes, the two brothers hauled the bicycle up to the porch and Bobby looked over the damage.

"Nothing we can't fix ourselves," he told Alex, putting an arm around the boy's shoulders. Alex held still for about four seconds, then shrugged off the arm and opened the screen door. Bobby looked at him with a slight grimace and said, "There's half a ham in the Frigidaire. Buttermilk. If you want something before bed."

"Good night, Alex," Mally said as he was going into the house. He paused momentarily but didn't look around at her. The steel ID bracelet he wore caught light as he closed the screen door. She saw both of his hands and noticed that the man's ring he'd been wearing earlier wasn't there.

Bobby came down into the yard, Mally waiting beside her old Dodge that needed repainting. There were a Plymouth coupe and a spiffy Packard Six station wagon parked on the double strips of concrete ahead of her own car.

"Mally, it's not to my credit I never let you know how bad I felt about William's passing."

"That's all right, Mr. Gambier."

"Daddy always swore "Highpockets" was one of the best infielders ever played the game. I saw him myself when the Bob Feller All-Stars took on the Memphis Red Sox in an exhibition game at the Memphis Chicks' ballpark. William could slug, too: drove in two runs with a triple that day. Daddy had a keen eye for baseball talent. He was a part-time scout for the Cubs."

"I never knew that."

"Sad news about Priest Howard. We heard from Rhoda how good you were about looking after him in his last days."

"It was going on seven months that he lingered. Poor suffering soul."

"So are you back in Evening Shade for good?"

"I really can't say, Mr. Gambier."

"All right, then. Nice seeing you again, Mally. Appreciate you dropping Twig off." He looked at her with a half smile, eyes resting on her casually but alert with the intuition good lawmen develop early. "Someday you might want to tell me what it really was Alex got up to tonight. Knowing Alex."

"Was pretty much the way I told it to you already." And she

added, realizing she probably ought to just keep her opinions to herself, "From what little I've come to know, he's a good boy."

"I hope you're right. He's reached an age now where he's—hard for me to understand."

"Mr. Gambier, pardon me for asking, please, but was he born that way, not able to talk?"

"No. He talked early and talked a streak after that; you couldn't get him to shut up. He could make up the tallest tales, but they were always worth a listen." There was a faint yearning within Bobby's smile. "Now he scribbles them down but won't let anybody see what he's writing. Anyhow, diptheria did a lot of damage to his voice box when he was four. For three years, either Mama or Daddy had him down to Memphis or up to Nashville, St. Louis a couple times, consulting with specialists. Alex had speech therapists too, and after a lot of hard work, Mama would write to me—I was in the army then— that he might relearn how to talk. But"—Bobby felt around in the pockets of his robe as if he wanted to smoke, but came up empty-handed—"then the fire took both our parents away from us and Alex shut up again, for good I'm afraid."

"Or closed up? What he's been through in his young life does bring a lot of anger to a child."

"He's probably going to a special school soon—another month or two. We're talking about it."

"You and Alex?"

"No, he doesn't know yet. Once we've got it all settled." The need for a cigarette was making him restless, Mally's cue that she'd overstayed.

"Well, good night, Mr. Gambier."

"Good night, Mally."

Mally got home feeling too edgy to sleep. The diamond ring missing from Alex Gambier's finger was right where she expected to find it, on the shelf above the wash stand in the bathroom. Grimy tape made it small enough to fit the boy's ring finger, although it was the kind of old-style ring men of substance flaunted on their pinkies. She left it where it was.

Habit more than anything prompted Mally to unpin her other nurse's smock from the clothesline on the front porch and iron it in the kitchen, as if she still had employment and would be going to the homestead at seven-thirty in the morning to relieve Priest Howard's night nurse. She hung the smock up in her bedroom chifforobe and returned to the kitchen of her four-room house. Cinder block and roof-shingle siding, well made, wouldn't leak through Noah's flood. She pumped water for the kettle. Mally was a coffee drinker in the morning and a tea drinker at night. Spearmint or camomile. With her tea strainer steeping in the cup she opened a jar of home-canned peaches, removed the paraffin plug, and carried everything to the screened porch, where she settled down in her bentwood rocker to enjoy the peaches straight from the jar. Traffic on Route 19 was light, whoosh of a car or small truck going by every thirty seconds or so. She heard jump music from the Negro tonk a quarter-mile down the road, what the sheriff's deputies called a "dinge joint." When the wind was right she could smell the gage they all smoked there. The tonk was one that attracted mostly the ill-natured and shiftless, and there was frequent knife play.

She heard a tom or maybe a bobcat yowl in the deep woods behind her house.

A big car went past the turnoff next to the boarded-up rib shack, traveling slower than most traffic on the straight road. Seconds later, Mally saw it again, backing up this time. Buick or Pontiac, she thought. A V-eight most likely. The car stopped; Mally studied it. Couldn't tell who might be inside, how many.

Evening Shade wasn't a bone-dry county, but liquor was legally for sale in only a single package store run by a sister-in-law of Sheriff Luther Tebbetts. So bootleggers abounded in the hollows and the hills. There were those white men who preferred the potent kick of 'shine to store-bought popskull. Even prosperous, churchgoing whites who drove nice cars and ought to have had better sense. It was strictly a case of know your bootlegger if you wanted to drink the stuff and go on living.

The black V-eight sedan moved again, turning onto the gravel beneath a live oak with the canopy spread of a revival tent. It came slowly toward her house, crunch of gravel beneath the whitewall tires. Lights on high beam. The driver stopped short of the timber bridge that crossed a drying-up streambed thirty yards from her porch. Mally lit up motionless in her rocking chair with her jar of peaches, face turned aside to avoid the glare.

Highpockets' old Fox 1912-model shotgun was just inside the door and loaded. Mally didn't want to kill anybody, but a load of birdshot aimed at the knees would be more than enough to rout any stranger who set foot unbidden on her porch steps.

No, mister, no 'shine for sale here; you've come to the wrong place.

Mally and whoever was in that big car waited. Then, after half a minute or so, they backed up slowly until the headlights swerved off of her. When she took another look, she recognized from the prominent hood ornament that it was a Pontiac, that Big Chief Indian profile. Moments later the car was gone and the night got quiet again except for owls, cicadas, and a lone bullfrog in a puddle lamenting his aloneness. A mosquito whined in Mally's ear.

A little later she went inside and locked the front door for a change, picked up the shotgun and carried it back to her bedroom. Shade rolled up on the window, but just outside there was a pretty willow tree hung like watered silk and filtering the light of the moon. Mally opened her steamer trunk with the brass fittings she kept polished and took a ribbon-tied packet of letters from a drawer. Then she lay down in her slip on top of the patchwork quilt on her narrow bed, holding the letters that she knew by heart in one hand. In near darkness, the only light came from the dial of her Crosley table radio, R & B, Fats Domino on WDIA from Beale Street down there in Memphis town, then Louis Armstrong with that voice like gargled chocolate, the music fading in and out, surf sounds, Mally dreaming deep inside William's letters from the Pacific, wearing the flimsy paper like a nighttime skin. The changes in William's tone as his ship steamed urgently into great battles. Guns pounding away at midnight, garden of unearthly blooms. In a calm dawn the sea a junkyard paved with oil. Fishing out floating men in life vests with heads brittle as coal. Eyeless, only gleaming teeth unburnt. Three of Mally's last letters to William had come back to her weeks before he appeared on their doorstep like two men side by side. Divided as his ship had been divided explosively and sunk. Old/new William. She never learned which of them had the secret death wish.

Priest Howard's last will and testament was read in his lawyer's office on the third floor of the West State National Bank, in which Priest had been the majority stockholder, at ten o'clock on Friday morning.

It went as Leland had predicted to himself. The homestead was Saxby's, with the provision that, should Sax and his family choose not to live there, the property was to be sold, proceeds held in trust for however many children Rose Heidi had the stamina to bear before calling it quits. Leland knew that Sax would have the homestead appraised and on the market before sundown that day. But it wouldn't be so easy to get shut of, a big old house in a somnolent community; probably it would still be sitting there unsold after probate was completed. Mixed blessings indeed.

Cash money and stock certificates were apportioned by the estate for the continuing care of Priest's third wife, who had outlived him, barely; she was confined to an expensive nursing home, brought down by a catastrophic stroke a year and a half ago, now helpless as baby Moses in the bulrushes. The loyal Burnell was to receive four thousand dollars, and there were lesser bequests to a housemaid and cook. Leland shifting a little in his chair, listening disinterestedly as the vault of his late father's largess was emptied, gold toothpick going from one corner of his mouth to the other. He didn't smoke anymore but it was occasions like this that made him sorry he'd quit.

Leland's father had been generous in his givings to his church and his alma mater, Vanderbilt University, and many charitable and other worthy organizations, down to and including the Boy Scouts of America.

Most of his mistresses, when he still could get the drop on some pussy, had been married women; all were spared the necessity of trying to make explanations for windfalls to their husbands.

After the lawyer had finished droning his way through the unnecessarily wordy four-page document, there was a drowsy silence in his office, all of the others present trying to avoid looking at Leland, who jauntily rolled that toothpick around on his lower lip. Sax was sweating. To Leland's mind Sax was the disinherited one, since birth. As for wit, unarmed; as for looks, beggared. Leland could afford his smile.

Rose Heidi fanned herself, content that her children were provided for, but some cash would have been nice too. The water cooler in one corner belched. A bluebottle fly was buzzing on a windowpane. The ugly black oscillating fan atop a bookcase behind the lawyer's desk smelled as if it were on the verge of burning up. Pages of the will stirred in the lawyer's chubby liver-spotted hand in the stale gusts from the tickety fan blades.

Leland, still smiling, popped his toothpick into a leather holder in his shirt pocket, reached for his hat and stood up.

"Fuck you too, Daddy," he said in response to Priest Howard's posthumous belittlement of him and strolled out of the office, no defeat in the angle of his head; like any good politician, Leland knew how to act the part of a man who has the fatted calf by the balls.

Behind him, Rose Heidi cut loose with a nervous, malicious-sounding giggle.

Friday noon Mally's second cousin, Verona, came around with a bushel of tomatoes needed putting up, not the kind of activity Mally was looking for on a day when the mercury in her nailed-up porch thermometer held steady at just under one hundred degrees.

No cross-ventilation and pots of tomatoes boiling, it was a steambath in the kitchen she and Verona needed to step out of every so often to keep from fainting. On the front porch and out of the sun the air felt almost cool. They unwrapped their soggy headrags, took off seedy aprons, and drank water with squeezes of lemon in it from a pitcher. Mally didn't have enough lemons to make real lemonade, and she needed all of her sugar for those jars of tomato preserves.

Her print cotton dress was wet down the back and clinging to her thighs. Verona fanned herself with a folded copy of the *Tri-State Defender* newspaper. All Mally wanted was to sit very still for a few minutes and breathe slowly.

They finished with the tomatoes at a quarter to four. Verona took a bucket bath and drove home with her half of the still-hot jars in an orange crate on the seat of a fuming '36 Ford pickup. Mally coaxed the temperamental pump in the wellhouse to deliver a tepid shower in her bathtub. Her cistern was empty and the well considerably down in a dry year. Then she used a lot of talcum, put on a T-shirt and a pair of overalls ragged at the cuffs. Barefoot on the porch, a bread board across her lap, she wrote her weekly letter to her father at the medical school in Nashville. All the gossip about people and relations he hadn't seen, probably hadn't given a thought to, in donkey's years.

She heard a bicycle bell, looked up and saw Alex Gambier in the yard beside half of a whitewashed truck tire that was planted with geraniums.

"See you got that bike fixed," Mally called. "Well, come on up." She had almost finished her letter anyway.

He leaned his bike against the wide stump of a long-gone gum tree and joined her on the porch. He had heat rash on his neck. Sweat rolled in big drops from beneath the unruly shock of coarse blond hair and down the sides of his face. Mally calculated the ride from his house was about nine miles. Overfar in such heat. No point in pouring him a tin cup of water; he was perishing. She just handed over the nearly full pitcher and watched him gulp. Then she took the pitcher away.

"Too much all at once gives you cramps," Mally warned. Alex nodded. She poured a little water into a cupped hand and sluiced his face, wiping it down. He held still for that, closing his eyes, licking lips that looked raw in places. "Now wait here," she said. "Rest yourself. When that water's run through you, you know where the outhouse is." He hunched his shoulders, remembering cobwebs in the dark two nights ago. Mally smiled.

She returned from her bathroom with cornstarch for the heat rash, petroleum jelly for his lips, and the ring he'd left there. He took it from her and put it on, looking not at all surprised where the ring had turned up. Mally read him plainly.

"If you want to come visit now and then, no need to go leavin' anything behind as an excuse." She paused, spoke again to chase the consternation from his eyes. "You're always welcome here. If you're just wanting a place to get away to."

He looked at her in rapt contemplation, looked away to where small green lizards had arranged themselves on rusty screen wire, a watchful hieroglyph.

"That ring belong to your Daddy? Must have kept it in a safety-deposit box; doesn't appear to have been damaged by the fire."

Alex nodded slightly, blinking, flash of curiosity in his humid face. She knew about that?

Mally handed him the jar of petroleum jelly.

"Fix up those lips, why don't you? And you better had avoid the sun next couple of days; got to take care of a fair complexion. All right with me if you want to stay on for supper; might cool down by then. Cornbread and butterbeans the best I can do. Some nice green tomatoes. Probably they feed you better at your house."

He made a wry face, dipped a finger into the petroleum jelly and smoothed it over his crusty lips.

"Now you can powder on some of that cornstarch to take the hurt out of your rash. Then if we don't have anything else to talk about, I could use some help cleanin' up the mess in my kitchen, I put up a bushel tomatoes here today."

Alex looked at her with terrific disdain. Mally put a hand on her hip and cocked her head.

"Can't ask you to do women's work? Well, summer's going fast, so maybe I could trust you to split me a big pile of stove wood 'thout chopping off your foot."

First time she'd seen him smile. Did wonders for him, Mally thought. And just maybe, deep down inside, there was laughter in him too.

M*ally didn't notice the writing tablet* Alex had intended that she find until after she returned from dropping him and his bike off at the ball field behind the Methodist church a few blocks from the Gambier house. He must have brought it in the saddlebag strapped to the back fender of his Schwinn, left the tablet beside the Bible in the front room that he assumed, correctly, she read almost every night before turning in.

The tablet looked well used. There were dried-out rubber bands around it that broke as she removed them, part of a child's inky thumbprint in one corner. On the first page inside the boy had written *Property of Alexander Gambier Fifth Grade West End School. Copyrite 1948 by Alexander Gambier.*

Knowledgeable about copyrights. Obviously something important was to follow. Mally sat on her bamboo sofa with a cup of spearmint tea, sunset flood on the pine-paneled picture wall behind her, an orange sea through which box-camera memories surfaced, shadow faces of the deeply drowned. She found a last Chesterfield in the pack of cigarettes she'd bought a week ago, lit up and leafed through several pages of the writing tablet without attempting to read, intrigued by his not-so-neat, blotchy handwriting, the impulsive scrawl of words on blue-lined pulp paper. Alex had had a story to tell, and Mally wondered if she was the first to read it.

THE RESCUE

by Alexander Gambier

Wyatt Sexton was the 7th child of Martha and Big Red Sexton who was so called because of the color of his hair that was likened to a prary fire seen on a dark night. They named the new arrival to the famly after the legendery sheriff of Tombstone Ariz. Mr. Erp himself, who was also proud to be the little boy's godfather. Everybody doted on little Wyatt specialy his sisters who took turns bathing and feeding him while the men of the famly tended all the cattle on ther fabulus spred. Wyatt could walk while he was not even one year old and rode his own paint pony by age two. He will be the best horseman in the famly you'll see! his proud father braged to one and all, and Big Red's word was never doubted at peril to your life. But that was before tragedy befell. It happened in the town where Wyatt, now five years old, was playing with other boys around the watering ~~tro~~ tank in front of the Mercantil Store. A waggen driven by a drunk man who should have known better lost control of his horse team which ran away. The waggen which he did not see coming ran over both Wyatt's legs. They were cruely mangled beneath iron weels! Wyatt was the unlucky one as all of the other boys were spared. When his terrible injuries heeled Wyatt could not stand up by himself any longer or take any steps with his crooked feet. He was a lifetime criple doomed to crawl on his belly like a reptil and boys who had been his frends now made jokes about him. That was worse than if he deid! His days on horseback were over and his heartbroken father sold Wyatt's paint pony. That was the most crushing blow of all! Wyatt was never destined to take his place at roundup time with other men of his famly. What use would he be? He wanted to kill himself. But that was no anser. Self ~~slot~~ killing yourself was reproved in the Bible. He would be condemned to a lost soul in limbo forever. Like Jesus young Wyatt felt the need to have time to think and be someplace where no other soul could find him. So one night when no one was watching he crawled away from the house into the desert one mile, then two miles until he became porched with thurst. All alone in the desert wolves howling and a big thunderstorm filing the sky all around poor Wyatt. What was he to do now as lightning flashed!

Climb to the top of the tall rocks a voice inside him said. Soon there would be a flood in the coolee where he lay and sweep everything from in its path. Wyatt was a criple scorned by many but there was not a cowerdly bone in his body. Bravely he made his way up the tall rocks where wolves waited with yelow eyes that had deth in them. What now? His anser came in a crash of thunder then the hevens opened! Down came a lightning bolt to cleve the rocks and send the wolves tumbling to certen doom. Wyatt could not beleve his eyes! Where the wolves had been now stood a magnificant stalion biger than the bigest horse in Big Red's remuda. Sixteen hands high glowing all over like silver. Are you real? Wyatt asked. You look like a silver ghost. But he knew when the horse nodded that "Silver Ghost" who he named on the spot was ment for him.

After it rained all night sunup was a welcome sight. Time to ride his new horse home. Silver Ghost knelled to make it easy for the cripled boy to mount him. Wyatt rode with both hands on the horses flowing mane and off they went across the desert. It was like flying! Soon they reached the Sexton spred but no fine welcome waited there. For the ranch house was under ~~atak~~ surrounded by feerce Apatches! There faces painted. Apatches on the warpath! They were the terrer of the fronteer. Not even Wyatt Erp himself dared to face a band of bloodthursty Apatches.

The house was on fire! Wyatt herd his sisters and mother screem inside. Where was Big Red? At the Gilded Cage Saloon in Tombstone no doubt, as wisky was his manly weakness. Drunk in an upstairs room while Apatche devils killed his loving famly. Wyatt and Silver Ghost were having none of that! His horse showed no feer of the redskin raders. The huge silver stalion scattered there own puny mounts as he galoped into the inferno. One by one Wyatt plucked his sisters from choking smoke and carryed them outside into the fresh air. The nabors cheered this act of curage while Big Red stood by weeping tears. Son I am so ashamed of myself to let this happen and I swear I will never take another drink of wisky in my life. You are a great hero Wyatt! Legends will be told forever about your curage and your marvolus silver steed. God bless you Wyatt Sexton everyone cried. Wyatt knew from that day on no one up and down the wild fronteer would think of him as just a boy with crooked feet.

Having read the pages Alex had given to her, and in reading come closer to the heart of him, Mally turned off the lamp and sat for a time in the front room while what remained of her cigarette burned itself out in a saucer, Mally staring through smokerise that divided the ghost square of a twilight window. Men were drinkers, it was a quelling thing in a torpid place like Evening Shade where even some preachers took occasional solace in gin or sin. She recalled that High Sheriff Robert Gambier had had a reputation for passing out on social occasions in someone's garden or down to his own cellar where, maybe, he kept the worst of his unconfessed demons.

Drunk the April night of the fire that swept through his house? Alex thought so.

Mally stirred and yawned and found, in the fruit basket in her kitchen, a browning apple. Leaning against the sink she pared the McIntosh slowly, cutting away the bad place with its deep-down curl of worm as the boy had excised his heart, speaking to her in his only voice of suspected guilt on the part of his father, planting in that raw place a fantasy to absorb his anguish, beguile him as he grew. Mally's heart felt like a cold seed deftly opened by the stroke of her knife so that she loved Alex Gambier not for what he could be to her, a thirty-two-year-old colored woman in her own prison of scars, but for who he was and what he continued to suffer.

She'll only be here for two or three days," Cecily Gambier said to her husband. "Until her own house has aired out. Mom just can't bear the paint fumes, Bobby."

They were in bed, aglow from pure sensation, their humid bodies still deliciously sensitive to the slightest touch. The lingering allure of youthful fecundity, her tangy skin tone and deft contours: Bobby was in the mood to give Cece anything she asked for. Even though he sensed that once his mother-in-law had taken possession of the guest room down the hall, a *For Sale* sign would pop up in the front yard of her own place. Which was why she was spending close to eight hundred dollars on painting and roof repairs.

"She'll be next to Alex," he reminded Cecily.

"I don't see why Alex couldn't make an effort to be civil to Bernie for a couple of days. Do you?"

Bobby was feeling sleepy in her arms. He didn't say anything. Cecily took his silence as assurance that the matter was settled. She kissed the bridge of his nose and after some deliberation plucked a single coppery chest hair—which had become a ritual of secret, loving significance (Bobby wondered what she did with them)—before slipping away to their bathroom to shower.

THREE

A Traffic of Mourners
Bernie's Wing-Ding
Night Visitors

On Saturday, *the last full day of Mally Shaw's life, she*

attended the funeral service for Priest Howard at the Evening Shade Presbyterian Church, which was on the opposite and lower side of the courthouse square from the Baptist church. The Baptists had claimed the high ground, but the Presbyterians' needle spire rose a good ten feet higher than the Baptists' spire. They also could boast of a few more pews inside, and a new education building.

Six hundred mourners were in the church by ten-thirty of another calm, hot, August morning. The tall windows on either side of the sanctuary were open, which scarcely helped relieve the heat inside but invited flies to the tiers of flowers behind the closed bronze casket in front of the altar. Hand-held fans were a necessity, downstairs and in the cramped balcony shared by the colored seating section, the choir stall, and the pipe organ.

Priest Howard had arranged every detail of his passing weeks before his subsiding heart sent a last tremor through his frail body. He had been a vain thin-skinned man who did not relish having anyone gawk at his remains. There had been no wake, and he had not wanted anyone to dwell on his mummified profile during the service. Better they should dwell on a four-thousand-dollar coffin that glowed in supernal light from the large, round, stained glass window behind the altar as the pastor, T. Lowndes McClure, and others whom Priest Howard had specifically designated, eulogized him.

Mally, crowded in among members of Burnell's big family, down to the newest grandchild in pink taffeta and beribboned pigtails, found her attention diverted from the expensive casket—a last expression of

67

Priest Howard's vanity—to the squarish jars of sealed tomatoes in a pristine row on a shelf of her kitchen, and her heart felt constricted in her breast. If she had been a fool, at least it was done with, and whatever dark mischief had been in the mind of the dying man would never be revealed.

Her attention shifted again, to the man whose vanity was in his walk and his style, his gold toothpick (not in evidence at this solemn hour), and his combers of blond hair. If hair could have swagger, Leland's surely qualified. He was seated in the first pew facing the bier with his visibly sorrowing brother and Sax's pregnant wife, sorrow and tears also not in evidence in Leland Howard's bearing. Most everyone knew he'd been disinherited. He bore this stigma with stoicism; his own father's distaste for him would be no problem with the voters statewide. Many men, and women, had never got along with their fathers.

Much of what was said from the pulpit had been printed in Priest Howard's lengthy obituary. He had "immersed" himself in community life while achieving success in the banking profession. Name the fraternal or charitable organization, and Priest had at one time or another been the head of it. His office walls were lined with brass-on-walnut distinguished-service citations. The Boy Scouts had awarded him their coveted Silver Beaver.

More appropriate, Leland thought, looking for a little humor to entertain himself on a depressing day, if it had been the Girl Scouts.

Pastor McClure reiterated with his own stab at humor that Priest had been an "avid" golfer not above "improving" his lies. He loved life, his family, his church, and his fellow man.

Long before the eulogies had been concluded everyone was restlessly anxious to move on to the cemetery.

At twenty past twelve, Priest Howard's burdensome casket was carried down the front steps of the church and stowed inside the old-fashioned horse-drawn hearse the deceased had ordered for himself. The director of Hicks and Baggett Funeral Home had spent ten days locating the hearse, which was found negligently stored in a southern

Missouri barn, and a week having the pigeon droppings removed and the brightwork restored at considerable cost.

The cortege, preceded by a Boy Scout color guard, moved slowly to Priest Howard's final resting place. A traffic of mourners in devil sun, all throats athirst. Death and interment a cool dream to the tormented living who found shade to be scarce at this hour in spite of oaks planted near the family mausoleum by Leland and Sax's grandfather Solomon, oaks with a sturdy lifespan to outlast all flesh and its histories of truth, rumors, and lies.

The mausoleum, already ostentatious (it stood alone among much humbler monuments in the twenty-acre cemetery) had been rejuvenated and enlarged for Priest's arrival. Another wretched expense, Leland thought; he was seated uncomfortably in the foreground of the family archaeology. Not to mention the time it took. Cremation was a far better idea, although Leland conceded that having your ashes scattered by the four winds was like spending your last moments on earth as dandruff. He unwrapped a piece of hard candy in his pocket and sneaked it into his mouth, pretending to cough. His face remained impassive but his mind seethed. Hating the dead wasted mental energy and clouded his view of actions that must be taken immediately to save his political future and, more than likely, keep him out of the Atlanta federal pen. But his patience did have limits. Women could cover their heads with appropriately somber wide-brimmed hats, but it was disrespectful for a man to wear his hat at a funeral. Consequently Leland's leonine head was overheated, his dark poplin suit soaking up more heat. The immediate family was seated beneath a canopy in front of the miniature Greek temple with its anomalous stained-glass windows, but the glowing canvas overhead afforded little relief. They all were edgy waiting for the final commendation of Priest Howard to God, Eternity, and scabrous decay. The casket was draped with an American flag. One more ceremony to be observed, VFW honor-guard rifles firing in salute to Priest and his family's modest military tradition. Grandfather Solomon, on Lee's staff, had fallen at Appomattox Courthouse. Priest had been assigned to the War Department in Washington during the First World War, where he lost his young wife (and Leland's mother) to influenza. After retiring as a major in the Army Reserve, he continued his patriotic mission by serving as the head of Evening Shade's draft board.

The family of long-time houseman Burnell and other Negroes employed through the years by Priest or his bank were strung out beneath a carnival array of parasols on a rise to the left of the main body of mourners and near the long line of parked cars on the road. Leland had no trouble distinguishing Mally Shaw in their midst. She was holding an infant he was sure wasn't hers, rocking gently side to side, probably giving the fatigued mother a break. Mally stood out from the others in beauty and in the mildness of her coloring, not high-yellow but definitely quadroon, with a sweetness of eye and demeanor that obviously had appealed to Leland's goatish if-no-longer-capable old man. As striking a woman as Leland ever had known in the flesh, during his wilder flings at Cotton Carnival in Memphis, New Orleans any old time. Mally appealed deeply to him on very short acquaintance, but there was uneasiness in his interest, an edge of caution or even, although he would endure torture rather than admit it, fear. He had been cursed in a way he didn't yet understand, and Mally Shaw was an instrument of that familial curse. Therefore she had power over him. Always a dangerous situation with women, including the two he had knowingly impregnated but avoided marrying at serious expense to himself.

He didn't know yet what Mally wanted. He could only be sure she wanted *something* from him. And it was important enough for Mally to bide her time, Leland thought, scheming all the while.

Alex Gambier, *well removed from the burial site,* idled on his bicycle in circles and figure-eights around homely tombstones while taking in the military-style funeral. He had nothing better to do except to go swimming. But this late in summer and after months of drought most of the popular swimmin' holes or ponds were low, scummed over or infested with cottonmouths. An exception was the only home swimming pool in the county, which was on the Swifts' place. They bred and showed Tennessee Walking Horses and had money. Francie Swift had invited Alex to a pool party once, her twelfth birthday, but the evening hadn't gone too well because Alex had scuffled with his chief nemeses, Charlie Tiller and Ben Hodge, Alex's usual hair-trigger response to being imitated when he got carried away trying to express himself with his hands. Ben should have known better because Alex had both height and reach on him, although he really hadn't meant to pop Ben hard enough to break his nose.

Francie was forbidden to invite Alex back to her house, but Alex had observed that all of the Swifts were at the cemetery. He also knew that a certain amount of socializing was called for after a big funeral, in this case a catered affair at the Howard homestead. The Swifts' farm was only about a mile cross-country from the cemetery, and Alex was perishing. The notion of riding over there and jumping in the pool for half an hour he found irresistible. And what if they did come home in time to find him there? His brother was undersheriff of Evening Shade, and that, he knew very well, generated tolerance for Alex.

Francie probably wouldn't mind seeing him. She usually had a smile, a genuinely pleased smile for him when they bumped into each other at school or around town. Although he wasn't always in a mood to acknowledge her.

B*ernice Clauson had brought her own sheets,* pillowcases, and extra pillows to the Gambier house, so her first order of business, even before she unpacked some clothing and personal items, was to remake the four-poster bed in the guest room. This was not intended, she assured her daughter, as a criticism of the quality of the linens Cecily owned; but she was partial to her own made-in-Belgium sheets because, frankly, anything of a lesser quality easily irritated her susceptible skin. Bernie offered all of her assurances with breezy good cheer immediately after noting defects in just about everything she came into contact with in her daily life, from the suspect freshness of a loaf of Sunbeam bread in the grocery store to pigeon poop on the marble threshold of her bank to the cleaning abilities of the Gambiers' maid, Rhoda Jenks: "Well, you know when they get older, and of course they're slow to begin with, they tend to leave *dust;* that's just something we all have to put up with, Cecily. And I know Rhoda is wonderful with Brendan. Although that does remind me—"

The only thing likely to spoil her little visit, cast a pall, really, was unfortunate proximity to Alex Gambier, who—frankly—Bernice loathed, although she was careful not to express the true depths of her animus even to Cecily. Knowing full well Cecily's own feelings; but there was a marriage to respect. Cecily was bringing her young husband along *very* nicely, inspiring him to better himself in the world; Bernice thought it would be tragic if the continuing presence of Alex Gambier in the household should lead to difficulties between Bob (she never called him *Bobby,* which in her view was not a fit name for a man, suggesting a lifelong streak of immaturity) and Cece, difficulties that could blight the purity of their love for each other. Bernie was doing her best to help Cecily find a way out of her dilemma. Willing to spare no expense. But Bob seemed unwilling to accept her generosity (pure stubborn male pride), reluctant to seriously discuss the considerable good a school for his brother, well away from Evening Shade, would provide.

But if her offer of financial assistance wasn't going to be enough to convince Bob that his brother would be better off in a different, structured environment, well, there were other ways to skin a cat. Frankly.

Once she had settled into the guest room, Bernice ventured into the bathroom next door that she would be forced to share with Alex.

Rhoda had cleaned to the best of her abilities, opened windows wide to what freshness a hot afternoon could provide. But, *really,* Bernie thought, looking around with a hand pressed over her heart.

This arrangement was not going to be at all satisfactory. There were lurid pulp magazines stacked untidily in a basket between the toilet and the claw-footed tub. A typical cover had a hawk-nosed westerner with blazing six-guns in each hand and a darkly tressed, ruby-lipped woman in a torn blouse cuddled in the crook of a protective arm. Such lamentable taste, when there were so many classic books to be enjoyed by a boy Alex's age. He simply had not been encouraged in the right directions.

Windowsills were scarred with cigarette burns. No effort for Bernice to picture Alex lolling in the tub, smoking, reading; or hunched naked on the commode, picking his nose (all boys picked their noses). Or, much nastier—as her imagination took a heated turn—engaging in self-abuse. Cecily had told Bernie about the semen-yellowed handkerchiefs, his *best* handkerchiefs—thrown under his bed. Only the worst sort of boys . . . but it went without saying Alex Gambier was not of a good moral nature.

Blond hairs in the soap on the wash basin. Little smudges of toothpaste on the tile backsplash. Bernie shuddered, then gathered up all of the pulp magazines so offensive to her eye and carried them into Alex's room, where everything looked slapdash and tribal to her. She was treading carefully, as if she were afraid of toads hopping out from under the bed. She couldn't find room on any of Alex's loaded bookshelves for the magazines and finally dropped them on his student's desk, where there was a portable Royal typewriter with a sheet of paper in it. Always writing something, Cecily had said. Often typing late at night. To Bernice it would be worse than hearing mice in the walls. She was a very light sleeper.

It was probably too much to ask, Bernice thought, that Alex be required to use Bob and Cece's bathroom while she was in residence. But there was a perfectly adequate little room with a toilet and shower partitioned off from the rest of the basement. Rhoda sometimes stayed overnight there when Cecily needed extra help with Brendan. Why, Bernice asked herself, couldn't Alex move to the basement for the short time he was to remain in the house?

Alex didn't have to be persuaded that it was a good idea, because it certainly wasn't up to him. Bernice could count on Cecily to be in agreement. Bob would say Alex was being evicted from his room, make a fuss about that, what had his brother done to deserve such treatment . . .

And of course he hadn't done anything, really; Bernie had to admit that.

She was looking idly around the cluttered room when she spied a jar of petroleum jelly on the table beside Alex's bed. The force of her inspiration nearly staggered her.

Now all she needed to do was work up a suitable amount of resentment in Alex toward her, for everyone to observe, but that shouldn't be hard. During most of her visits to the house, Alex never even looked at her, sensing in the way of children a natural enemy.

Bernie turned to leave, and there was Alex in the doorway to his room as if on cue, looking daggers at her. She was startled. Recovered with a smile that had an edge of its own. She heard Cecily down the hall with Brendan.

"Well, hello, young man," Bernice said to Alex with a lifting of her heavily plucked eyebrows. "You do have a way of sneaking up on people." As if she wasn't the intruder. Bernie was a small woman, but even her normal speaking voice carried like a sawmill's whistle. "I was returning some of your reading material that I found in the bathroom. The paper of those pulp magazines attracts all sorts of insects, so since we'll be sharing the bath for a few days, I'll ask you not to leave them lying around in there." Alex just stood there with a displeased expression that hadn't quite matured into a glower. His sunstreaky hair falling every which way and his clothing, what little he had on (didn't he ever button his shirt?), looking damp, as if he'd been swimming. "I will be staying," Bernice went on, "until the paint fumes are completely aired out of my own house. I am already somewhat acquainted with your, hem, creature habits, but I would like for you to know what I require from you, so there will be no misunderstandings."

Alex was looking around for his magazines, saw them on the desk. He couldn't walk into his room without walking into Bernie, and she wasn't giving ground yet.

"As you know, I'm asthmatic, so if you must sneak a cigarette, please be aware of my condition and do it outside. Hem. Now, about my bath schedule. Mornings at seven and again at nine-thirty in the evening unless dinner is unusually late, before I retire. I'm sure that Cecily will find a little table for my bath things, which I kindly ask you not to touch. As for when you bathe, you must leave the tub *absolutely* sparkling clean—"

Cecily appeared in the hallway behind Alex, carrying Brendan.

"Mom, everything okay?" she said, anxiety-niche between her eyes. Giving Alex the once-over as if with a wire brush.

Brendan broke out in a smile and reached for Alex with both hands. Alex's expression changed, and he turned to take the boy from Cecily, but she put a shoulder between them, saying, "No, no, Brendy, Alex doesn't want to be *bothered* right now." The moment of pleasure left Alex's eyes. He turned his face away from everyone, chest tightening as he took a deep breath.

"Oh, we're fine!" Bernice said. "Alex and I were having a, hem, getting the rules clear so we're not bumping into each other up here. I'm surprised you haven't told him that I would be your *guest* for a few days."

"He's not around long enough to tell him anything," Cecily said with a curtness inspired by Brendan's outcry at being kept away from his uncle. Alex looked at him again, then reached past Cecily's protective shoulder to touch the baby's button nose with a forefinger. He walked away as Brendan's fuss turned to chortle. They heard Alex taking the stairs down two at a time, hitting the landing with both feet together, giving the women a mild seismic jolt.

"Oh, my," Bernice said with a vague smile.

"That's what I mean," Cecily said and grimaced to sum up all of the tension that she felt Alex brought to their house.

"Couldn't you have let him hold the baby for a few moments?"

"No," Cecily said.

"Well. Frankly, under the circumstances—there's just so much hostility in Alex. You see that, don't you, dear?"

"I only wish Bobby did."

Alex *was in the garage* before supper cleaning his bike, applying a little 4-in-1 Oil to the chain, when Bobby strolled in, still wearing his sheriff's department khakis and black gunbelt rig. He leaned against his workbench with folded arms until Alex, crouching, glanced at him over his shoulder.

"How's everything, Twig?"

Alex shrugged slightly, then nodded toward the house.

Bobby lighted a Lucky, blew smoke.

"Yeah. I know. She 'Berns' me up too." He grinned encouragingly. "But I think we can both get along with Cece's mom for a few days."

Alex shrugged again.

"I got a call today from Berk Swift? Said you were over to their place using the pool today when nobody was around except the stable hands."

Alex nodded indifferently.

"Said it wasn't so much he minded you in their pool, but if you had an accident and drowned with nobody to help you, then they'd be liable."

Alex got up, took the broom leaning at the other end of the bench and a dustpan and swept up some of the sawdust from the concrete floor where oil had dripped. He might leave his underwear and soggy towels on the bathroom floor, but he was meticulous about keeping the garage neat, tools hung correctly, not a stray nail anywhere. It was *their* place, his and Bobby's.

Bobby handed the Lucky to Alex, who took a drag and gave it back.

"Don't want to let it turn into a habit," Bobby cautioned routinely.

"Half pack a day, that's all I allow myself. What I'm asking, summer's over another month, so unless they do the invitin', stay away from the Swifts' pool."

Alex smiled cynically.

"I know; you can swim like Tarzan so drowning's not the issue. What I thought we could do, get up early tomorrow morning, take the boat over to the Tennessee River for the day."

Alex looked toward the house again, where Cecily, her mother, and Rhoda Jenks were all in the kitchen laughing about something.

"Just the two of us," Bobby said. "Sound like a winner?"

Alex gave him a thumb's-up sign, then took a double handful of sawdust from a barrel and spread it on the floor where he'd been working. He looked happy.

Bobby stubbed out the Lucky in a Folger's can on the workbench. Half a pack a day, and never smoke one all the way down.

"Supper," he said. " 'N I could eat the ass off a barely singed cow."

H*alfway through the evening meal,* Bobby was called away from the dinner table. An accident involving a truckful of hogs had tied up a highway bridge over the Yella Dog halfway down to Memphis, and there was a fatality; Luther Tebbetts being away on the third honeymoon of what Cecily called his "romantic career" Bobby was needed.

After supper Cecily fed Brendan, who was still on the breast, in the nursery while Alex and Bernice ate peach cobbler on the front porch. Bernie keeping up a cheery dialogue about this and that, although she was largely talking to herself. But she had never minded the sound of her own voice. Alex nodded a couple of times while wolfing down his dessert but avoided looking at her.

Alex's second cousin Denny Limber came by on his bike with his best friend Jess Robinson, as Denny was apt to do a couple of times a month, prodded by his mother, who felt sorry for Alex. They were going to the Gem picture show which was playing *Red Mountain,* a western with Alan Ladd. Alex made a quick decision to tag along. He seldom passed up a Western picture, and Alan Ladd was a big favorite of his. If he could have any voice he wanted it would be Alan Ladd's. Pleasant baritone timbre, manly. Alan Ladd wasn't tall, but he was someone who meant business. Alex sprinted upstairs to change his shirt and withdraw fifty cents from his hidden allowance cache.

Once Brendan was tucked in for the night, Cecily went outside with her own postponed dessert. A mild wind had risen at night's renewal, freshly starred. Through tall poplars and shagbark hickories in the side yard she saw heat lightning. It was well to the north: no rain was expected in their vicinity.

Mother and daughter passed a half hour together with gossip and random reminiscences, avoiding touchy subjects. Then Bernie, almost on the dot of nine-thirty, excused herself and went upstairs to draw her second bath of the day.

Cecily rinsed out her dish in the kitchen, left it on the drainboard of the sink, then went up the back stairs to look in on Brendan. The filmy curtains at his windows billowed from the wind that had been consistent enough to cool down the house. The lightning seemed closer, more prolonged, and there was thunder. Brendan slept with little knowledge of the world to trouble him. She went into their bedroom wondering if Bobby would be gone half the night, feeling a little sore about that. And then he planned to be up early and off somewhere with Alex and the boat, probably for the whole day. Displeasure was hardening into resentment when she heard a knock.

She opened the door to find her mother in the hall wearing only a pink lace negligee and a tight hairnet, hand at her throat, looking ill or faint from terror.

"Cecily, ohhh, Cecily!"

It was all of the talking she seemed able to manage. Through increasingly frantic gestures, she urged Cecily to follow her down the hall to the bathroom between her room and Alex's. Breathing heavily by the time they got there, Bernie motioned her daughter inside while leaning against the doorjamb, still clutching the root of her throat. Forcing blood into her cheeks as if she were decorating a cake with a pastry gun. Cecily looked around the brightly lit bathroom not knowing what to expect, but everything appeared perfectly in order.

"The tub," Bernice said with an erratic flap of one hand. "Look."

Cecily inspected the bathtub with its finely cracked porcelain and eyelets of blue iron where the porcelain was chipped away, then looked around at her mother in utter confusion.

"Mom, I don't—"

"Slippery. It's all slippery. He wanted . . ."

Cecily got down on one knee beside the high tub and looked more carefully at the bottom. The stopper was in. Bernice had run about an inch of water.

". . . me to break my . . ."

Cecily reached down and drew a finger across the tub bottom. Scummy; no, slick from something. Add a little water, and—

"Thank my lucky stars I didn't run the tub full before stepping in! I might've hit my head and drowned."

"I am not believing this," Cecily said slowly, rubbing her thumb and forefinger together, feeling stunned and apprehensive. Had to be petroleum jelly. And it completely coated the bottom of the tub.

Bernice sat splay-legged on the toilet seat and announced, "I'm going to be hysterical."

"Mom, no you're not; please try not to get all worked up."

"I want to go home! I want to be in my own house! How can I stay here another minute? He's a young maniac, and he'll murder me in my sleep. I have never been anything but gracious to that unfortunate boy, but you see what he's done!" Bernie began to drum her heels on the tile floor and flap her hands. "Why are you *doing* this to me, Cecily? Don't you love me? How could you *allow* this to happen?"

Cecily had been exposed to such outbursts before. If she touched Bernice during a wing-ding, then her mother would pummel her in a frenzy. Making the point that everything that was wrong in Bernice's life was Cecily's fault as an imperfect daughter.

"I ought to kill myself and be done! That would be best for everybody, isn't that what you're thinking?"

Hysteria had no logic; she would continue until she burned herself out, with the neighbors hearing and wondering what the hell. Cecily got up grimly, half-filled a pitcher of water, and let Bernice have it full in the face.

"Sorry," she said and left her mother sputtering and keening to go into Alex's room. If Brendan didn't wake up, it would be a miracle.

She didn't have to do much looking around. The nearly empty jar of petroleum jelly was at the bottom of Alex's wastebasket beside his desk, covered with the tissues he'd used to wipe his hands clean.

Cecily just stood there looking down for the time it took disbelief to yield to heart-thumping rage. How much time she couldn't have said. But when she returned to the bathroom, her mother, prostrate and heaving on the floor with her negligee in total disarray, was in the latter stages of her fit, wailing incoherently. The wailing would taper off into moans and sobs, and then with the help of a sedative she could be expected to drop off and sleep soundly the rest of the night.

She pulled Bernie to her feet and helped her into the guest room.

"Don't know what it's like to get old and not be wanted anymore."

"You're not that old, and you know I love you."

"No, no, I can't stay here!" Bernice said, looking wildly around.

"Yes, you can. You don't have to worry about Alex. He won't be spending the night in my house. Or any other night if I can help it."

"Bob protects him."

"That's over with. Even Bobby will have to see there's something seriously wrong with his brother."

"You and Brendan are all I have left in the world."

"I know, Mom. Let me get you into these pajamas."

"You won't leave me? You'll stay right here? I'm afraid, Cecily."

Cecily was afraid too, but couldn't let on. Her turn to do the mothering, to be the brave one.

Bernie calmed down as Cecily helped her into silk pajamas.

"You're such a dear. Always so good to me. I've never regretted not having other children, because none of them could have meant as much to me as you have. I've been blessed."

"Yes, Mom," Cecily said, her mind on another track.

"Would it be too much trouble to fix me a cup of tea? I want to take my pills."

"Of course not."

"I'm so anxious. To think . . . Does he hate me so much that he hoped I would slip and fracture my skull or break a hip? I'm not a young woman. It's what I most dread, living out my life as a helpless cripple in a wheelchair. And what a burden to *you*." In spite of her arthritis, Bernice managed a solid grip on one of Cecily's wrists. "You know, I've heard that young people with severe . . . mental disturbances do things that are spiteful or dangerous, but later on they have no recollection. They are subject to blackouts. Hem. Remember when Alex climbed the WDOK tower? To this day we don't know what he was thinking. Ask him about the Vaseline in the tub, undoubtedly he'll deny any knowledge of it. Blackouts." Bernice produced an expiratory moan as she slipped into bed and laid her bedraggled coif on a feather pillow. Cecily pulled up the sheet, smoothed it over her mother's breast, and rose from her side. Bernie made a last effort to cling. "Where're you going?"

"Downstairs. To fix your tea and call my husband. I don't care about that wreck on the highway, I want Bobby home *now*."

"And isn't it about time for Alex to be home from the picture show?"

"Depends," Cecily said, pulse picking up again, a flurry of light behind her eyes like the hard jewel of a migraine exposing itself. "I'll be back in a few minutes. I'm closing the bedroom door, Mom. Don't get up unless you're feeling sick to your stomach."

"Leave the lamp, and would you turn my little radio on? Ted Weems and his orchestra are broadcasting from the Drake Hotel in Chicago right after the ten o'clock news. I have such memories of the Drake Hotel. Your father and I spent our first night together there after we were married." She closed her eyes, smiling faintly. "Men and their urges," she said. "But it is over with rather quickly; otherwise I had a splendid time."

Cecily stopped by Alex's room for the wastebasket with the discarded jar of petroleum jelly in it. She hurried downstairs to lock the front door.

The house she loved suddenly seemed cursed, imbued with a deadly menace; Cecily didn't know if she was locking it out or locking it in. She stifled a splurge of tears on her way to the telephone on the hope chest in the center hall. There she cleared her throat and made her voice steady before she spoke to Arlinda Kellum, the night dispatcher in the sheriff's department.

"Tell Bobby to get here as fast as he can."

"Are you okay, Mrs. Gambier? If it's an emergency, I could have Tuck or Owen over there in two shakes."

"It's really family business. I only want Bobby."

To the kitchen.

The key to lock the back door hung on a cup hook beside the keys to her Plymouth coupe. In the two years they'd lived on West Hatchie, Cecily had never locked any door. This lock was old, and the key wouldn't turn. Maybe some oil . . . but she would have to go out to the garage, which was twenty yards away. The speed of her heart dizzied her. She worked the key frantically in the frozen lock. Not only wouldn't it turn, now she couldn't pull it out.

Behind her in the kitchen the refrigerator door opened.

She looked up and saw Alex reflected in the glass half of the kitchen door, taking a quart of milk from the top shelf.

He was already in the house—where, basement?—and she hadn't known.

Her choices now were to confront him—Alex was looking at his wastebasket that she had brought downstairs—or open the door, walk outside, and wait for Bobby in the yard. And that was the same as be-ing run out of her own house by this . . . *boy* who didn't belong there in the first place.

Cecily stayed by the door, her hand on the knob. "Yes, I found it," she said. The migraine jewel inside her head winking again like a lighthouse mirror, so hurtful she squinted her eyes.

Alex looked blankly at her, and again at the wastebasket. Standing there with the fridge door open, milk bottle in his hand, little smear of chocolate bar bought at the picture show in one corner of his mouth.

The phone rang.

Bobby, she thought. His presence, although at the other end of a telephone wire, still distant from the house, gave her courage.

"Put that milk back and get out of here," Cecily said, taking a step toward Alex. "That's Bobby calling. And when I tell him what you've done . . . Get *out*. Now. I don't care where you go. I never want to see you again!"

His flaky lips parted in astonishment. He started to shake his head, then shrugged, confused and defensive.

Now Cecily, urged on by the ringing phone, continued through the kitchen as if stalking him, and Alex backed up, staring in conster-nation at her overheated face. Upstairs, Brendan let out a wail, proba-bly disturbed in a dream: He usually slept through wet pants. But Cecily jumped to another conclusion.

"Were you in the nursery? *What did you do to Brendan?*"

Alex found this new accusation—although the other one was a mystery to him—unnerving, and Cecily's own nerves, her show of incoherence, panicked him. He turned to the message board on the wall beside the fridge and the pencil hanging there on a string and began to scrawl on the notepad fixed to the board. In his haste he lost his grip on the bottle of milk. Some of it splashed across Cecily's bare feet. Cecily kept moving toward the telephone in the hall. She had cleared the doorway when Alex caught up and pulled her back into the kitchen. He wanted her to read the note he had ripped from the pad, but Cecily rounded on him in a panic equal to his and slapped him hard across the mouth, splitting his lower lip. Blood flew, but still he wouldn't let go until she screamed in his face.

"If you ever hurt my mother or my child, I WILL KILL YOU!"

Her fury staggered him, and his grip slackened. Cecily tore free of Alex and stumbled into the hall, stubbing a big toe on the doorjamb. She hopped twice and fell to her knees by the hope chest, lifted the receiver from the hook of the upright telephone.

"Cecily?"

"Bobbbbbbyyyyy."

"What's wrong?"

Crouched beside the chest, she looked in terror over her shoulder, thinking the worst: Alex now with knife or cleaver in his hand instead of a pencil, intent on shutting her up. But she didn't see him in the kitchen. The back door stood open. She heard her mother in the hall upstairs. Cecily's head was exploding, and she sobbed.

"Bobby, it's Alex. He went crazy tonight. Tried to kill my mother. And he . . . put his hands on me. Bobby, Alex put his *hands* on me!"

For the early part of the evening on that Saturday night, Mally Shaw had had company: a middle-aged man (late fifties probably was more accurate) who had notions of courting her. His given name was Herschel, but he had been called "Poke Chop" all of his life. They were related in some vague way Mally had never troubled to sort out. In the colored community Poke Chop had status: he was a 'cumulating man. Until recently he had been a letter carrier earning good Federal wages until fallen arches prompted his retirement. Among his accumulations were farmland, thirty beehives, fruit trees, a good well, a sound house filled with Sears Roebuck furniture and a late-model Oldsmobile. His most recent wife had gone to her rest two years ago; adult children had migrated to the big cities and he was lonely. Poke Chop had a wide rubbery face like a deflated inner tube and a picket-fence grin. He brought Mally treats such as pickled pigs' feet or comb honey when he came to call, and played his banjo for her. Mally recopied in a good hand the letters he wrote to his scattered brood with a carpenter's pencil and served him spice cake.

There was no chance she was going to marry him, should he get around to popping the question, or marry anyone else, but following his visits Mally always felt a little down in the dumps, adrift in the vacancies of her life.

There was now a heavy stirring in treetops that had scarcely moved for the better part of a week of swelter. The sky lighting abruptly behind those trees like gunfire from ambush. Thunder. Rain was pushing in, a belting storm. Mally felt the effect of falling barometric pressure in her sinuses. She wrapped up what was left of the spice cake and stored it in her breadbox, then went to the bathroom to wash up, sitting on the edge of her tin bathtub to shave her legs.

The glass in Mally's bedroom window was vibrating, and the willow tree thrashed outside. Her Crosley radio was full of static, and so was her hair when she brushed it, finding herself lugubrious in the tarnish of the dressing table mirror. She put on cotton pajamas and a Chinatown kimono her father had bought for her when he attended a medical convention in San Francisco right after the war.

She went to the front of the house to close windows, and in a spray of atmospheric electricity discovered Alex Gambier on the front porch, chest heaving as if he had just finished the *Tour de France*, his young face kinetic with strife.

Of all nights, Mally thought. But hadn't she asked for this?

"Best bring your bike up to the porch if you're coming in," she said, trying not to sound put-upon.

She went to the kitchen and unwrapped the spice cake again. The cake went well with a tall glass of buttermilk, which he drained without pause while sitting on the edge of one cushion on her bamboo sofa, tilting the cushion up behind him. He winced as the cool milk bathed the serious cut on his swollen lower lip. She poured a second glass and re-covered the crock with cheesecloth. Sat opposite Alex while approaching thunder gave some of the framed pictures on her wall the heebie-jeebies.

When Alex had drunk his fill and seemed calm enough to describe to her the events that had him racing to her house again, she gave him the bread board, her writing pad, and a mechanical pencil. He laid the board across his knees and hunched over it for several minutes as if he had committed to composing another epic tale. Writing with such vehemence he broke the pencil lead twice. Mally wished for a Chesterfield, but she had to be careful what she spent her money on, with no immediate prospects for employment.

Alex handed her the pad suddenly and got up to pace. The air outside was momentously still for half a minute or so. Then big raindrops spattered down like pennies on the roof. Mally gave Alex a thoughtful look before she began to read his page and a half.

"If you've got to go," she said, mindful of the quantity of buttermilk he'd put away, "you can use my toilet. You'll get soaked to the skin outside."

Nearly as soon as she'd spoken, the wind rushed into the hollow where she lived, bringing with it a crackling deluge.

While he was in the bathroom, she read all that Alex had wanted to tell her. Mally put the pad facedown on the oval table next to her chair and thought, *Lord 'a mercy, what goes on in that house?* It seemed to Mally that Cecily Gambier had smacked Alex in the mouth for no good reason. Otherwise Alex was outright lying and mooching around looking for sympathy where he could find it. Which contradicted most of what she instinctively felt about his character.

Mally wasn't given time to think about that. She heard the swash of a car approaching the house. Bright headlights were almost on top of her porch. She had other visitors.

B*obby Gambier walked downstairs* after looking over the ogre-footed tub in the guest bathroom, seeing that carefully slicked-over bottom for himself (the small amount of water Bernice had run into the tub had slowly leaked out). Power was off in their house and up and down the street; the storm that had swung their way to break the heat if not put an end to the drought was still pounding them after almost twenty minutes.

Cecily and Bernice were together in the parlor, where Bobby had got a camp lantern going. Cecily rocked the fretful Brendan, hiding his face from the lightning. The two women looked at Bobby, who didn't sit down. His face was grave.

"I could never have believed that of Alex."

"Haven't I tried to warn you?" Cecily said, too emotionally sapped to put any sort of recrimination behind her words. It was a simple statement of fact.

Bobby turned to leave the parlor.

"Where're you going?"

"Find my brother, Cecily."

"And leave us alone here?"

"Les Owen will be sitting outside in his prowler while I'm gone."

Bernie put a hand on her daughter's arm while Bobby walked out.

"We'll be all right, darling. This is between Bob and Alex now. Let it be settled tonight, for everyone's sake."

Cecily, her brain lurid from headache, handed Brendan over to her mom, turned, and buried her face in a tasseled pillow. So Brendan wouldn't be further upset, hearing his mother weep.

Bernice joggled the baby against her breast, looking calmly around the parlor during the eerie winks of lightning, thinking how best to rearrange the furniture to accommodate her baby grand piano. Which she couldn't play anymore; but she could teach, and she'd observed that Brendan had the hands to be a fine pianist. Start him early enough, who could tell how far he might go in competitions?

FOUR

Ten Big Ones
Catahoula Leopard Dogs
A Style of Murder

Two men wearing *hats and slickers came out of the car* in Mally Shaw's yard and, leaning against the slash and flash of the rainstorm, holding tight to their hats to keep them from flying off, hurried up her porch steps.

Mally looked out through the oval glass of her front door, which was covered with an opaque curtain, saw revealed by lightning the Pontiac Eight that had briefly visited two nights ago, and picked up the shotgun that was nearly as tall as she was. With her other hand she hooked up the chain latch and backed away from the door.

Thumping of their booted feet on the floorboards of the porch.

"Mally Shaw!"

"Who are you, and what do you want?"

"Sorry to be bothering you this time of night, Mally! It's Leland Howard! I need to talk to you."

"Take off your hat," Mally called back, "but stay where you are! I have a shotgun."

"All right now, Mally, all right. No cause for alarm. Like I said, just want to talk to you."

She already knew his voice, but she wanted to see his face. When the hat came off his wavy blond head, that vanity pompadour flattened some, she pulled back one side of the curtain to look more closely at him. Rain light on his face, drops falling from the end of a hound-dog nose. No way to avoid getting wet out there. She couldn't tell anything about the tall man standing behind and sideways to Leland Howard, perhaps looking over the homely things collected on the porch. And the blue-and-white boy's bicycle.

"Who is that with you?"

"Oh, it's just my man, Jim Giles. Does most of my driving for me."

"Have him go back to your car and wait there, Mr. Leland."

"Why sure, Mally. Whatever will put you at ease."

When he turned his head to speak to Jim Giles, Mally had a quick look back over her shoulder. Alex Gambier wasn't in sight; the bathroom door along the short hallway to the kitchen was still closed.

The light of the single lamp in her front room, metal shade painted Gay Nineties style with a hanging fringe of cut glass beads, had gone dull orange, as if the slender wire connecting her to the rural electric line alongside Highway 19 was about to be whipped loose from its pole.

"Mr. Leland, I wish you would come another time, if it be all that important!" Flustered now, wondering why he hadn't made himself known to her on Thursday night—or had it been only his man Giles in the Pontiac, sitting silently and watching her on the porch?

"Surely wish I could do that, Mally! But I need to be in Knoxville by tomorrow afternoon. I'm campaigning over that way most of next week. I'm only asking for a few minutes of your time after we drove all the way out here in a gullywasher." He opened his slicker and reached inside. "Got something here I need for you to sign off on."

Jim Giles had left the porch and was down in the yard, lit up by the headlights of the Pontiac. Mally shifted her attention to Leland Howard again, not feeling easier about all this. She saw a white envelope in his hands.

"This is yours, Mally! What I have here is one thousand dollars cash money my Daddy left in a desk drawer in his study at the homestead. You can see your name's here on the envelope? Money I expect he wanted you to have for all the good care you gave him, without having to wait until probate closes!"

Mally flinched at a sear of light, opening her eyes to find herself in the dark. In more ways than one. A thousand dollars! Priest Howard had never uttered a word to her about that.

Leland, the disinherited son, opened the envelope to show her, when the sky flared again, what surely looked like ten hundred-dollar silver certificates. But Mally still found such a windfall difficult to believe. She was down to sixty-eight dollars and change in the Chase and Sanborn coffee can she kept under the floorboards beneath the metal stove-wood box in the room behind her. Barely a month's keeping if she was especially frugal. But she had to take a couple of courses soon to renew her nursing certificate, and that was fifty dollars gone right there.

Leland Howard thumbed the wheel of a dented steel Zippo lighter he might have carried with him in the war. In the shielded light, his fleshy but good-looking face seemed unthreatening. His smile and benign blue eyes did not begrudge a penny of her good fortune.

"So if you will kindly sign a receipt for this money, then I can be on my way."

"Mr. Leland, the power is gone; I'm needing to fetch a paraffin lamp from my kitchen!"

"You go right ahead and do that, Mally," he said, dropping the lid on the tall lighter flame and putting his hat back on. The porch roof in the onslaught of rain was now leaking steadily in several places.

She came back with the lamplight bobbing in darkness, having intuitive moments of regret, just before she unlocked the door, about not taking time to put on clothes. But she was still awestruck by the sight of all that money in the envelope. Not thinking as clearly as she ought to have been thinking. First off, when had Priest Howard had the strength, during the last weeks she was taking care of him, to rise up from his bed and go downstairs to his study? At night, when Mally wasn't there? Not likely.

Hail pattered on the roof and struck the windows on the north side of the house. Leland Howard stepped inside as Mally retreated to set the paraffin lamp on the Franklin stove top in one corner of her front room. The crown of his hat hit the underside of the door frame, pushing it askew on his head.

Leland grinned and took the hat off once more.

"I'm tall myself, but ol' Highpockets must've bruised his forehead a few times coming through this doorspace."

Mally didn't reply, just stood by the stove holding her lime green kimono tight together with one hand.

Leland shut the door behind him and looked around. They were both aware of the shotgun at the same time. Mally had left it leaning against one end of the bamboo sofa to go to the kitchen. Leland grinned bigger and picked it up, looked it over with an eagle eye.

"Fine old piece for bird shooting," he said, then broke the shotgun open and pulled out both shells, which he dropped into a raincoat pocket.

"Wouldn't want an accident to happen while I'm here," he said with what looked like a wink; or maybe one of his eyes had begun to twitch from some pent-up anguish or fury. He hung his hat on the twin barrels and leaned the shotgun against the sofa where he'd found it.

Mally knew she had been a fool for letting him into her house. Worse, the money he'd flashed at her was a ruse; it would stay in his own pocket. She knew what he'd really come for.

When she made a break for the back of the house and the kitchen door, she learned that for a big man he had speed and good reflexes, snatching her back into the front room by an elbow, almost lifting her off her feet. She stumbled against the whatnot cabinet. Teacups and figurines rattled around on the shelves.

"Don't be putting your hands on me, Mr. Leland!"

He didn't let go. "Mally, I just think you've got some wrong ideas about me. Let's settle down now, have us a civilized conversation. If you're forthcoming with me, I like what I hear, I'll leave the thousand dollars and be on my way."

Leland pulled her closer. Soft whisper of Chinese silk and bourbon on his breath; she saw a little flare of excitement in his blue eyes.

"Here I am dripping all over your parlor floor. What I expect you to do now, sit over here on this sofa while I get out of my raincoat;

I'm stifling already. Don't try and run off on me again. James got his eye on the house where he is. He's a mean sumbitch, but I'm not one to do you harm."

"Let go of me then," she said.

Leland put more pressure on the nerves above her elbow with that unpleasantly calloused hand; she let out a gasp. Then he released Mally and with the flat of his other hand nudged her toward the sofa. She sat down, rubbing where he'd hurt her. No harm done though, was that what he thought? And his hand had been on one of her breasts. Mally was scared but made her voice level.

"I won't run. But there's nothing we have to say to each other, Mr. Leland."

"That so?" He rubbed his heavy jaw that would be jowls in a few years, faintly grinning, eyes preoccupied as he stared his way around the little room again. Just the two of them and already overcrowded. But he found the space to prowl, stopping in front of her to graciously offer a piece of hard candy from a crumpled sack he had in his coat pocket. Mally shook her head. Leland unwrapped a piece for himself. Balled the cellophane and let it drop to the floor.

"Always wondered, did William blow his brains out in the house, Mally? Or did he have the courtesy to spare you the sight?"

"In his truck," Mally said after a few moments. Parked behind the rib shack. Three o'clock in the morning. She'd heard the shot, of course. Knowing it was William, and what he'd finally done, as her head jerked up from the pillow. Hatred of Leland Howard for mentioning William's sad end rose in Mally's breast like a blister from a hot iron.

"Did you ever come across that secret recipe of his for rib sauce? That sauce was something all-fired special, Mally, the couple times I took out a plate of William's ribs. His sauce recipe would be worth money to you nowadays."

"He never wrote it down."

"Oh, too bad." In his prowling, Leland picked up the writing tablet from the oval table by the sofa. Mally thought of Alex Gambier shut up in the bathroom, wondering if he'd heard when she raised her voice to Leland Howard, hoping Alex had enough sense not to show himself now. Leland looked closely at the words on the tablet, but there wasn't light enough to make for easy reading.

"Letter to my daddy I was writing," Mally said helpfully. Blood throbbing in her temples.

Leland nodded and dropped the tablet on the table. Looked down at her with fuming eyes while he sucked candy clotted on his back teeth.

"What does old Ramses do now, practice medicine in Nashville?"

"No, he teaches at Meharry."

"There's a colored man had the moxie to make something of himself, give credit where it's due." Leland tugged at the knot of his necktie, loosening it. "Getting close in here," he said. Mally was already about to choke on the closeness—his roiled blood, her desperation—in spite of the calm way she sat there meeting him eye to eye.

Leland mopped his forehead with a handkerchief, put it away, came up with a gold-capped silver hip flask. Tilted it high to finish off the bourbon she figured he'd been drinking most of the evening.

"It's been a hard day, Mally," he said, as if he were apologizing for drinking in front of her.

"Yes, sir, I know that," she said, her words barely audible.

"It's not like I'm going to miss the old bastard. You don't have any idea what it was to grow up with somebody had the balls and gall and mean bent of my daddy." His mouth crimped, as if, like a cruelly hazed child, he was close to tears. "And how he must have schemed this past year! Watching me rise up in the world of national politics without his help. That's what he hated most about me; I never asked his help *one* time. When my mama's money ran out, I just took what I wanted and needed from him. Knew he would find out but I didn't care; because what could he hope to do except cover my tracks at the bank? You understanding me, Mally?" His look both begged and demanded her understanding. "Priest Howard's weakness—and I always knew it—was his good name. He would never allow anything or anyone to bring dishonor to *his* name. Now, that made him, and his fuckin' bank, easy pickings. Oh, but you know all this. He would've trusted you, told it to you a dozen times lying up there in his bed with the knowledge his life was over but determined to wreck mine. Bided his time, didn't he? Waited until I was about to enjoy the fruits of my success."

"Mr. Leland—"

"It's all right, Mally. I'm not here looking for your sympathy. You've had it hard yourself, I appreciate that, why I had the desire to help you out with a little of my own money. Scarce as I find it to be these days. On account of I knew Daddy Priest was too stingy to re-ward you. So here it is again . . ."

He pulled out the now-damp envelope with the money and flopped it down on top of the writing tablet.

"Yours alone. Pick it up, feel it, count it, missy. There's ten big ones. Shoo, dog! All you need do to justify keeping that money is hand over what Daddy left behind in your hands to ensure my ruina-tion."

Mally was deathly still during multiple lightning flashes like cam-eras at the scene of a traffic accident while the scent of blood was fresh and strong. An accident in which she sat pinned in wreckage looking out with stunned eyes for a rescuer to arrive.

Leland Howard dragged the back of one hand across his mouth, staring at her, seemingly perplexed by her lack of gratitude.

"Mally?"

"Mr. Leland—I just don't know what you mean."

"Copies of the altered accounts is what I mean. Those investment accounts I jiggered for a year, thirty-five thousand dollars' worth, so I could get out of his bank and his clutches and enjoy a free life! And I suppose he prepared his own account of what I stole and how I did it. I'm a thief—as he correctly named me in his last hour, with you standing by and not missing a word of it."

"But he never mentioned to me, Mr. Leland, what you did! It wasn't my business—"

"Don't think I'm a fool. There was nobody else as close to him in his dying days. Sax? Sax was clear the other side of the state running dealerships Rose Heidi inherited. But Daddy never would have left my fate in Sax's hands for the simple reason Sax never had the nerve to cross me. Burnell? A good soul who couldn't pour pee out of a boot and get it right. No, he chose you. You're bright; you've got education. You were like an angel to the old fucker. So what if you didn't know what you were messing with? I expect he kept his instructions simple. Take this little package, keep it for me. When I'm gone, put it in the mail to the state bank examiner's office. Or the Nashville *Banner.*"

Leland's mouth was spitty from an excess of fervor as he envisioned these possibilities for his eventual downfall. He wiped his mouth again, a hard glitter in his blue eyes.

"That's right. The *Banner,* the *Tennessean,* or the *Press-Scimitar,* that muckraking reporter they got on their political beat. Any goddamn newspaper would print the story! And my ass would be barbecue."

He moved closer to the sofa where she sat trying not to cower and leaned down with a smile.

"But you didn't send it yet, did you? Because you're too bright, and natural curiosity prompted you to open the package. Oh, yeah. I felt this afternoon like you were sending me a message, out at the cemetery."

The tricky light, a flurry of her eyelashes, he interpreted as conspiratorial agreement.

"As the Lord is my witness—" Mally began.

"Now, Mally." He would not be put off.

"I don't." A lick of her lips. "Know anything. Or want a thing from you. I'm not plotting against you, Mr. Leland. Don't want your money. There is—" She had to massage her throat to force more words out. "No way. I could hurt you. Please believe."

"Mal-ly." His face close to hers, reddened, glistening. She could smell him. Talcum, Vitalis hair dressing, sharp perspiration. And something stronger, vile, a disease she couldn't name. Disease of the soul. Strongest of all, the male musk that his blood was heating up. Mally herself drenched in fear. The tension between them had acquired a new tone. Both of them recognizing this at the same time.

"You just tell me what it is you're looking for, Mally." His confident, persuasive, politician's voice. "Anything. I'm an agreeable and willing man. And I can do plenty for a bright, pretty woman."

He raised his eyes, looking over her head at his own face in misty reflection on the glass of the framed military portrait of William Ulysses "Highpockets" Shaw. Taken before some horrid, forever inescapable moment of the war had stopped his emotional machinery like a rifle bullet can stop a pocket watch. The confidence in the man's face inspired Leland's lust to take a turn into deviltry, a raw desire to deface something William had held sacred, although he was long past knowing.

Leland looked back at Mally with a little nod and a wise smile. His face inches from hers.

"Sure. You want us to get better acquainted before we come to terms. That's all right. Been my thinking too, Mally. You haven't had a man to take care of you in a while. How long? Since William shot his head half off?" He put a hand on Mally's thigh. Words whispery now. "Good news is, Mally, my white snake, you could ask around, is the equal of any colored boy's blacksnake you ever went straddle on."

She dropped a hand to his wrist and tugged. In his obscene excitement he was bull-strong. Fingers clutched higher inside her tender thigh.

"I swear on my Bible—Mr. Leland. I'll leave tonight. Won't ever come back to Evening Shade."

"No, Mally. That won't do. I'm needing you too much now that you've got me in a lusty way. Have a look—no, down here you honey." Caught her wrist adroitly and moved her hand toward him as he leaned, bulked up in his trousers. His mouth slackening as he made Mally feel him. She saw the tip of his tongue, bright orange from the candy he'd eaten. "Gal, we are going to be so fine together. Couch isn't big enough for both of us; got yourself a bedroom back there? Are the sheets clean, Mally? I like to have clean sheets. Get yourself naked right now, or I will by God—" backhanding his mouth again, that unpleasant excess of saliva—"tear those nightclothes off myself. You honey. You sweet brown bitch."

Long after the rain had ended—Alex didn't know how much time had passed—he saw Leland Howard and Mally Shaw leave her house by the front porch. Close together, arm-in-arm it looked like, Mally wearing a dress now, and sandals, but she was a little awkward going down the steps, as if she were half-asleep.

He'd last seen both of them as he surreptitiously left the house by the back door. Mally's humiliated body on her bed with cute pillows she'd made, her arms flopping as if useless while he thrust away, Mally just taking it, her eyes closed, both bodies streaming sweat. Alex had been numb from the shock of what he'd witnessed before he fled to the privy twenty yards from the house and sat hunched inside breathing fetid air, rain blowing in through the many chinks between the boards.

He had lingered outside the bedroom door long enough to see that it was ugly, and knew without a doubt she was being raped. He'd heard Mally earlier between thunderclaps, pleading. Mally had called him "Mr. Leland." Alex knew who that was, his face on at least two billboards outside of town. What made it all so bad in his mind as he trembled and chewed a thumbnail to the bloody quick, there wasn't a thing he could do to help her.

When the rain slacked off he moved cautiously out of the privy and made his way down to the boarded-up rib shack and hid again, behind the concrete-block garbage pit that smelled faintly of old burned meat deep down in the ashes. The man who accompanied Leland Howard to Mally's house was smoking inside the Pontiac, the driver's door open and his feet on the running board. Alex could see his face in profile when he drew on his cigarette. He looked country, and rough.

The man got out of the Pontiac and flicked his cigarette away when the screen door squeaked open on the porch. He met Leland Howard and Mally halfway under the spread of still-dripping oak boughs. Leland took something out of his coat pocket, put it in his mouth, and made a sucking sound.

"Mally's going with me up to the farm," Leland said. "We'll take her car. Mally's in a state right now. Can't remember what we need to know or doesn't want to talk. She'll get over it. Meanwhile go inside there, see what you can find. But don't tear the place up."

Leland turned Mally in the direction of her old Dodge. He was half-carrying her, as if Mally were drunk or wounded, or scared half to death. She didn't make a sound. The other man went back to the Pontiac and took a big chromed flashlight from the trunk.

Alex got down lower where he was while Leland coaxed the sluggish Dodge past the rib shack to the highway. He had wanted to see Mally's face but didn't dare to look. He had gooseflesh on his forearms. He felt sick to his stomach.

The man with the flashlight was in Mally's house for a long time. Alex stayed where he was because the only other possibility was to walk away from there, and he wasn't going to leave his bicycle. His lower lip was swollen and sore. He kept thinking about it, that scene in the kitchen when he was trying to get himself a glass of milk and all hell, in the person of Cecily Gambier, broke loose. No idea what she was carrying on about. He hadn't gone near Brendan's nursery, was just home from the show and had been down in the basement looking through his tackle box because he and Bobby—

Then his thoughts jumped to the other scene he wasn't going to forget no matter how long he lived, Mally being raped and the sheer size of Leland Howard, his penis like Popeye's or Dagwood's or Mandrake the Magician's in one of those "Eight-page Bibles" a few boys at school circulated and let certain girls have peeks at, as if their reactions would provide an accurate assessment of their willingness to experiment. He wondered how Francie Swift looked bare-naked and what it would be like to feel her up. Tumult in his groin. Thinking about sex behind a garbage pit while he watched the stealthy beam of the flashlight in Mally's house, another violation of her that he was powerless to do anything about. He had to let Bobby know what had gone on, but would his brother even listen after Cecily gave him an earful about Alex's supposed transgression? He was desperate to be home and in his bed, but what if Cecily had gotten her way finally, told Bobby a big-enough lie so Alex wouldn't be let back in the house? Trouble with that was, he had liked Cecily in the beginning, before the birth of Brendan changed things, his own status. And he didn't believe she was a liar.

Alex dozed off with his back against the fake-brick siding of the rib shack and presently dreamed of his sunny afternoon in the Swifts' pool. Francie was there too, blond hair slicked back, bewitching in her soft-spoken way. They were just lazily cutting up, but Alex was embarrassed; he'd lost his suit somehow, and his own incredibly sized hard-on kept popping up out of the water. Francie was merry about it though; she thought it was the *cutest* thing and wanted to . . .

W*here are we going?"* Mally asked, breaking her silence after fifteen miles of driving. Leland Howard had done the talking, being genial, liking the sound of his own voice probably. Or he was one of those men who just couldn't keep shut for longer than ten seconds. Full of observations and opinions and of course a favorable, boastful slant on his own unique self. ("I've got my little flaws, Mally, Lord knows; but who among us is without human failing? When you get to know me better, you'll learn that I'm a caring man.") Before turning off the hard road onto a rutted and twisty wagon track, barbed wire rusted and sagging on one side, a greenskin slough on the other, Leland had spent a few minutes trying to get across to Mally that there were no hard feelings on his part that she had aroused him to such a randy pitch he just couldn't control himself. Like a little kid with a bedwetting problem. Mally knowing he was going to rape her again, only a question of when and where. No difference to him that she was leaking a little blood, her period coming on days early after his assault. Some men liked that.

The bad road was murder on her old Dodge. She thought the radiator might be leaking again; there was steam from under the hood. She could jump out now and probably not be hurt. But Leland had made her take off her sandals once she was in the car. If it came to a foot race, he had the advantage.

"The farm here," he said, answering her, "was my mother's legacy to me, which I took over when I reached my majority. I was only sixteen months old when she was swept away by the influenza epidemic during the Great War. I blame my old man for that; the bad climate in Washington, D.C., where he did his wartime service, was not agreeable to her."

Mally had no sympathy. Her own faithless mother had run off to Atlanta on the brink of the Depression with a tenor-sax man, never to be heard from again. Severely annoying Mally's father; he had been sour on women and romance from that day on. Sometimes Mally wasn't sure he loved her. Ramses had always been dutiful toward her, kind in his fashion, but she had never heard him say a loving word. In spite of that, at the moment she missed him fiercely.

"I lease out most of my acres," Leland went on. "It's just a place I get up to now and again, use it mostly during quail season. Keep my dogs here. You a dog fancier, Mally?"

She glanced at him; he didn't look as if his mind was on dogs, but on what was still unfinished between them. A farmhouse had come into view, a high barn with a peaked roof over the loft doors, a pond in a meadow. There were poplar trees around the house with their leaves still turned silver-side to the cooled night air. The hard rain passing through had left puddles and a false sheen of health on acres of stunted corn.

Leland parked the Dodge near the front stoop of the house and left the engine running. In the headlights' throw, Mally saw his rangy dogs kenneled beside the large barn. They were running and leaping, rattling the chain-link fencing that enclosed them. But for the most part they were silent, which made them all the more formidable. They were shades of black and gray with plentiful white markings. Because of flop ears and bobbed tails, they resembled some pointers Mally had seen, but their eyes were like blue frost. Those pale whetted eyes, the power in their long legs and deep chests, and most of all the habit of silence gave her a strong chill.

"They are Catahoula leopard dogs," Leland said pridefully. "Spanish war dogs that found their way to the Gulf Coast on some of the early expeditions three centuries ago. Catahoula Indians in the Louisiana Territory got hold of a couple and crossed them with wolves. Nowadays they're bred to track wild boar through the swampland. But they will track anything that moves, Mally, and not make a sound. Like bloodhounds on the scent."

He took out another piece of hard candy. He'd been snacking on the candy since he'd sat up naked and all wrung out on the side of her narrow bed and, no longer tantalized by her liquorish darkness nor moved by tearshine, the low sick sway of her head as she clung to the edge of the bed beside him, told her brusquely to put clothes on. This time he offered candy to Mally, but she looked away. He unwrapped the piece, which turned out to be lime, not his favorite. Popped it into his mouth anyway, beside his rainbow tongue.

"Needing to go round back now, kick on the generator. Turn the house lights on. You can get out of the car if you want. Have a closer look at my dogs." He paused to emphasize what came next. "Let them have a closer look at you." He made the sucking sound she'd learned to despise, savoring his candy. Watching her. She gave him enough of a look to let him know she understood what he meant. Leland nodded. "I thank you for being sensible, not wanting to cause me any trouble."

"No. I wouldn't want to cause you trouble."

"Well, I like the sound of that. We have a ways to go in our relationship, but I do believe it's going to work out fine for both of us. That's so, Mally?"

After a few seconds Mally nodded. "Yes, sir."

A politician's cocksure smile, all the necessary votes in his pocket. "Why don't you just call me Leland from here on?"

Not waiting for her to reply. He backhanded his mouth as if the candy was making it water again and got out of the car, walked around the side of the house calling jovially to his dogs. Three in all. They had girl names, "Tootsie" being one Mally caught. The bitch Catahoulas romped along their concrete run, sensing release from boredom, the far-ranging freedom of an imminent hunt. Mally felt a shrinking of her heart as she crossed arms over sore breasts. Thinking about what she would have to do soon to Leland Howard. Wondering if she had the nerve.

B*obby Gambier walked into his house* at five minutes to two in the morning. The power was still off. Hurricane lamps burned in the parlor and the downstairs hall. His loved ones and his mother-in-law, he supposed, had long since gone up to their beds. He picked up the lamp from the cedar hope chest and continued to the kitchen, opened the fridge and pulled out a beer.

He sat at the table with the bottle in one hand, staring at the lamp flame and his reflection in the chimney. Then he looked at Alex's wastebasket on one of the ladderback chairs around the table. After a couple of minutes he reached for the wastebasket and inventoried what was in it without touching anything. Shriveled apple core, couple of seeds like mouse eyes staring at him, pencil shavings, wadded pages of yellow copy paper that had been typed on, greasy tissues, and the nearly empty jar of petroleum jelly. Bobby got up, opened a cabinet drawer where they stored grocery sacks from the Piggly Wiggly, and dumped the contents of the wastebasket into the sack, which he folded down from the top a couple of times. The kitchen door wouldn't open; a key was stuck in the lock. He went outside by way of the front door and put the Kraft paper sack on the back seat of his station wagon, which had been his father's and nearly new the night of the fire that had buried Sheriff Robert beneath charcoal beams in the cellar and, days later, finally killed Bobby's mother, who was lying comatose and wrapped like a mummy for delivery to the saints in a room of the Baptist hospital in Memphis. The Packard had been parked in a carport beside the house, but volunteer firemen had rolled it to the street before it burned up too.

Lights in the neighborhood came back on while he was in the driveway. When he returned to the kitchen, Cecily was there, elbows on the table, holding an icepack against the right side of her head.

"I heard you come in," she said. "Can't sleep."

Bobby kissed her and was aware of a whiff of vomit on her breath.

"Bad one?"

"Yeah. Bobby, did you—?"

"No sign of him." He pulled a sack of potato chips out of the breadbox, sat down at the table opposite her. Cecily could barely open her eyes; they looked as if they were drowning in headache pain. He drank the rest of his beer, looking sympathetically at her.

"Alex will turn up, won't he?"

"Sure."

"What then?"

"Tell me what he did to you, Cece."

"Grabbed me. On my arm."

"That's all?" Bobby said, wolfing chips.

"Yes."

"Why?"

"He, I think it was, he wanted to get my attention. I was already off the deep end, you know how I—"

"But he didn't hurt you."

"Bobby, what difference now? It's what he did upstairs that matters. That was deliberate. As if he's totally lost his mind."

Bobby pushed the potato-chip sack aside, rolled the beer bottle between his palms.

"What time has it got to be?" Cecily asked.

"After two."

"Everything's closed, even the pool hall. Where could he have gone?"

"I don't know. Do you care?"

"Please don't take that attitude. We have to do something about him. *For* him. I know Alex isn't a mean kid, but if he's having these—wrong impulses, where he can hurt somebody or maybe himself, then we have to get help for him right away."

"What has your mother had to say about all this?"

"When she calmed down and we talked it out, she agreed with me. Just a question of money, Mom told me, don't give it another thought. She's ready to write a check tomorrow for professional help, you know, psychiatric care in a *good* place, not the awful asylum down there in Bolivar."

Bobby put the beer bottle down and rubbed smarting eyes with a knuckle, feeling overcome by a grim sense of inadequacy and fear for his brother.

"If you love me," Cecily said, "and you love Brendan, then you have to do what's right."

"Got to find Alex first."

"You're not thinking about going out again?"

"No. The deps on the twelve-eight are on the lookout for Alex. Maybe he'll show up here. What the hell, I don't know. Let's go to bed, Cece."

"I'm so nauseated. I was this morning too. Bobby, I'm not sure yet, but I may be pregnant again." She laughed, then sobbed, looking to him for help, for his love. His eyes were no longer bleak, just amazed and a little bewildered. A daddy times two.

"Now you quit that, you hear?" Bobby said, smiling and blinking away a tear of his own.

"Listen to w-who's talking."

Bobby got up to kneel at her side and cradle her head in the hollow of his shoulder.

Mally *caught Leland Howard* on the right side of his head with the heavy, butt end of the brass fireplace poker. He'd been standing sweaty naked with his back to her getting a cigar going. He hadn't fucked her this time in his own bedroom—not sure of the condition of the sheets—but down on a blanket thrown over some davenport cushions in the living room. Just before she struck him he had a rosy look of satisfaction, puffing away with head tilted to the ceiling, no doubt pleased with his stamina and her own spiritless compliance. Quite sure he'd worn her out as she lay there with a lax hand lying on her pudenda. Facing the brick fireplace.

So Mally reached out and lifted the sooty poker from the rack of fireplace tools, reversed it as she twisted around in a catlike crouch, uncoiled with her well-aimed swing. Years ago William had shown her how to hit a baseball. The same principles applied. There was a loud, meaty smack but no underlying deadly crunch of bone in his hard skull. The blow staggered Leland sideways, cigar flying from his fingers. He fell on one knee, then pitched against the wall beside the fireplace, his eyes haphazard, closing as she crouched again, taut and wild, with the poker raised and back for another swing.

But he was out, and the only sound she heard was a slow fart as Leland's body settled inertly, knees under him, head upright in the angle made by the wall and the side of the fireplace.

The surge of adrenaline, her heart knocking, then the contents of her stomach coming up. Mally projectile-vomited, and for a minute afterward was so dizzy she had to sit down on the cushionless davenport to collect herself, fright stirring up her mind. What if she'd killed him? She stared at a blue welt an inch below his temple, blood oozing from the ear on the side where she had hit him. Then at his chest, which rose and fell in a shallow rhythm. Her gaze dropped to her own body, knees wide apart, the mess clabbering her inner thighs, her blood and his dribbled stuff. She choked and thought she was going to heave again, her sore stomach trying to turn itself inside out.

In the kitchen she wet a dish towel and held onto the counter with one hand while she cleaned herself. She wanted to lie down somewhere and just go to sleep. Instead she tossed the bloody towel into the sink, ran water again and filled her bitter mouth from the tap, rinsed and spat three times.

When she returned to the living room one of his legs was moving and an eye had peeped open like a speck of blue sky in his grayish face. Mally was terrified. He was looking at her but not as if he knew who she was or what had happened to him. Mally had attended to enough accident victims during her hospital training to know that he was a long way from being fully conscious and ambulatory, which helped her calm down.

She dressed quickly while Leland Howard continued to stir ineffectually and make hurt little moans. Then she went through his jacket and trouser pockets looking for her car keys. Couldn't find them. Terror again. Leland's head lolled and his eyes opened wider but remained insensate.

She came across the money in the envelope he'd baited her with, hesitated, then took one of the bills, enough money to get her to Nashville and the safety of her father's house. Safe for a few days at least, while they decided what she must do.

If she couldn't drive her car, then he wasn't going to drive it to chase her down either.

Outside she plunged a bread knife from the kitchen into bald spots on the old front tires. Retrieved her sandals, kept the knife, and jogged down the farm road, calculating how far it must be to the highway. Not more than a mile. She had good wind and felt that she could cover the distance, dodging mud puddles, in under ten minutes. No hope of transportation, a bus, so late at night. She would have to find herself a cabin on another farm, friendly folk to take her in.

The stars were out, the night quiet except for the harried sounds of her breathing, slip-slap of sandaled feet. The cooled air freighted with sharp wild odors of fields and low-standing water and her own, human heat and mistings that only a hound's nose could raise. She could see the moon bobbing out of the corner of her eye at the level of scarecrow trees along the owl-haunted slough. Careful about her footing, but she slipped twice and muddied herself. Tasted a swallow of blood from her tongue. She had to pause, once the farmhouse was well behind her, and snatch some breath, leaned-over and holding her knees, fear using her up faster than she had anticipated.

Mally looked back once and saw nothing, looked back again as she resumed her jog and saw the Catahoula dogs coursing in her tracks, coming twice as fast as she could hope to run in mud-caked sandals. Not a sound out of them, only the icy wolfen shine of their eyes by bold moonlight, and that was the horror of it.

Past tangled barbed wire in a pasture to her left she glimpsed a tree she could climb and a few cows standing beneath its low boughs. She tore her flesh getting over fenceline the dogs would leap across with ease and ran for the sanctuary of the spreading oak as the cows, alert to her fear and aware of dogs on the hunt, began to lumber off. Mally stumbled over a snakelike root and fell into cowshit, lost her grip on the bread knife. She groped for it, jumped up again thinking that if she could only get her back against the broad trunk of the tree, then—

Alex woke up with a chilling start when a cockroach skittered across a bare instep. He shook his foot and heard the Pontiac's engine rev up with a series of roars as if the man driving was stomping-mad about something. After turning the car around he cut out of there spewing gravel from beneath the whitewall tires. A small rock skipped over the top of the garbage pit, hitting Alex near the left temple. The pain and injustice of being unexpectedly struck again caused him to flood.

When he had cried himself out and thought it was safe, Alex got up to retrieve his bicycle from Mally's porch. He didn't know what time it was and couldn't locate the moon; it seemed to be low behind the trees west of the house. He heard a car on the highway as he was taking his bike down the steps. His blood turned cold enough to start him trembling. He dropped the bike and crouched beside the steps, but the car went past. He recognized one of the homely '49 Fords from the sheriff's department, important-looking chromed bullet lights above the windshield. Momentarily he thought it might be Bobby out looking for him. More likely it was only one of the rookie deputies on the boring midnight-to-eight-a.m. shift.

As he was about to get on his bike, it occurred to Alex that he didn't have anywhere else to go. Dead of night, he was nine miles from the house on West Hatchie and at least a million miles from anyone's good graces. Tired as he was, still he'd manage to peddle to the house, but then what? Would he be given a chance to justify himself? The older he got the more he needed to speak, and the more distant that possibility became. He hadn't tried for over a year, and then, prompted by the goodwill of a teacher he had admired and wanted to please, he had strangled on a single syllable in a roomful of tittering classmates. Turned red and just died there in his seat, furious, helpless.

All he could think of was that he might have given Cecily a bad scare, but it wasn't as if he purposely had sneaked up on her in the kitchen.

Reminding him: What was his wastebasket doing there? What did she mean, *I found it*? The expression on her face like he was in the habit of doing dumps in his own wastebasket. *For Chrissake,* as Holden Caulfield would have put it. Alex had recently discovered Holden as a soulmate, and, although *Catcher in the Rye* was six days' overdue at the library, he was reading it for the second time.

Whatever Cecily's problem was, it was all *her* problem, and Alex took small comfort knowing from past incidents he had more or less innocently precipitated that it should all settle out given enough time.

He looked back at the house with a quick flare of anger. This thing *wouldn't* settle out. If he ever had the chance, one chance to get even with Leland Howard for what he'd done to Mally tonight—

But it was Bobby who would deal with him. Bobby was the Law, and the Law was more powerful than a man with his face on billboards.

Thinking of his older brother with the gold badge pinned to his uniform shirt pocket, Alex felt proud and confident of the doctrine of just desserts.

He yawned. Couldn't know if Mally would return tonight, but he doubted it. Even when she eventually did come home, probably it wouldn't bother her knowing he had stayed there. For cry-eye, Mally had enough to be upset about already.

James Giles arrived at Leland Howard's farm to find Leland in a rocking chair in the yard looking as if he had survived a bad accident and got drunk afterward. There was crusty blood in his hair above his right ear. The front of his white shirt had blood all over it. He was barefoot, having discarded his shoes. Which were bloody as well, as if he had danced the night away in an abattoir. The fifth of Old Crow he'd been working on was three-quarters empty. His face was dirty, with tear tracks through the dirt.

Giles looked him over carefully and looked at the dogs in the kennel, either asleep or just lolling, as if they'd been run hard. Before Leland spoke Giles already had a chilling idea of what had happened here.

"James, James, it wasn't my fault! I don't know what to do, James."

Giles walked closer to the man who employed him and could send him back to Brushy Mountain Prison on a whim and took the bottle of Kentucky whiskey away from him.

"What happened?"

"Mally hit me with a poker when my back was turned and ran off."

"After that."

"Well, she—I didn't know which way she'd gone."

"Turn the dogs loose then?"

"It's not my fault! I didn't know they would—"

"You damn fool," Giles said in his customary low-pitched voice, no special emotion in this assessment. "Ever one of those Catahoula bitches is in heat. They can be mean cusses then. The nigger woman have blood on her?"

"I think she did, James. I *think* she was into her period. Not fly-ing the flag, but there was a bloody dish towel in the kitchen she might've used on herself. I let the dogs have a whiff on it."

"You damn fool," Giles said again. He took a kitchen match from his shirt pocket and chewed on the wood. It helped his thinking. "You'd have done the woman better to pour gasoline over her and light her up."

"I didn't know, I didn't think!" Leland cried, rocking furiously. "I didn't know so much blood could come out of a human body. She's dead, James."

"Most likely." Giles looked around and didn't see a corpse. He looked at the Dodge nearby, wondering why Mally had been afoot. But there were two flat tires. "Show me where they caught up to her."

"I can't go back there! I can't look at her again. You don't know what those Catahoulas did once they got ahold—"

"Yes, I do." Giles tilted the whiskey bottle and emptied it, slung the bottle high over the roof of the house. He put a hand on Leland's shoulder and bore down, squeezing until Leland gasped in pain. "You ready to quit that damn rocking now? Listen to me?"

"Jesus, I've got a whopper of a headache. I think I need to go to the doctor; I'm still seeing double."

"No doctor." Giles looked down at the gold lozenge of the Bulova watch on Leland Howard's left wrist. "Three, maybe three and a half hours to sunup. And you don't want her body found any-wheres near your place."

"What can I do? No matter what, I'm a ruined man!"

"Start with, get up out of that granny rocker." When Leland didn't obey, Giles lifted him out of the seat by his shoulder. Leland began to weep again. Giles slapped him on the undamaged side of his face, fingers stinging like bony whips.

"You're still a man. An important man. Don't go throw it all away count of some trifling nigger woman."

"But they'll say I killed her!"

"Not if we do this thing right. Shut up your blubbering. Go in the house and clean yourself up while I get a couple tarps. You didn't kill nobody. Can't call it murder necessarily; reckon it's a style of murder. Dogs got after her; well, that's just how they'll say it was. Pack of wild dogs. Nobody's fault less'n hers for being in the wrong place tonight. You never got seen with her; that puts you in the clear." He gave Leland a shove toward the house. "Hurry it up. I need to get two spares on that old Dodge and butcher a hog. Twenty minutes, you better had be sober enough to drive."

"Why are you doing this, James? Why are you helping me?"

"Two months since my parole, you never lorded it over me. Reckon when you make it to the high station you're bound for, a pardon won't be out of the question."

"That's right. Whatever you want, James. Whatever's in my power—"

"I never did have no big wants. Like to get my name clear, that's all. Now get going, Mr. Howard." Leland had taken a couple of steps when Giles remembered. "By the way. Didn't find such as you told me to look for in the woman's house. But that there be a problem for another day."

In his dreams Alex was exploring Mally's house and finding rooms he hadn't known were there. One was exactly like the reading room at the Evening Shade Public Library where he spent a lot of time: shelves of reference books and a couple of maple tables with green-shaded lamps on them. The placid old soul of a librarian behind her desk, distance in her eyes, listening to her books like a sailor listens to the sea. He wished he could settle down with a good novel by Ernest Haycox or a *Saturday Evening Post* serial by Luke Short, but he caught a glimpse of Mally in the stacks and followed her instead.

Then he was inside the boarded-up depot at Cole's Crossing, where no trains had stopped since before the war. He could recall having been there only once, when he was about three years old. The trains that had stopped were sooty locals with antiquated rolling stock, mixed baggage and coach. Only a handful of passengers, nearly all of them colored, getting on or off.

In his dream he was looking up at the familiar octagonal clock with Roman numerals above the closed ticket window. The clock seemed not to be working. Bobby stood on a tall ladder taking it apart, finding the works clotted with old pink bubblegum. He didn't have time to talk to Alex, who felt guilty. Although he knew it wasn't his bubblegum. He wasn't allowed to chew gum in the house, another of Cece's rules.

Cecily and Bernice were playing hearts in a corner of the depot. Cece was naked, as she often was in his dreams. They were using a coffin for a card table. Alex's mother lay in the coffin. He was furious with Cece and Bernice. Such disrespect. Why didn't they close the lid? He could smell the stuff they'd put on his mother's burns. And coal smoke that poured from a black locomotive standing on the tracks outside the depot.

Mally Shaw was on the platform. When she saw him, she shook her head as if she was annoyed about something he'd done. Everybody had rules where he was concerned. Maybe it was because he had slept uninvited in her house. He started to run down the long platform toward her, but his feet like Wyatt Sexton's were on wrong. Wherever he willed himself to go, he stumbled in another direction. Mally boarded the grim-looking train while he flopped around with misery in his soul. Alan Ladd came along leading an Indian pony by the reins and told Alex it was ten cents to ride for ten minutes. Alex found himself on the pony's back, but he was three years old now and scared. Just trying to hang on while the pony broke into a trot. But there was no saddle, and he was slipping slowly off the back of the pony, going upside down beneath its belly before finally falling . . .

Alex woke up on the floor beside the bamboo sofa. He sat up and although it was still dark and his eyes were tearing he saw Mally in the hall down by her bedroom looking around at him.

"It's over, sugar." she said. "Go back to sleep." She went into her bedroom and he heard the door close.

He tried to lie down again on the cushions with his knees bent the way he had made himself almost comfortable earlier, but now he had a crick in his neck and he needed to pee.

When he passed Mally's bedroom the door was standing open, although he was sure she'd closed it. Moonlight filled the little room with its rumpled bed, reminding him of what he'd seen going on there during the rainstorm. Some clothing strewn about, her intimate things.

Every corner of the room was alight, and Mally was not there.

Nor was she in the bathroom, or the kitchen, or standing outside on the back porch where he ultimately chose to relieve himself, arcing into the weeds around the cistern while listening pensively to peepers and the early staccatos and trillings of birds in the back woods.

When he was inside again, he spoke her name a couple of times but knew the house was empty except for himself, although he had clearly seen Mally for a couple of seconds, heard her voice. Then heard the closing of the bedroom door. The hidden rooms of Mally's house had existed only in his fretful dreams.

Now he was alone, but he had not been alone.

Go back to sleep, she had said, fondness in her tone.

Alex rubbed the prickling skin of his forearms.

Not much chance of that.

FIVE

Secret Pleasure

The 4:10 from Nashville

Showdown at Pee-Wee's Good Eats

The closest parishioners *to Little Grove Holiness*
Church were Elder Ike Thurmond, his wife Zerah and their eight
children. They lived on a farm less than half a mile away from the
church and graveyard at Cole's Crossing. Ike and two of his brothers,
who had made their break away from furnish and shares in '37 with
the aid of loans from FDR's Farm Security Administration, now
leased some good bottomland along the Yella Dog. The brothers
made out fine on the eighty-odd acres of corn in good times and
squeezed by on the proceeds from a sawmill and a machine shop they
also owned when the rains didn't fall in dry years like this one.

Ike had just begun to stir in his bed, as always—Sundays not
excepted—anticipating his Dominecker roosters by about five minutes, when he heard something he hadn't heard for going on twenty
years: the deep sound of the old iron church bell at Little Grove Holiness. It had been so long since that bell had rung he'd all but forgotten its particular tonal quality.

He was a good six foot six in spite of the shrinkages of age and
numerous infirm joints, and at seventy still had a grip on all his precious faculties. So he wasn't imagining this nor hearing another
church bell carrying from a greater distance in the stillness before
dawn. Next closest church was New Life Baptist in the Adair community, four and a half miles down the Southern's main line. White
folks' church. But a cracked bell on a rusted vertex didn't just ring
out suddenly, any more than he could jump out of bed as spry as if
he were nineteen again. It took plenty of Sloan's Liniment, applied

by Zerah, and four packets of Goody's Headache Powder just to get him down the stairs for that first cup of coffee.

But he was hearing a bell all right; if not *the* bell, then one that tolled like it.

His wife reached out for him suddenly with cold, wrinkled fingers; at fifty her own impairments were hypertension from salty food, a common complaint of the women in her community, and fading eyesight due to cataracts.

"What's that I hear, Ike?"

"Church bell."

"Like it was just down the road."

"Must be."

"But."

"I know."

"It ain't rung in how long?"

"We hearin' it spite of, that's all I know, 'cause I ain't deef and you ain't crazy."

Zerah uttered a low, adulatory moan with a religious fervor that had the sparse hair on his crown wanting to stand up. "Sweet name of Jeee-zuss! You don't reckon?" She gripped him fiercely.

"The Lord's done us a wonder?"

One of the younger kids had appeared in their doorway rubbing her eyes.

"Church bell woked me up."

"Get in the bed here," Zerah told her, "and go back to sleep. Ike?"

"I's gwine," Ike, not such a ready believer in miracles, said with a shudder of apprehension. Church bells tolled for many reasons, but seldom in a dark hour of a new day. "What did you do with my Goody's?"

"Put your Sunday suit on," Zerah told him, still in the grip of a fervor willing to become full-fledged ecstasy. "Never know what you'll meet up with."

"Mean *who,* don't you?" Ike said, with another shudder that tormented his painful lower back.

Sunup, *and just east of Lexington, Tennessee,* traveling through the middle of the state on the long haul to Knoxville, Jim Giles had to pull over again so Leland Howard could be sick in the weedy ditch beside the two-lane blacktop.

He climbed back into the Pontiac Eight gray as Caesar's ghost and sat in a semisprawl with his eyes heavy-lidded, breathing through his mouth. Giles got them rolling again. Leland squinted and flinched at the first influx of sunlight.

"I've had bad hangovers. This one's like I went over Niagara Falls in a barrelful of cannonballs."

Giles grunted something. He was chewing one of his kitchen matches.

Leland marveled at his calm. How he took the worst of things unflinchingly, expression seldom changing. He was a thick-lipped country man with a brutalized nose, hard knocks all over his face, gray eyes deeply countersunk beneath a jut of brow, strawberry hair fading to a widow's-peak frizz.

"You ever been sick-drunk, James?"

"No. Never had no fondness for the alkyhall myself."

"Well, I'm swearing off. Taking the pledge. Know I've said that before, usually after a hellacious Mardi Gras, but this time I mean it."

"Yes sir, Mr. Howard."

"Eastbound, we'll have the goddamn sun in our faces a good six hours." Leland adjusted the pillow behind his head with a series of pokes. "When do you think they'll find her, James? Wouldn't have found her already, would they?"

"Couldn't say. What does it matter?"

Leland shielded his eyes with one hand as if searching for a penetrating insight into the future and peeped sideways at Giles.

"Then you . . . still think we're going to get away with it?"

"No reason why not. What you need do now is put it all out of your mind. Try to get some sleep."

Leland winced as he swallowed. Sleep? Not with his case of nerves. And his throat was sand-dry. But if he took a drink of water or coffee from one of the thermos bottles they had with them, the next time the Pontiac gave a lurch on the lumpy highway his stomach would throw it back at him. Better to suffer the dryness for now.

He wondered just what kind of fiendish death he looked like at this hour. But nothing could best how Mally Shaw had appeared, the glimpse he'd had of her remains by flashlight rolling out of that tarp at the cemetery's threshold before James Giles went to work with the one Catahoula dog they had brought with them and the gallon jug of fresh pig's blood to, as Giles put it with his tight, sardonic smile, make it more real than anyone, even lawmen accustomed to accident scenes, could bear to look at for long.

With a passion in his breast that was akin to worship, Leland said, "I don't know what I'd've done without you, James."

Giles rolled down his window and discarded his chewed match into the slipstream, reached another from his shirt pocket.

"That's all right, Mr. Howard."

Leland closed his eyes again and tried once more to make himself comfortable.

"What I want you to do is, after you leave me off in Knoxville, get on back to Evening Shade and hang around for a while, keep your ears open. Don't worry about me; one of the campaign volunteers can do the driving next few days. Then I'll be back in Nashville for the big rally at the Parthenon before the primary Tuesday week. We'll meet up there."

After a few moments Giles said, "All right, Mr. Howard."

"Of course if anything comes up—"

"Don't reckon there will be a problem. What else is there to make of a nigger woman got herself mauled to death by wild dogs when she was paying a visit to the grave of her dead husband?"

"I tend to be a worrier, James."

"She's meeting up with the Lord this minute."

"Are you a churchgoing man, James?"

122

That sardonic smile again. "No. Don't believe in the afterlife nei-ther. It was just a manner of speaking."

"I learn something new about you every day, James. Now, I've often wondered. You're forty-two years old—"

"Forty-three."

"Did you ever get in trouble over a woman?"

"I leave the women alone, Mr. Howard."

"Except for an occasional visit to a whorehouse?"

"Never have set foot in a whorehouse. Them kind of pussy don't appetize me."

"Wish I could stay out of whorehouses, 'sall I know. Could be my fatal weakness. But what do you do, pardon my asking, when you get cravings, if you don't like women all that much?"

"There's boys," James Giles said.

"Boys?"

"Not saying little squirts. Boys. When they are just full-hung but not shaving yet. Maybe oncet a week they shave. Those are my meat, Mr. Howard."

"Oh," Leland looked away, his mind hopping off that touchy subject like fleas abandoning a dead dog.

Giles said, "There's a truck stop up the road apiece, this side the river. Recollect they don't never close. I could do with a stack of buckwheats and a pot of black coffee, fried ham and gravy drippings on the side."

Leland's stomach cramped at the thought of all that grease.

"I'll get along without breakfast, but stop whenever you feel like it, James."

"Well, all right, sir."

Alex Gambier had the rest of Mally's spice cake and most of her buttermilk for breakfast. He hung around her house until about eight-thirty Sunday morning and then, growing restless, got on his bike and rode toward town, intending to return later in the day to find out if she'd made it home okay and if there was anything he could do to help her out. Also he was sure that Bobby would want to talk to her as soon as Alex told his brother about the rape.

He had pedaled a couple of miles beside the highway when a sheriff's department car pulled even with him and the deputy driving motioned for him to stop.

The deputy was Skip Stallworth, to whom Alex was related on his mother's side. Skip was beefy, crewcut, and took petty authority too seriously. He was still screwing high-school girls, and obviously he had gotten himself some the night before: There were fresh hickeys on his neck, as if he'd been set upon by a toothless vampire.

"Your brother said if any of us was to meet up with you this morning, run you straight over to the courthouse 'cause he needs to talk to you."

That was unusual, because Bobby didn't work Sundays even if Luther Tebbetts was out of town.

Alex wrestled his bike into the back of the Ford and joined the deputy in the front seat.

"Been awhile," Skip said. "Seen you around town now and then. You still not talking? What is that anyway; you got a bad stuh-stuh-stutter you don't want nobody to hear?"

Alex shot his cousin a birdie.

"Spit on it and sit on it," Skip advised, grinning and going heavy on the accelerator because he liked driving fast and scaring the bejesus out of other motorists even when there was no emergency to respond to. "So keep your fuckin' mouth shut, have the little gals feelin' sorry for you, but garntee the only ass you'll ever get will have VD or feathers all over it." He whistled a little tune, added words. "'Take it away, I don't want it; slept all night with my hand on it.' By the way, Bobby's in a cussed frame of mind, so I'd watch my step."

Alex looked Skip over.

"Well, one thing, he had to come in to work of a Sunday. There was a body found out by Cole's Crossing early this morning. I ain't too clear if it was a hobo fell under a freight train or maybe set upon by wild dogs. Come to think, Dispatch said likely it were a woman's body." He returned Alex's look. "Ever see a dead body? Hell, I forgot. They done pulled old Shurf Bob out of your burned-up house a few years ago. That must have been a sight to behold."

Alex crossed his arms and stared through the bug-sprinkled windshield. For the fun of it Skip wound the Ford's mill up to a snarling ninety until they reached the edge of town, where the highway made a sharp up-and-downhill curve around the Evening Shade waterworks and he had to slow down. Also he had been trying to see if he could make Alex flinch, but got no reaction. Alex's eyes were slits, his pulses calm. He had no fear of machines or events that could kill him. Alex had faced down the *Dixie Traveler,* and that was just sport to him. Knowing that Skip would have shit himself royally—if he had the nerve to be on the track in the first place—filled Alex with secret pleasure.

T*he Sheriff's department and county jail* were in the court-house basement where some daylight sifted in through chickenwire-reinforced windows that were partly above ground level, the lower halves enclosed by gravel-lined window wells.

Bobby Gambier was out of uniform, drinking coffee and talking on a phone by the dispatch bullpen when Alex came down the steps by way of the parking-lot entrance. Without comment or a clue to his mood, Bobby pointed Alex to his office. He joined Alex a couple of minutes later, closing the door behind him.

"Had you any breakfast?" Bobby said, sitting on the edge of his cluttered desk and sipping coffee, regarding his little brother with a combination of wariness and skepticism, not liking the role he had to play right now.

Alex nodded.

"That lip is where Cecily popped you?"

Alex touched his sore and puffy lower lip and grimaced slightly.

"Well, I'm sorry she did that, and by now she probably is too. You know Cece; she lets things get out of hand way too easy. Not to make light of the stunt you pulled to bring it on."

Alex shrugged and shook his head, still having no idea of what the hell.

"Jesus name, Twig, where did you get such a damn-fool idea, smear Vaseline on the bottom of the bathtub? Was that in some library book you—"

Alex leaped out of his chair just as the door to Bobby's office was opened. A deputy looked in and said, "Ready on your call to Nashville."

Bobby motioned to Alex, *stay put,* ignoring the boy's outraged, boiling-over expression, and sat down behind his desk. He picked up the telephone receiver, tight-lipped, and leaned into an old strawback support cushion with springs popping out through the sides.

"Mr. Val Gene? This is—oh, *doctor,* I see, and Val John is how you—well—this is Bobby Gambier. I'm undersheriff here in Evening Shade? Yes, that's right, he was my father. The reason I'm calling this morning, I'm afraid I have some bad news regarding your daughter, Mally Shaw."

Alex's expression changed again as he stared at Bobby, one hand flexing at his side, his lips parting as if he were subvocalizing Mally's name; then his face seemed to freeze from dread. Bobby didn't look at him. His eyes were fixed on his inky, scrawled-over desk blotter that was filled with doodles, names, phone numbers, while his mind was fully occupied with the difficulties of a bereavement call. He scooted his swivel chair closer to the desk and picked up an uncapped fountain pen.

"Yes. Unfortunately that's how it is. She was uh discovered dead early today near the Little Grove Holiness church, in the cemetery there, you're familiar with—? No, not murdered. But it was a terrible thing I'm sorry to say from all we know of it. Seems Mally got jumped by a pack of wild dogs while she was paying a visit to her late husband William's gravesite. I don't know how to put it any more—uh-huh. Reason we figure why she was out there at such an early hour was she had a vase of flowers with her; we found them scattered—. How's that? No, we—I'm not understanding the reason you asked me that, it surely is not a very pleasant—. Well, if you truly feel the need. Yes. I do appreciate that you want to be satisfied in your—. No, certainly wouldn't be much trouble for us to do that, I'll see to it. Yes. Um-hmm. Sure. They are still in business. Godsong and Wundall are the only colored undertake—. I'll look up their phone number for you in just—. No, couldn't say for sure. You would have to ask them that yourself."

Bobby paused in his doodling, responding to a draft from the hall, where the big standing fans at each end already had been turned on although it was only a few minutes past nine in the morning. Another scorcher on the way. His office door was wide open. Alex was gone.

Cecily *came into the kitchen*, where Bobby and Brendan were having a disagreement about the goodness of the Gerber's carrots Bobby was trying to spoon into the baby's mouth, and said, "Alex is outside in the street on his bike, riding around in circles and staring at the house. What do you want to do?"

With his little finger Bobby scooped a dribble of spit and carrots off Brendan's chin and said, "Talk to him. If he'll just quit running off whenever I try." He made another attempt with the carrots and Brendan made a face. "Is it always this hard getting him to eat?"

"You have to sort of play with Brendy when it comes to vegetables. What you do is, mix those carrots up with some applesauce."

"I like them better that way myself."

"You didn't say a word about my new dress."

"It's a winner. What do you call that material?"

"Organdy."

"What's your mother wearing to church this morning, sackcloth and ashes?"

"Ha, ha. Wish you were going with us. Everybody thinks you're a heathen."

"I'll repent on my deathbed, Cece." Bobby twisted the cap off a jar of junior applesauce. "Okay, Booger, try this."

"Bobby, I just wish you wouldn't call him that."

"I wish you wouldn't call him 'Brendy.' Sounds like a kid who's signed up for dance school."

Cecily let that one go by. Her mother called from the front of the house, "Cecily, it's six minutes to eleven! Our pew will be full before we get there!"

Bobby got up to give Cecily a kiss. He liked the scent she had on this morning. It came off the nape of her neck when the swivel head of the fan on the sink counter turned toward her.

"Where'd you say you and Bernie were going after church?"

"Visitation. We're taking the casserole I made and some magazines out to Midge Prechter; you know that hip of hers just refuses to heal. Are you sure you won't need me until, say, three o'clock?"

"Huh-uh."

"Just a little bit of carrots and the rest applesauce is how you get it past him," Cecily reminded, giving Brendan a buss on the forehead where he hadn't managed to splash any of his food.

Bobby smiled and patted Cecily's midsection with his clean hand.

"You going to say anything to your mother about what we suspicion?"

"Sus*pect*."

"I know; I went to college too. That's just my down-home courtroom talk. You never want a jury to think you're smarter than they are. Got to lead 'em to the conclusion you want them to make."

"No, I don't want to say anything to her about another baby. It's just between us, if it's true. Bobby, are you going to let Alex in the house while I'm gone?"

"Yeah."

"Just keep an eye, all right?"

"Sure."

"And you *are* going to tell him?"

"Well, it's come down to that, hasn't it?"

"I know how hard this is on you, Bobby. But it's none of your doing. You know that Alex has been asking for it."

Alex *watched Cecily and her mother* drive away in Cecily's Plymouth instead of walking the four blocks to the Methodist church, whose bells and the bells of three other churches around town were tolling eleven o'clock, an all-points summons to the tardy and a reminder to the doubters and backslid few of the community that their sloth or disbelief would not go unreckoned with.

Neither Alex nor Bobby Gambier had been big on churchgoing since the cruel death of their parents. Just the way it was.

Bobby came outside with a cleaned-up and freshly diapered Brendan and put him down to crawl in the grass. He put a booted foot up on one of the painted wagon wheels, covered with climbing roses, on either side of the walk. He had a smoke, compounding his spiritual felonies on the Lord's day.

Alex parked his bike against the low rail-and-lattice fence and came over, reeking of dried sweat. Bobby offered him a drag.

"Now get inside and wash. Change your clothes and don't leave a mess. I'll wait for you on the porch; we've got serious talking to do."

Alex shook his head, held up two fingers together, nodded toward the house. Brendan scrambled toward him and latched onto an ankle, began pulling himself up Alex's leg.

"What do I need to go with you for?" Bobby asked.

Alex gave him a steady look. *Because.*

Bobby shrugged and looked at Brendan. "Want to carry him?"

Alex nodded.

"You two get along, don't you?" Alex lifted Brendan and swung him onto his shoulders. Bobby followed them into the house and up the stairs. Alex's shoulders were getting tired. He handed Brendan over to Bobby and went into the bathroom. Bobby dangled Brendan upside down for a few seconds, which he never did when Cecily was watching, then turned the baby right-side up. They both laughed. "Remember how I told you your eyeballs would fall out if I did that?" Bobby said to Alex. "You believed me too."

Alex had other matters on his mind. In the bathroom he pointed at the tub, then pointed to himself and shook his head vehemently.

"So you didn't do it."

No.

"Guess it must have been Rhoda or maybe the Antichrist then."

Alex took a shaker of talcum powder from a shelf and got down on one knee to spread the powder on an eight-by-eight dark blue tile. He wrote in the powder with a forefinger, *She did it dumbass.*

Brendan wanted to get down and play in the powder too. Bobby draped him casually over one shoulder, holding him by the ankles, forgetting that Brendan had just had his lunch.

"Bernie, you mean."

Alex looked up, nodded.

"I can hardly wait to tell that one to Cecily. 'Hey Cece, your mom greased the tub so she'd slip and bust her head open.'" Bobby grimaced after he'd spoken, and he looked away from Alex, staring through the opened windows above the tub, higher than mosquitoes ordinarily traveled. Alex knew the look on Bobby's face. He got up and dusted his hands on his shorts, unbuttoned his fly, and stood over the toilet. He looked back at Bobby while he was whizzing.

"No, guess that's not why she would've done it," Bobby said, swinging Brendan back and forth like a pendulum. Brendan squealing with delight until he spit up. Bobby held him upright again and wiped Brendan's mouth on the sleeve of his old Evening Shade High athletic jersey. Dancing school, Bobby thought. Over my dead body; he's a football player.

Alex flushed the toilet, let his shorts drop. As usual in summer, he wasn't wearing undershorts.

"Bigger than when I saw it last," Bobby commented. "About to beat me out there, you know that?"

Alex smiled a little self-consciously, kicked off his moccasins and stripped his polo shirt.

Bobby held Brendan against his chest and gave him some sugar.

"Don't be calling me dumbass ever, or I'll kick your skinny butt sideways. I already figured it had to be Bernice. I've always been knowing you better than that, and even Cecily needs to admit her mother's got sneaky ways."

Brendan *was pushing himself* around on the porch in his baby walker when Alex came outside eating a roast-beef sandwich he'd made for himself in the kitchen. Bobby sat in a lawn chair with his back to the painted cement steps to keep Brendan from pushing himself off the porch. Alex sat on a swing and looked at his brother.

"There isn't anything I can do about it," Bobby said. "Because it puts you and me against Cecily and Bernice, and I'm not about to let that happen."

Alex chewed slowly, swallowed, looked at the floorboards and shrugged dispiritedly.

"But Bernie's not coming into my house full-time, made up my mind about that."

Alex looked relieved, for the moment.

"Made up my mind about something else too," Bobby said. "This is about you. You're not a kid anymore. Few more years and you'll be a man. I wouldn't be any good to you as a brother if I didn't think about that. You and me communicate okay, but how do you communicate with other people? Write down everything you feel or want to say? Easier just to pass on by, isn't it, ignore anyone who looks the wrong way at you. Well, you're going to be fourteen. Bad news for you. Life just gets harder. It's already past time when you ought to be learning the language of others who don't hear, can't speak. There's good schools where they'll teach you sign language. Closest one is Louisville. I want you to go there, Alex, because otherwise you won't stand a cut dog's chance. You've got to become part of the world, always improving yourself, not just drifting and living on the edge of things. You can't speak, but there's plenty worse things can happen. The Forney kid is in an iron lung for as long as he lives because he can't do his own breathing. Compared to him, you're lucky. You can see, hear, run, play ball. You're not shut off from two-thirds or all of the world. The world's waiting on you, Alex, to get the chip off your shoulder because you got bad cards once. If it's up to me, which it is, what Cecily thinks or wants doesn't enter into my decision: You're gonna pitch in and get on with life."

Alex sat with his head down, lips parted, breathing through his mouth. Then he gave Bobby a look dense with fear, loathing, and despair. He raised both hands and began waggling fingers in a parody of sign language, grinning hatefully. Bobby stared him down.

"You're scared to be called 'dummy.' But the only way you'll get over it is to share what you're afraid of with others who are like you. You're going to Louisville, Alex. I'm driving us there to the school Monday week, get you signed up, settled in."

Bobby looked at Brendan, who was sagging over in his walker, eyes closing. Nap time. Bobby picked him up and carried him into the house, glancing at Alex, at the back of his head. Feeling a little shaky himself, sympathetic, but glad he had got it over with. Now it was time for Bernie to write that check. Thinking she'd won something. But the answer to that might be in Cecily's belly this minute. They were going to need a lot of room in their house, all the room they had, for boys and girls to grow up. Bernice could spend her winding-down years with men and women her own age, once her arthritis got so bad she couldn't feed herself or brush her teeth.

When he went downstairs again after putting Brendan in his crib, Alex was gone, off somewhere on his blue-and-white Schwinn. But Bobby had expected that. His brother had thinking to do, reality to confront. Grow up a little. Bobby smiled (*I've been wrong, but now I've got it right*), took a deep breath, and saw a sheet of paper under a windshield wiper of the Packard station wagon in the drive. He went down the steps and across the lawn to retrieve the obvious message: "Screw You," probably.

The paper had been folded small enough for Alex to carry in his back pocket. It was a campaign flyer he had pulled off a telephone pole, Leland Howard's smiling confident face on one side. *Leap Ahead with Leland!* There was, of course, a lot of talk about the young candidate from courthouse loafers and pundits in an election year, the consensus being that Howard was a comer, and if ever a post-Reconstruction Southerner had a chance to be elected President, then—

Bobby turned the flyer over. On the blank obverse, Alex had printed in red crayon

I SAW HIM <u>RAPE</u>
MALLY SHAW LAST NIGHT!!
WHAT ARE YOU GOING TO DO ABOUT IT?

Along with a few other passengers, Ramses Valjean got off the 4:10 from Nashville at the Southern Railway's depot two blocks from the courthouse square. Ramses wore a red polka-dot bow tie with his dark blue sharkskin suit, which appeared to hang on him as if his weight had crash-dived in recent weeks. The trousers were held up by red suspenders. His hat was a twenties-style cream-colored straw fedora with a wide black band. He was not a sightless man, but he wore the glasses of the blind, little round lenses dark as India ink to fit the orbits of his eyes. Ramses had a lion's head on his gaunt body and sported a short beard with a pure-white crest in it. He carried a pigskin valise in one hand and a black medical bag in the other.

He set his valise down on the station platform, took off his glasses, and rubbed coalsmoke-sensitive eyes with thumb and forefinger while he waited, like a man of import, for the crowd of mourners who had met the train to come to him. There were relatives of all ages, such as Mally's second cousin Verona with her brood, friends like

Herschel "Poke Chop" Burdett, and a son of one of the owners of the funeral establishment, a plump, dapper young man named Dorsey Wundall, equally as well dressed, if in a more somber tone, as Ramses.

He had been away for a long time: since the early thirties. Most of the faces he recognized, some only at second glance. A couple of great aunts plucked at Ramses' sleeves while weeping, but no one embraced him. Ramses did not have the bearing of a man given to embraces in public.

He thanked them for coming. Dorsey Wundall introduced himself with appropriate condolences. Ramses looked sharply at him.

"Did your father receive my telegram?"

"Yes, sir. May I drive you to—"

"I would first like to see where it happened. Then you can take me to my daughter."

Ramses handed his pigskin valise to the undertaker and looked in annoyance at another young man, this one standing apart from the circle of mourners with an eager expression. He was wearing a hard-crown straw boater with a press card in the ribbon headband, holding a Speed Graphic camera in both hands.

"Dr. Val Jean, I'm Eddie Paradise Galphin from the *Tri-State Defender*? Reckon could I get a—"

"It's Val-*zhon*. I don't want to be photographed." Ramses took off his straw fedora as if to shield his face should the young man ignore his wishes. Hatless he showed a full head of relaxed, pomaded hair that he dyed black and wore styled like Ellington's.

"Well then, if I could talk to you for a few minutes about your—"

"No."

"This is a sorrowful day," young Wundall snapped at the *Defender*'s man. "Show some respect for a bereaved father."

"Yes, respect his privacy," one of the elderly aunties said.

A few of the mourners accompanied Ramses and Wundall to the mortician's Cadillac as if to protect him from further indignities proposed by the presence of a reporter. Eddie Paradise Galphin remained on the station platform smoking a cigarette; when Wundall drove

Ramses away from the depot, Galphin hurried to his own car, a vintage rumble-seat roadster, and followed them.

S*heriff's deputy Olen McMullen* had been on duty at Little Grove Holiness Church since about nine-thirty that morning, keeping everyone who attended the Sunday service and later the morbidly curious away from the cemetery hollow where Mally Shaw's body had been discovered at dawn by Ike Thurmond. McMullen was tired, surly, and bored stupid while waiting on a relief dep. He had read the sports pages of the Sunday *Tennessean* three times. Much of the sports was devoted to the Summer Olympics that were about to get underway. Few people in Evening Shade cared anything about the Olympics; and where the hell was Finland anyway?

The two-car procession, one highly polished Cadillac and one dilapidated roadster driven by Eddie Paradise Galphin, newshound, arrived, and both cars parked on the Yella Dog side of the road opposite the church and not far from Mally Shaw's Dodge. Wundall the mortician remained by the Caddy while Ramses, carrying a brown paper sack, made his way along the gravel path to the cemetery gates. There was no wall around the cemetery, only a pair of wrought-iron gates with hinges rusted open.

Deputy McMullen wiped his brow again with a soggy handkerchief and sauntered over to intercept Mally's father a few feet from the gates.

"What can I do you for, uncle?"

Ramses paused, and his bearded chin came up in the manner of a thoroughbred horse confronted by a broken-down old plug.

"I am Dr. Valjean. My daughter, I have been given to understand, was found here this morning, slaughtered—according to a preliminary investigation—by wild dogs. I have the permission of acting sheriff Bobby Gambier to view the general area."

"Oh uh yeah—I heard you might be coming. But I should warn you it ain't a pretty—"

"I am a doctor of pathology. I now teach at Meharry Medical College after many years as chief of staff at Hubbard Hospital in Nashville. I have, you might say, seen almost every terrible thing that can be visited upon a human being. Has anyone other than law-enforcement personnel come through here since Mally's body"—here he faltered, but only for an instant—"was removed?"

"No uh sir," Olen McMullen said, the first time in his life he had ever sir'd a Negro. And looked around guiltily as if he was afraid he'd been overheard.

Ramses looked at the deputy's perspiring red face and smiled sympathetically.

"It's very hot, isn't it? Have you been here long?"

"Practically the whole friggin' day," McMullen said.

Ramses opened his paper sack. "Well then, it was fortunate that I stopped at the mercantile back up the road. Would you care for a Coke or perhaps Grapette?"

"Ohhh—sure, wouldn't mind atall. You said grape?"

"Yes." Ramses handed the bottle of soda to the deputy, reached into a coat pocket for a large staghorn knife which contained, in addition to two sharp blades, an assortment of gadgetry that included a bottle opener. He popped the tops on the bottles, and they drank together, McMullen sighing with enjoyment, the surly knit of his brows relaxing.

"Real nice of you, Doc."

"My pleasure." Ramses took out his gold pocket watch. The time was a few minutes before five p.m. That left him, he calculated, half an hour at best before he would need to seek isolation and refuge. He closed the watch. "Now, if I may—"

"Surely." McMullen looked up to the road. "Who's that with the camera?"

"A representative of the press. If you wouldn't mind asking him to keep his distance for now while I am—engaged in prayerful solitude, then I may agree to have my picture taken next to the church. I believe that should satisfy his mania for, ah, 'getting the story.'"

"Okey-dokey."

Ramses set his Coke bottle down as the deputy walked toward the road. He removed his suit jacket, folded and laid it on the front seat of the sheriff's car parked beside the gates. Then he walked the gentle downslope of the wide path into the burial ground. He could see just where the carnage had taken place while he was still a hundred feet away: A headstone with torn-up turf around it was splashed with blood that still attracted flies.

Ramses approached the site, where for several minutes he was motionless, moving only his head as he surveyed every inch of a gruesome scene. He heard a train whistle; soon a long freight rumbled by a hundred yards north of the cemetery. He felt the ground tremble beneath his shoes. When the train had passed, he noticed a boy on a bicycle riding along the platform of the abandoned Cole's Crossing depot. A white boy.

He returned his attention to the death scene, where he slowly began to walk around, sometimes dropping to one knee for a closer study. Sniffing deeply a few times. Carefully parting tufts of grass. His mind was fully in clinical mode as he repressed all emotion. He saw clots of blood, insects, pieces of a dress. There was a vase with spilled and wilted flowers not far from the blood-soaked headstone. It was still possible, to his trained eye, to tell where Mally's body had lain and in what position. Around the beaten-down grass and pods of dried mud there were paw prints and men's footprints. Five or six different men. There was a chewed sandal in grass and weeds ten feet from the vase and flowers.

Ramses kept his back to the gates and the deputy who was with the mortician and the reporter. He pulled on a pair of white cotton gloves and began to pick up bits and pieces of things that interested him. He wrapped each separately in tissue paper he'd also purchased at the general store and placed everything in the brown paper sack.

Before leaving he picked up Mally's sandal, holding it by a torn strap. The leather was darkly dappled with blood. He was interested in what was on the sole. He carried the sandal out of the cemetery and met Deputy McMullen coming down from the road.

"I wonder why this wasn't removed along with my daughter's remains?"

"Prob'ly they just overlooked it this morning."

"If you think it would be all right, Deputy, I'd like to take it with me."

"Much as it was your daughter's, can't see no reason why not." McMullen looked at the folded-over paper sack in Ramses' other hand but didn't say anything else. He was curious, though, when Ramses took time to study tire tracks both on and off the pea-gravel path.

Ramses retrieved his jacket from the sheriff's car.

"Thank you for your kindness, Deputy."

"Well, it were a terrible thing happened, and I feel right sorry about it. Those pack dogs been a problem 'round these parts since I was a kid. Killed a old woman over to Palermo, let's see, four-five years ago, believe it was. Just have to track 'em down and shoot 'em."

Ramses nodded, looking as if the heat and horror of what had befallen Mally had worn away his defenses. There was a trudge to his step as he went up to the road and beckoned Eddie Paradise Galphin over for a brief conversation. McMullen watching and thinking that here was some nigger all right; not like any other buck or uncle he had run across in Evening Shade or the military service. If there was a difference to most of them it was the difference between dirt and mud in McMullen's estimation; but Ramses had disturbed this complacent equation in the deputy's brain and he wasn't happy with the suspicion that forevermore he might have to deal with it.

Every place of business in Evening Shade was shut tight on Sundays except for the Tropical Breeze ice-cream stand that was open summers only and Pee-Wee's Good Eats, both across the road from the brick factory where eighty-odd local people were employed making Hanes-brand underwear. Pee-Wee almost never closed except for Christmas day; he lived in two rooms in the back of his cafe and if you were hungry at two a.m. you could go around and rap on the back door and if he knew you and thought you might have some fresh gossip to reward him Pee-Wee would get up and put the coffee on.

All Southern communities with more than one traffic light have a Pee-Wee or a Shorty, and most run true to type: Mickey Rooney–size, born standing up and talking back and, in the case of Evening Shade's Pee-Wee, minutely knowledgeable about all on this earth that is worth living for: fishing, hunting, politics, and sports in their seasons; the brag and mythos of male sexual prowess.

Around six in the evening. Alex was halfway through a cheeseburger soggy with mustard and ketchup when Bobby came in to the tinkling of the bell over the front door, yelled at Pee-Wee, who was wrapped in an apron that looked as if it had been through an auto-da-fé, old Pee-Wee wreathed in stinky fry-grease smoke behind the counter and yelling back at him. He had the face of a cranky fetus. Bobby slipped into the initial-scarred high-backed booth opposite his brother, having another look around the cafe to check on who was there and not given to minding his own business. But Pee-Wee's clientele was nearly all families with small ones, a couple of whom were whiners or liked to crawl under the tables. Except for a smile or a wave of greeting, nobody paid further attention to Bobby.

Pee-Wee had Sara Sundeen waiting tables this Sunday and an elderly coachwhip Negro named, obscurely, True Willie Nebraska working alongside him, handing the burgers and Cokes out the Jim Crow window. The Negroes ate their meals at picnic tables in a restful grove of persimmon and chestnut trees between Pee-Wee's establishment and the Tropical.

"What you fixin' to have, Bobby?" Sara asked him. She was fifty, give or take, still maintaining a rawboned beauty in spite of the puckered skin under-eyes like misplaced vaccination scars. She had carried on with his daddy once upon a time, among other things Bobby knew about her.

"Coffee black; let's see uh toasted cheese, whole wheat. I still got to eat dinner home later on."

"Catch up to them wild dogs yet?"

"No, but we're out there looking."

Alex paused with a mouthful of burger and raised his eyes to his brother's face.

"Lord, that does give me the shudders! Poor thing. She was a pretty one. Educated too."

Bobby glanced at Alex's face, the wad in his jaw he wasn't swallowing, and wondered.

"Heard she was looking after Priest Howard in his last days. Reckon what she was doing in that cem'tary come crack of dawn?"

"No telling. Might just have been something she liked to do, Quiet that early, nobody else around to bother."

"Well, sure. God bless 'n keep her."

When they were alone, Alex pushed one of his spiral-bound notebooks across the formica tabletop to Bobby and resumed eating. Chocolate malt and french fries backing up the burger.

Bobby read Alex's account of the rape of Mally Shaw, his face settling into an expression of gloom.

Before he could ask questions, Pee-Wee paid a social call.

"Ad-lay!" he said with a derisive twist of his little mouth, summing up the previous week's high point in national politics and his own distaste for the Democrats' choice to lead their ticket in November. "Sure did think old "Cowfever" had a lock goin' in, but Truman's hard-on has always been for Stevenson. Ad-lay against a war hero, it be a sho'-nuff perscription for losin' the White House."

"Pee-Wee, you know you got to provide a decent burial soon for that old apron of yours before I declare it a public nuisance."

"Like hell you will!"

"How's your boy making out with that new wife of his?"

"Reckon it'll be a good marriage. They been together eleven days already, and she ain't left him but twice."

"Your grill is on fire again."

"True Willeh! Throw some flour on that, gosh dang it! 'Scuse us older boys here a minute, Alex. Bobby, you heard why scuba diving is like sex with a tall woman?"

"Haven't heard that one."

"No matter how big your tank is, you can't never get in deep enough!"

"Speak for yourself, Pee-Wee. Your ex-wife told Cecily yours didn't have no more twang to it than a one-string banjo."

Pee-Wee chortled. "How would *she* know, her root cellar was tighter'n a gnat's navel. Damn if I didn't almost go broke paying for those lube jobs just so's I could get me a little somethin' come Satiddy nights." He winked. "'Scuse us again, Alex, that wasn't meant for your tender ears."

When Pee-Wee returned to his chores Bobby looked at Alex and said, "What were you doing over to Mally's last night? Looking to diddle her yourself maybe?"

It was his angry tone more than the off-base accusation that alerted Alex; Bobby was deeply troubled by what he'd read. Alex calmly shook his head although his cheeks were reddening and stared his brother down. Bobby looked at the notebook under his right hand.

"Okay, that was—I know Mally Shaw wasn't uh—so what were you and Mally all about anyhow?"

Somebody used up a nickel at the jukebox to hear Hank Snow's *Rhumba Boogie.*

Alex leaned back in the booth, wiping his fingers on a paper napkin. Not taking his eyes off Bobby.

Bobby looked up again uncomfortably.

"This uh story of yours—"

Alex shook his head again, very deliberately, his lips clamped together.

"Okay. You heard and saw most of it. Mally let—him—in her house when she should've known a sight better. Then one thing led to another while you were hiding out. Probably the only smart thing you did last night. Let me tell you. The man's reputation is, he's always been Woody Woodpecker with a big set of balls. Takes 'em and leaves 'em. So what do you want me to do? Arrest Le—the man on your say-so? Know how far I'd get with that? Hell, you're old enough to know the score, Alex. Rape is a booger to prove anytime, and when it's a nig—shit, forget it. Even saying she was still alive, Mally wouldn't dare open her mouth in her own behalf. I'd be out of a job in an hour with mouths to feed, and six months from now I'd be gone fishing and like as not never turn up again. Until maybe the concrete blocks they wired to my feet slipped off the bones. That's how they play it—man who has friends with a big stake in his future."

Alex was very still with cheeks fully fired up, causing his eyes to water a little from the heat of his disapointment and dismay. Then he reached for his notebook, but Bobby slid it away from him.

"Uh-uh. I'll just hang on to this, get rid of it when I can. Now tell me: There a chance anybody saw you out to Mally's last night?"

Alex half-rose from his seat to try to wrest the notebook from Bobby's grip.

"Sit down," Bobby said grimly. "I'm after looking out for your welfare, and all you ever do is think up new ways to make it hard for me. I said *sit down,* asshole!"

Alex's sore lips trembled. There was such pain and disillusionment in his brother's eyes that Bobby had to look away for a moment.

That's when Alex stuck his left index finger down his throat, triggered his gag reflex and vomited all over the table and Bobby as Sara Sundeen approached with Bobby's pot of coffee and his toasted cheese.

Alex had finished barfing and bolted from the booth before Bobby, looking at the undigested burger shotgunned across his shirt front, could recover from his astonishment.

"Oh my," Sara said, reaching for the wipe cloth tucked under her belt. "We'll just take that one off the bill."

SIX

Of Shadows and Phantoms

NOW *in the blue hour*
Beneath a gemmy cusp of sky
In that landscape of surcease
Known as Little Grove churchyard
The boy lingers with more
Anguish than any boy can be prepared
To know,
Sun sinking west like a homesick
Heart
Gilding him with the hint of a halo
In a stoned church window.

The wind sighs in the vernacular
Of the estranged. There in uplifting
Night he stands ready once more
To welcome the *Dixie Traveler.*

It is the cloudless time
Between the limepit noon of summer
And the mockingbird's dark,
Time of crossings and recrossings,
Of going and returning—of
Shadows and Phantoms that appear
To the occult eye as dew
Gathers on blades of grass,
Pallid Sisters and Brothers

Rising to the occasion
From little houses of the dead,
Sepulchres of the shattered
Grail.

The rusted bell tolls. But he, lusting
Now for more than antics, for the
Bravest step of all, cannot hear
Beyond the *Dixie Traveler's*
Iron thunder. His heartbeat
Swells, his mind is filled
With a bluesy reckoning:

If you don't have what it takes,
Some pretense of folly,
There can be no love lost or gained.

He is kindled by the headlamp
Of the *Traveler;* studies it
With the pierced, deep look
Of the entranced. Night seals
His world. The stars
Grow older, but slowly.

Surcease. Tears at his grave
(He knows) will settle
Like a melancholy rain. O
The fickle-hearted! Now he trusts
Only the entrancement, mirrors
That reflect inward.
The *Traveler* is here, and it is
time for him to board.

He steps forward and puts a foot
on the shining rail to meet
His Titan—

—*Steps forward*—

Alex Gambier, what the hell* did you think you were doing?"

From where he lay on his back in gravel seven or eight feet from
the now-empty rails, stunned as if swept back from the wheels of the
passing train by a blow from a wing of an angry angel, Alex blinked
to clear his cloudy vision and looked up into the eyes of Mally Shaw,
who was standing over him, hands on hips in a scolding attitude. No
wings but anger to spare. The moon, the stars in their appointed
places becoming visible to him past Mally's squared shoulders, bright-
est around her head, coronal.

At first thought he was dead, then, *no,* dreaming. But the dead
knew no pain, according to the preachers. As for a dream, you didn't
hurt from scraped elbows while dreaming.

"Go and throw your life away like that, for *what?* Don't you know
what I would give, just one more day, one *hour,* even, to get out of
here, have me a deep breath of air, eat corn on the cob just dripping
with melted butter—I never figured you to be so dumb."

"Get out of where?" Alex said, hearing the last rattle of the club
car of the *Dixie Traveler* as it cleared the long trestle over the Yella
Dog, then belatedly hearing his own effortless words in his mind even
though the voice was not familiar. He scrambled up off the right-of-
way ballast, away from the figment, the apparition his brain was trying
to pass off as Mally Shaw. Not doing such a bad job of it, actually: she
was perfect in form, not scarred like an ancient obelisk nor bloody
from hounds' teeth, wearing a dark blue dress with moonflowers on it
he'd seen her wear before—his body was moving, but his head reeled;
Alex did a spin and fell again and heard her laugh.

"Oh boy. Better just to take it easy for a little while, get your balance back."

"You're supposed to be—in the Promised Land." That voice that must be his.

Mally looked around with amused skepticism. "I'm sure enough not, punkin," she said. Her expression sobered. "How much more time do you need to get used to that notion?"

"Well, if you're not dead—"

"Oh Lord. I'm plenty dead all right. Can't take that back."

He tried to get up but his head wasn't ready; he fell hard on his butt.

"Then what are you doing here?" Alex cried in exasperation.

Mally gave him a long look.

"Don't know for sure. But it's bound to have something to do with you, Alex. And maybe some unfinished business of my own."

SEVEN

Jean Valjean on the *Pegasus*
New Gunslinger in Town
True Obsessions

Eddie Paradise Galphin *had finished throwing up* under the catalpa trees behind the delivery entrance of Godsong and Wundall's funeral home and was halfway through a cigarette when Ramses Valjean came outside, put down his medical bag and Eddie's Speed Graphic camera, and stood in the driveway of the one-story frame building rubbing his sore eyes. The sun had set, but the sky was still alight at treetop level. What breeze there would be to make the coming night bearable stirred the leaves above their heads and smelled of fresh-cut hay from a nearby pasture.

Eddie strolled over with a show of cockiness to the man who had seen him run from the room in which Mally Shaw's body still lay in all of its shrunken ghastliness on a zinc-top table—but Eddie was going to put that image out of his mind. He was going to . . . Sure. In about six months, if he was lucky.

"How long will you need to develop the photographs we've taken?" Ramses asked him.

We've taken was being generous; Eddie had managed with panicky heart and rising gorge to get one shot at Ramses' direction before abandoning his camera and quitting that room with its morbid airs on the dead run. No telling how many other plates Ramses had exposed. Or of what use they were to him. His own daughter? If he wasn't such a cool customer and a doctor to boot, Eddie might have entertained dark suspicions about Ramses Valjean.

"I've got my own darkroom, so soon's I make it back to the house—"

"Do you have a wife, Eddie?" Ramses seemed momentarily

staggered, as if by a sudden zephyr, and put out a hand to a post of the fence that lined the gravel drive. Finally getting to him, Eddie thought with a twinge of sympathy. Eddie had spent much of the last four hours with the enigmatic Dr. Valjean at the Little Grove cemetery, then on a visit to the farm of Ike and Zerah Thurmond, finally this stop at the mortuary. Eddie the willing chauffeur; Ramses might have had the use of Mally's old car, but he had never learned to drive.

"Married? Not hardly. Not on what the *Defender* pays. I not only write for it, I got to deliver it to make ends meet. But it is journalism, and you got to start somewhere." Filing daily items about life and events in Evening Shade, such as his account of Mally Shaw's death. Half a column for sure, maybe a two-column head in tomorrow's paper. But Eddie, having met her father while doing his follow-up, sensed that a bigger story was happening here that, once he had the complete lowdown, could pave his way to a salaried position as a staff reporter, not a lowly stringer. And not necessarily with the *Tri-State Defender.* Eddie had his sights set on Chicago and the Negro journalist's Olympus, the great Chicago *Defender* newspaper. All he had to do now was stay close to his source.

"Dr. Valjean, you look done in. Which under the circumstances who can blame you? Wonder do you have yourself a place to stay while you be in Evening Shade?"

"I haven't given that any thought, Eddie," Ramses said, gripping the fence post with one hand, looking up at the stars and breathing deeply as if he were trying to inhale one or two. "I should stay the night at Mally's house, if you know where that is. In the meantime I have more to do. The sheriff, what was his name? Gambier. I need to see him, although I'm sure I won't find him in his office."

"Lives on West Hatchie. He's acting sheriff while Luther Tebbets be out of town the next week or so. Had my druthers, rather deal with Sheriff Bobby than old Lute."

"Could you drive me to his home, then?"

"No problem at all," Eddie said with a gracious smile.

With Ramses in the rumble seat of the red roadster and Eddie driving, conversation was awkward but Eddie gave it a try, looking back and raising his voice so that Ramses could hear him over the noise provided by a bad muffler.

"Lived here all my life! But I don't recall any Valjeans hereabout!"

"My father's name was Russell."

"Be plenty of Russells in Evening Shade. How did you come by that name of Valjean?"

"I changed my name after adopting France as my native country. If you drive more slowly, I would be able to hear you without your having to shout."

"Oh, right!" Eddie throttled back to twenty-five sedate miles an hour. "You been to France, then? When was that, during the Great War?"

"Long before. I spent fourteen of my first thirty years in Paris."

"No fooling? I'll bet that's a story."

"Yes, it is, Eddie."

"Changed your name and everything. So if you don't mind my asking—"

"Ask away," Ramses said, brushing a flying insect with diaphanous wings from his beard.

"Where did 'Valjean' come from?"

"From a famous novel I read, or taught myself to read in French, when I was a cabin boy aboard a merchant marine vessel. *Les Misérables.* I identified very closely with the unfortunate hero of Hugo's novel. Have you read it?"

"No. How did you happen to—"

"When I was fifteen, I fell in love with the notion of going to sea." Talking seemed to be something he needed to do right now. Words helped him breathe properly, which was useful for repressing the feelers of pain finding their way around the roadblock from his last injection of morphine. And language called up memories to replace other memories of the grim hour he had spent in the mortuary. "I was one of a barefoot gaggle of farm children, and the only sea I knew in reality was a green sea of corn rows in a good year. My father said he couldn't spare me, so I simply ran away. To the Mississippi River, and down to New Orleans by barge. This was in 1906. I was a handsome boy in rags, yet I carried myself well. I survived around the docks until I came to the notice of Captain Jack Marsh of the *Pegasus*. He happened to be an educated man who kept a small library, in four languages, aboard his vessel. To which I was eventually allowed access during my four lengthy voyages aboard the *Pegasus*."

Ramses stopped there, thinking as he had not thought for some time of Captain Jack. Who had, in addition to education, proclivities Ramses was willing to indulge in exchange for the tutorials he received. Already knowing it was a world of give and take. He was never abused. Shame or guilt didn't enter into Ramses' calculations of his personal worth. It was a thing of bodies that he also found gratifying most of the time.

Nearing retirement and landlocked sunset years with his wife, Jack Marsh turned his cabin boy, now a mature French-speaking seventeen-year-old, over to a scion of the shipping line's founder in Marseilles. That young lady applied her own veneer of manners and polish to her pet Negro. When she became engaged to a wealthy older man, she recommended Ramses to a male cousin, a Parisian physician and drug addict who fell in love. Provided for Ramses in his will, money which came to Ramses only eight months later, when his benefactor was separated from many of his body parts in a motorcycle accident. The inheritance was sufficient to allow for a decent existence and put Ramses through medical school at the Sorbonne.

He might never have left France, but a desire to present himself to the homefolks in the full dignity of his station prompted Ramses to return to the United States in 1920. He needed a radical change of pace and scenery after serving in the French Army Medical Corps for two and a half years, never far removed from the battlefields.

Accustomed to the laissez-faire racial attitudes of cosmopolitan Paris, for Ramses traveling to West Tennessee was like being shipped to a penal colony. One week only and he would never return, Ramses vowed. Then, on a visit to Nashville for a series of lectures at Meharry Medical College, Ramses encountered an irresistible force named Dawn Bird Hollins.

Alex Gambier *walked slowly* along the platform of the decrepit depot at Cole's Crossing, sane, he thought, but with a nervous apprehension muttering around his heart. Mally Shaw was beside him, out of touch but still a comforting presence like the soul of a candled saint, perfectly realized by her own mysterious light in the deep darkness around them.

"You can't just leave here if you want to?"

"No way that I know of," Mally said with the sorrowfully perplexed expression she'd had from time to time. When she was alive.

"Have you tried?"

"Oh, yes. Cemetery at Little Grove is as far as I get."

"What stops you?"

"Nothing I can explain. It's not like running into a wall. There's nobody with a stop sign like a crossing guard at school. I just feel the need to turn back."

"But you've been to the cemetery."

"Since my remains were taken away, yes, I did go."

"Is something down there that I uh can't—"

"No, sugar. There's just little shrunk-up corpses wearing the fine clothes they were laid to rest in. Souls have all moved on. Even my William's spirit, which I hope is not so tormented anymore."

"Well where did they—"

"This place is a Crossing between worlds, which is all I know about it so far. Maybe I ought to be someplace else already, 'stead of walkin' up and down this platform keeping you company because you don't seem to understand it is way past your bedtime."

Alex snorted. "I stay up all night lots of nights. And this is . . . I mean, I don't want to go. *You're* here; it's the most incredible—"

"Not going to pee in your pants again, are you?" she teased.

"Hell no. Don't make fun of me! We've got to get to the bottom of this."

"'Kay. I'm game if you are, and I don't have anything else to do."

"I thought maybe you can't leave here for the same reason you can't touch me and I can't touch you."

"I don't know," Mally said, shrugging as if she'd lost interest in phenomena. She had another interest, looking down at herself. "Wonder where did I get this dress from? And did you notice, Alex? My fingernails and toenails, they're done ever so nicely."

"I noticed."

"Well, and I did wonder could it be what Alex thinks or remembers about me or—wants me to be, that's how I'm going to look to both of us when I'm with him? Although you never did see me in my lifetime with my toenails done up." She smiled impishly. "You like women, girls, with their toenails painted? Your brother's cute wife? Might be you have a crush on her?"

Alex looked uncomfortable. "I'm over that."

"Oh, sure."

"Sometimes I did think about her when I was—"

Mally cut off his confession with a wave of her hand. "No need to be completely honest with me, Alex. Boys are gonna be boys, and there's no shame in it."

She folded her arms across her breasts, frowning as if she felt a chill or sense of alarm, and darted a look over one shoulder.

"What's wrong?"

"Better had step away from the track. Train's coming in."

Alex looked around too. "What train?"

"There is one. But it might not stop here. Depends on who's waiting for it."

She turned her face aside and hugged herself tighter, closing her eyes. This went on for at least ten seconds. Then she seemed to relax and stared at Alex.

"I was right. Wasn't anyone here ticketed for that one."

Alex grinned. "Come *on*. A train just went by us?"

"Baby, this has been a busy place for trains all night so far, and I don't count the *Dixie Traveler* that was a short whistle away from mowin' you down."

"But I told you. I had it timed. I was gonna sprint across in front of it at the last second. It's how well you gauge the speed and depth perception and—"

"And if you did chance to time it a little bit wrong, still you could call it a brave thing, die a hero's death? Oh, Alex. That was part of what was on your mind, sure enough. The rest of it was just wrong thoughts that are bad for your soul, whether you remember it all or not."

Alex validated her slant on the matter with a shrug. He did know the mood he had been in at the time. Soreness remained in his heart, but the morbidity had gone away because of his intense excitement at being with Mally, an eerie buoyancy that had him feeling as if he were floating in and out of a dream state. He didn't want to think about anything except being there with her, the wonder and delight of hearing his own voice. And of course, whenever he looked at Mally he was reminded of how much he hated Leland Howard.

"I told Bobby how you got raped in your own house. But Bobby said—"

Mally nodded wisely. "Said how he wasn't about to stir up a hornet's nest that could get him stung to death just on my account, 'cause what did it matter anyway if I was dead."

"Yeah, but when I tell him what else went on up there at Howard's farm—"

"Oh, you can't do that, Alex."

"Like to know why not!"

She gave him that deep, thoughtful look of hers, ending in a rueful smile.

"There's a couple good reasons. Just where you gonna say you got that story from?"

Alex had a familiar burning heaviness in his throat, as if he'd swallowed a handful of rock salt. He struggled to get words out, although he'd been fluent moments before.

"Cuh-couldn't B-Bobby—"

"Talk to me himself?" Mally gave Alex a meltingly sympathetic look. "Haul him down to the depot, say '*There's* Mally, didn't I tell you; listen to what she has to say and then go 'rest Mr. Leland Howard?'" She smiled. "You can talk to your brother about Mally Shaw, but all he will ever see of her in his own life is what is left over at the funeral home. You can't show me to Sheriff Bobby or anyone else. We seem to have some sort of special arrangement ourselves, Alex. Maybe we'll know eventually how it happens, or did happen this one time—who knows how long our 'arrangement' will last? Oh, the other reason you can't tell the real story how I came to die—nothing's changed for you. After you leave here tonight, you still won't be able to speak a word no matter how bad you need to."

"Don't say that! How do you think you know so damn much!"

Mally shuddered slightly and crossed her bare arms again.

"Another train's coming. Maybe this will be the one." She walked a few steps away from Alex, walked back. "No. Probably too soon for me. But the Crossing is busy tonight."

"What do you mean, 'busy'?"

"There are others here, just swarms of folks passing through. I can barely make them out myself. They ignore me. Guess we're all strangers everywhere, no matter what world we find ourselves in."

Alex shook his head unhappily, looking around the platform, empty to his eyes. There were tears on Mally's face. He heard a dog barking, and it raised hair on his forearms, the skin goosing up.

"We have to figure out what to do about Leland Howard."

"He doesn't matter to me now."

"That low-down polecat set his dogs on you! He deserves to be—I don't care if Bobby *is* scared to do anything; I'll do it myself!"

Mally looked worriedly at him.

"Your mind is tired, Alex. You've been through a lot this weekend. And it would be hard to beat what I suffered. Will you let me rest now? It's time for both of us to take a break."

He wiped sweat from beneath his eyes, blinking. She was losing definition, like a streaky image on a rainstorm window.

"I'm not tired," he said sulkily. "I don't want you to go. I'll never see you again."

"Can't be sure of that, it's true. But for now, please let go of me."

"What do you mean?"

"I can't do this all by myself. *Let go.* Turn your back on me, walk away. Don't look around."

"*No,* Mally."

"Tomorrow night, then. Be waiting here when the *Dixie Traveler* returns. Stay away from it, hear? But take its power deep into the marrow of your bones. That's how you'll likely find me again."

"I don't—"

"And Alex?"

"What?" he said despairingly.

"Almost nobody ever scores even in a lifetime. Either you get better than you deserve or, like most folks, a whole lot worse. There's nothing you can do to Mr. Howard he won't do to himself eventually."

B*ernice Clauson came into the kitchen* and said to Bobby and Cecily, who were going over household accounts and making out checks for the first-of-the-month bills, "There's a blind nigra man coming up your front walk. I think he must be blind. He has on those glasses they wear. A young man is with him, and he has a camera."

Cecily looked at Bobby, who shrugged and got up to go to the front door.

"Hello, Eddie," Bobby said, recognizing the *Defender's* man in Evening Shade as he walked outside on the porch. His hunch was that the older man was Mally Shaw's father with the French name from Nashville. He wore dark glasses all right, and his suit was too big on him.

"Dr. Valjean? Can't tell you how sorry I am about Mally; she was well liked here in Evening Shade. It's a terrible tragedy."

"Thank you, Sheriff Gambier."

"Acting sheriff is all, rest of this week and the next. Eddie, you doing a story? You know I don't care for having my picture taken out of uniform."

"Yes sir Sheriff Bobby, just carryin' it around gets to be a habit with me."

"Hot night. Would either of you like a drink of water?"

Ordinarily he wouldn't have made the gesture; Negroes didn't call socially on the Gambiers, and if there was some official although after-hours business to be done, it was a Sunday night and he didn't want them lingering. But under the circumstances Bobby felt that Dr. Ramses Valjean was deserving of the unusual courtesy.

Ramses turned him down, however, with a curt shake of his head.

"Well then, what's on your mind I can help you with?"

"I've come to ask you to accompany me to the Godsong and Wundall funeral home," Ramses said.

"Why should I do that, Dr. Valjean?"

"To view my daughter's body."

"Done that this morning."

"Let me make the assumption that you have not seen all that there is to see; of course you could not, sir, further assuming that you have no training in pathology."

"What are you getting at?"

"Among other things, although there can be no doubt that she was mauled to death by dogs, Mally could not have been killed where her body was found."

"How's that?" Bobby said, a moment ago feeling a little sleepy, now with a yellow caution light blinking in his head.

"It is so obvious that her body was moved there from another site, and that an effort was made to make it appear as if she were attacked in the Little Grove cemetery—a poor effort, by the way—it surprises me that no one in the sheriff's department has raised any questions about the attempted deception."

"Wait a minute." Bobby glanced at Eddie, whose eyes were wide, as if he were hearing Dr. Valjean's theory for the first time. "I was at Little Grove myself. Didn't see a thing would back up this sort of speculation. The ground had been trampled by dogs, and there was blood all over. Pieces of her clothing and—"

Ramses nodded. "Yes. Pieces of her flesh. I found what your deputies may have missed."

"Then what gives you any reason to suspect—"

"I can prove what I suspect, if you will accompany me to the funeral home, and if you are willing to accept the truth of my observations."

Eddie looked at Ramses and up at Bobby as if he couldn't believe this was going on, Bobby stone-faced now and certain he had just been called out by a new gunslinger in town, one who possibly held him in contempt. Colored man holding *him* in contempt. Eddie was forgetting how to breathe.

Bobby said, "I'll go with you." He looked at Eddie. "Eddie, go on home."

"All right, Sheriff Bobby."

"One word of this shows up in any newspaper across the State, one *whisper* gets back to me at the courthouse, I'll put a kink in your tooter."

"Oh no no no no. You can depend on me."

"You been standing there too long already."

"I'm gettin'," Eddie said, backing down the walk with a look of apology meant for Ramses. But Ramses seemed to have lost all awareness of him.

"I need to sit down," Ramses said in a quiet voice, and did so without permission, right there on the second step up to the porch, taking off his blindman's glasses with shaking fingers. The orbs of his eyes were yellow as egg yolk. Some hidden catastrophe of the flesh was etched on his grave handsome old face; seeing it gave Bobby pause before he went back into the house to let Cecily know where he was going.

When *Bobby saw Ramses Valjean's hand* go to the handle on the front door of the passenger side of Bobby's Packard station wagon he was about to say something like *I don't drive colored folks around town in the front seat of my car.* No temper, just a casual statement of fact, as if Ramses was befuddled by events of the day and hadn't realized what he was about to do. But he heard in his head what it sounded like before the words came out, and, curiously, it occurred to him how he would sound to Ramses. Never in his life had Bobby had second thoughts about how he spoke to Negroes. Or care what any damn one of them thought of him. Because, except for a couple of noncoms raised in Harlem who had some of that jive-stepping manner even Southerners generally were amused by and could excuse them for, Bobby had never met a colored man who needed instruction concerning who he was and how he'd been born to behave. This made him uneasy. Ramses Valjean was a man of medicine and had achieved distinction in his field; that, in Bobby's opinion, entitled him to more respect than the average indentured farmer or the courthouse janitor. And his daughter had died a cruel death.

So what Bobby said was, as Ramses was opening the car door, "Like for you to take a seat in the back, Dr. Valjean."

Ramses said after a few seconds, during which he was motionless but not hesitant, "As you wish." Not much inflection in his cultivated voice, certainly not a trace of arrogance. But Bobby felt as if he had just been scolded. Made to feel a little foolish. Then Ramses said, "I have always found it easier to talk to a man when I am, more or less, face to face. And obviously you are interested in what I have to say."

No denying. Sunday night, the Gambiers were as usual a little short of paycheck money to settle bills and would have to cash in another government bond before its time. Alex was giving him fits, and now Ramses Valjean had showed up and dumped a mess of an unknown size and complexity on his doorstep. He was both afraid and eager to hear more about it.

Bobby said wearily, "Okay, let's get this done," and nodded his permission for Ramses to occupy the front seat with him.

The woman Leland Howard took back to his hotel in Kingsport, Tennessee's Fort Henry Hotel was a devoted campaign worker, a divorcee who earned her living in the Sullivan County Clerk's office. Leland's friend and mentor Estes Kefauver had recommended her highly for a night's entertainment. Her name was Bitsy Beauregard. Mid-thirties, five feet nothing with frosted blond hair and a dazzling jut of teeth that prevented her lips from ever quite closing, which gave her a look of unquenchable avidity. She had a fund of tacky chatter and wouldn't shut up even while she was taking his pants down. She carried some extra weight on her hips, but her breasts had a nice blush and were firm as wax fruit.

Bitsy proved herself to be sexually inventive, but to his mortification Leland just couldn't follow through. Both his mind and his blood were sluggish. Whenever Bitsy's sweaty efforts were about to pay off Leland would think of what had gone on between him and Mally Shaw less than twenty hours ago and his penis would slide limply away from Bitsy's fierce clutch.

As Leland was phobic and never gave head, Bitsy finally left the suite determined to act cheerfully nonchalant about his bungled fuck. But obviously she'd got herself plenty worked up and was about to go nuts. He had always satisfied his women with the girth of his member and his stamina; this singular failure, which he alibied as exhaustion from the rigors of the campaign trail, depressed Leland. He hoped she wouldn't tell on him the next time she was intimate with Estes.

He didn't have the stomach yet to take a drink. Figured a hot bath might relax him enough to sleep. He opened the taps and turned away from the tub to take a gloomy pee, and when he looked into the tub again he saw that the pipes had coughed rusty water like the color of Mally's blood washing off his own body the night before. It gave his heart such a wallop he nearly fainted.

Leland turned off the bathwater. Catching sight of himself in the mirror of a half-opened cabinet door, he stopped and stared as if he were a case of mistaken identity, no longer solar in his status. He breathed through his mouth as he shuffled back to the bedroom. Heart going like kettledrums. The side of his head where he'd been hit by Mally ached ferociously. The more air he sucked in, the more starved for oxygen he was. He fell across the four-poster bed. Panicked. He needed a doctor! But in spite of sickening pain he was wary of calling down to the front desk. Word would get out. There'd be something in the papers tomorrow. *Leland Howard stricken.* Everyone would be thinking heart attack. His man Jim Giles was already on the road back to Evening Shade. His campaign manager was in Oak Ridge with the campaign's advance man. There was no one he could call on for help.

Blood roiling in his ears. His heart would not slow down.

Knock at the door. Leland staggered up and put on a robe.

There was a middle-aged colored woman outside.

"Everyone will know what you did," she said.

Leland backed away from the door. *"What?"*

She looked startled, afraid of him. He still smelled of another woman's perfume and pussy.

"Does you be wantin' me to turn down your *bed*?"

This time Leland heard her correctly.

"No. No, I was half-asleep already."

"Sorry for botherin' you then, Senator."

"That's all right."

She was halfway down the hall before he closed the door.

Calling him *Senator*. He felt revived, yanked out of the doldrums by her expression of respect. Well, he was all but there, and everybody knew it! Little more than a week to go. His closest primary rival trailed him by twelve points in the polls. Sinking like a leaky rowboat. Didn't matter a damn who the Republicans offered up in November. Steady course now, stick to the script, nothing to worry about.

Except for what Mally had known about him, and what she had done with the information his old man had provided to humble an unloved son.

Back in bed, he washed down three aspirin with warm Coca-Cola.

The preliminary search of Mally's house, by flashlight, hadn't turned up anything, but he knew Jim Giles was right. Even a small house like hers had so many rathole hiding places it would be necessary to take it apart board by board to find the incriminating documents.

Giles had come up with an ideal solution, and Leland agreed immediately.

Eventually he fell asleep with a comforting vision of flames in his head, Mally Shaw's remains atop the pyre, all of his potential troubles vanishing in smoke.

H*alfway to the funeral home,* a pain hit fiercely and Ramses Valjean doubled over midsentence as if a rifle ball had buried itself in his gut.

"What's wrong?" Bobby said.

Ramses gestured for him to pull off the road.

"Pain."

"What is it?"

"Cancer. My medical bag. Morphine."

Both his valise and his medical bag were in the back of the station wagon. Bobby helped Ramses out of the front seat and around to the tailgate, eased him down inside. Ramses took off his jacket and rolled up his shirt cuff while Bobby found his supply of morphine ampules in the medical bag. Two dozen of them. Stood by to block anyone else's line of sight while Ramses wrapped a piece of rubber tubing around his arm just below the bared elbow, held it tight with his teeth. Shot himself up, then sagged for a couple of minutes, legs dangling.

"How long have you been doing that? Morphine."

"About three weeks. Before that, codeine tablets. Eight, then twelve a day."

"Where's the cancer?"

Ramses was able to take his first deep breath in a while.

"In my pancreas." He looked up with the starry pupils of morphia.

Bobby couldn't help wincing. Ramses smiled slightly.

"Inoperable, of course. But it does have the virtue of being swift." He rolled his shirt sleeve down, buttoned the cuff. "Thank you for your patience and courtesy. We can go on now."

"How long is that shot good for?"

"Up to four hours. Although the duration shortens every day."

Bobby closed the tailgate, and Ramses walked without assistance to the front seat.

Bobby didn't restart the engine right away. A few cars passed on the road.

"How long, do you think?"

"Three months at best. Or worst."

"Did Mally know?"

"I hadn't told her. There wouldn't have been anything she could do for me until close to the end, a matter of a couple of weeks."

"Mind my asking, how was your relationship with Mally?"

"Cordial. But she felt closer to me than I to her. Shouldn't we be on our way? I told them at Godsong and Wundall that I'd be coming back; they're waiting."

Bobby drove. Ramses said, "Unfortunately, I've lacked the normal capacity to be close to anyone. Even my own daughter. I left most of her raising to my in-laws in Nashville and returned to France when she was ten. We didn't see each other again until she was a sophomore at Fisk."

Morphine had relaxed Ramses' tongue, unwound whatever inhibitions he ordinarily would have about revealing much of himself to a white lawman less than half his age, whom he had known for half an hour. But that was Bobby's strength: It was his nature to invite confidences, uncover the secrets of men who had the most reason to dissemble and attempt to conceal themselves from him.

"What about Mally's mother?"

"Were we close? In a morbid sense. She was a naked obsession. The inevitable doom of a man who cannot love, should he be so unfortunate as to meet a *fille méchante* like Dawn Bird Hollins."

"I don't speak the French language, but *may*-whatever doesn't sound good."

"Dawn Bird was privileged, for our race. Half-Choctaw, adopted by a prominent Nashville family. She was a hotheaded beauty with an undisciplined brilliance, wanton and often mad. Also incapable of loving. I was proud and too arrogant to believe she could ever matter deeply to me. As we carried on our *affaire maudite,* I believed that I was keeping my distance. Even as I was consumed."

"How long did it last?"

"True obsessions are forever," Ramses said with an aficionado's bitter smile. *'Solitary griefs, desolate passions, aching hours'*—to quote a fellow sufferer whose name I have forgotten. I last saw Dawn Bird twenty-one years ago next month. Although I returned to France during the Depression, I woke up each day with the expectation that today she would be coming back to me."

"So *she* left you."

"Once she had explained, quite reasonably to her mind, that if she did not leave she would soon kill me while I slept. Acting, no doubt, on the advice of her Spirit Guide, some demon of outer darkness. Oh, there was another man by then, of no real consequence to her. Perhaps he slept well during their relationship, but I have my doubts."

———

Before he pulled back the rubber sheet covering the body on the autopsy table, Ramses offered Bobby a small blue jar of Vicks. Bobby wiped a gob under his nose and handed back the jar. Ramses likewise anesthetized his sense of smell. Two loud window fans were going in the dreary basement room where the cracked concrete floor, painted over many times in various shades of green, sloped from all sides to a central drain.

"By the way," Ramses said, looking over one shoulder at Bobby, "what has become of Mally's car?"

"Towed this evening to the county's impound at Starke's Body Works. Was there something inside that you wanted?"

"No. I believe I found everything of consequence when I examined the Dodge earlier."

"What were you looking for?"

"Evidence that Mally did not drive her own car to Little Grove."

Bobby nodded, grimly curious. "I didn't see a need to look over every inch of her vehicle. Keys in the ignition was all I needed to know."

"I've labeled the glass containers lined up on the table there. The quart jar contains scrapings from the brake and clutch pedals of the Dodge, as well as the rubber floor mats front and back. They appear to be dried gumbo mixed with field detritus and cow manure. There were also two Brach's candy wrappers. Envelope number one. The cigarette butt in the ashtray had lipstick on it, probably Mally's. Envelope two."

Bobby looked over the items on the long table and picked up the quart jar with part of a Hellman's mayonnaise label stuck to the clean glass.

"The largest crust of gumbo, from the accelerator, contains an imprint that may have been made by a steel toe plate. There also are impressions of heavy-duty stitching that don't match the stitches on the sole of Mally's sandal, which is wrapped in cheesecloth at the end of the table."

Bobby unwrapped the sandal, found it caked with the same material that Ramses had collected in the mayonnaise jar.

"In the second jar you'll find scrapings of mud that contain bits of grass and weed from the Little Grove cemetery parcel where Mally's body was discovered. It looks very different from the field gumbo and manure mixture."

Bobby took a long breath.

"No matter how closely you examine the sandal, you won't find a trace of the mud from the cemetery on it, which would be the case if she were fighting for her life to escape a pack of wild dogs."

Bobby's face was getting hot. He didn't know if he was angry at Ramses Valjean for his dry, critical lecturing tone or himself for being a poor observer of a death scene.

"Those are your reasons for thinking she was brought there and dumped?"

"There is other evidence of what I conclude to be a fact. During your investigation, were photos taken?"

"That's our procedure if there has been a death, accidental or not. They won't have been developed yet."

"I had Eddie Paradise Galphin take a few pictures as well." Ramses held up a hand at Bobby's wrathful change of expression. His face was so charged with blood now it felt as if the roots of his hair were on fire. "Only as a precaution, should something go awry with the county's documentation. Not for release to any news organization."

"For your sake I hope not, Dr. Valjean. What else was there I should be aware of myself?"

"I am in no way offering my findings as a form of condemnation. I quite understand what your reaction must have been when you arrived at the cemetery early this morning. A multitude of paw prints in soft earth and on her torn body, the blood. You felt no need to look further for the cause of Mally's death."

"Now you're going to tell me it wasn't dogs?"

"No. That's what puzzles me. She was mauled, and by several large, vicious dogs. There in the smallest jar is a broken canine tooth I extracted from one of the deeper wounds between her ribs. But it couldn't have happened, as I've said, at Little Grove. Oh, a dog was brought there. But only one dog, I'm sure, probably on a short leash, made to trample the soft ground before her body was . . . dumped."

"One dog?"

"Every paw print I found was exactly the same size."

With that Ramses turned and folded the rubber sheet down to Mally Shaw's waist.

"As you must already have observed, the rip in the side of her throat, tearing the left carotid, was responsible for Mally's blood loss." Bending over her, he seemed at a loss himself for several moments. When he straightened and looked around at Bobby there was distance in his yellowed eyes and he had his classroom voice back.

"Do you recall the pattern of blood across the face of the tombstone closest to where the body lay?"

"No. I mean, there was no pattern."

"The absence of one is significant. Blood spurts rhythmically from an artery as the heartbeat pushes it through a severed end. This forms a distinctive stippled pattern on a relatively flat, blank surface such as the limestone grave marker. All of our photographs will show that the stone in question was all but washed in blood, like cleaning water tossed from a bucket. I think analysis will show it was animal, not human, blood. Everything we were bidden to look at in that little plot of cemetery ground was staged. Why?"

Bobby nodded, looking at a drippy faucet in a sink, the rattling window fans that were getting on his nerves. And Mally's corpse's face, a gray clayish thing with dark coagulate everywhere, bone showing near a sinkhole where an ear had been.

"Go on, cover her up again Dr. Valjean; for God's sake cover her up now! And if you don't have the love in you and can't cry for her, then leave her to those who knew her best, leave the grieving to them!"

Pee-Wee Cobb was undressed down to his underwear shorts, listening to the Cards' announcer Harry Caray in a delayed broadcast and studying the major-league baseball statistics in *The Sporting News* when Bobby came around and knocked on the back door of Pee-Wee's Good Eats.

"Bobby, you hear about that one-arm hermaphrodite stripteaser down in Naw'luns, calls herself 'Penis de Milo?'"

"Must be a handful," Bobby said, not cracking a smile while Pee-Wee guffawed. Then he said, "Need a bottle, Pee-Wee."

"Sure! Be your pleasure, Dickel or Beam?"

"Dickel."

"Want to drink it inside?"

"No. Got somebody with me."

Pee-Wee looked past Bobby at the dark figure of Ramses Valjean standing near a couple of fifty-five-gallon garbage drums.

"Who's that there?"

"Mally Shaw's daddy. Pee-Wee, you never saw either one of us tonight."

Pee-Wee cocked his head. "What's that? Did I hear somebody? Naw, must've been a old hooty owl." He disappeared for a couple of minutes and returned to hand a square fifth of sippin' whiskey and some picnic cups past the screen door.

"Little short tonight," Bobby said.

"Pay me Tuesday." Alert to some nuance in Bobby's expression, he amended, "Tuesday week I'm talkin' about."

After sharing half a fifth of whiskey and no conversation under the stars, Bobby looked up and across the picnic table in Pee-Wee's Colored arbor and said to Ramses, "Finding a body and not reporting it, call that a mortal sin but there's no statute applies. Removing a body to another location and trying to cover up what

171

you've done is a felony. Somebody needed to take a big risk."

"Why?" Ramses's eyes looked amber in the glow from the cigar he drew on.

"I don't know. Pour you another, Dr. Valjean?"

"If you wouldn't mind, sir. Also if you don't mind—Ramses, please."

"Half-French and all, would've figured you for a wine drinker."

"I can only claim to be a Francophile, and, yes, always wine with a good meal. But serious down-home drinking requires the presence of Mr. Dickel or Mr. Daniels of Lynchburg."

"Big amen to that," Bobby said, savoring his own fine Havana cigar, which Ramses had produced from a traveling humidor in his pigskin valise. The leaves of the chestnut trees stirred above their heads and they could faintly follow the progress of the baseball game on Pee-Wee's radio. Pee-Wee had stayed discreetly out of sight behind the pull-down shades of his two rooms. The game seemed to be in extra innings, but Bobby had lost track of time.

"Whoever moved Mally needed help. That's my thinking right now. One man just couldn't have done it all, and then where did he go? Left the car there, so he would've been on foot, and Cole's Crossing is a good long hike from anywhere."

"Two men possibly. Two vehicles, one of which might have been a pickup truck. But again, what could have been the motive for moving her?"

"They weren't wild dogs. They were somebody's dogs that got loose and attacked Mally. Matter of liability then."

"Who keeps dogs with the potential for attacking human beings?"

"Who doesn't? Even good dogs penned up long enough can turn savage if they're running free and something provokes them. Like a scared woman on the run herself."

"From the dogs? Or from men?"

"You have a reason to suggest that?" Bobby said sharply.

Ramses had put down his cigar; his face, his expression, was no longer readable in the darkness.

"No. Not yet."

"Maybe I need to get over to Mally's place first thing, have a look around."

"I should go with you. There will be effects to dispose of. I believe Mally owned the house, which will be a matter for probate."

"Where did you plan to spend the night?"

"Eddie Paradise Galphin kindly offered accommodations while I must be in Evening Shade."

"Oh, he did? His mother's house? Passel of half-grown kids using up the accommodations there, a mattress on the porch is the best you'd get. In your condition . . . Anyway, I'm liking you to stay away from Eddie for a couple days. I don't trust his ambition."

"I suppose I could beg shelter for the night from one of our local preachers."

"Uh-huh."

"I'm not a religious man. I would find it difficult to accept a preacher's hospitality and have to participate in rituals from a 'sacred' text made up of equal parts of myth, superstition, and wishful thinking. Are you a religious man, Bobby?"

"Off and on. And don't be calling me 'Bobby' anywhere there's a possibility somebody else might hear you."

"I thought we had settled a little something between us with this bottle of good sipping whiskey."

"Well, yes and no." He had the sense that Ramses was smiling. "I drink with any man anytime and anywhere I please, and that's nobody's business. I respect you as a man and I'm sorry for your loss even if you don't realize yet how much you've lost, and I'm sorry for—"

"My fate?" Ramses suggested.

"That too. Just respect me for who I am and need to be." Bobby took another drink. "My daddy was sheriff twenty-three years and they called my daddy Robert. Goddamn it, they call me Bobby."

"I understand."

"The mattresses are thin down to the jail, but it's quiet Sunday nights."

"Is that where you want me to go now, Bobby? To spend a night in jail?" There was no denying the amusement in Ramses' voice.

"No," Bobby said. "Tell the truth, I just don't know what to do about you."

Bobby sneaked into the conjugal bed hoping Cecily wouldn't wake up, but she rolled over and put the back of a lax hand against his cheek, a caressing moment.

"Thought I heard you talking to somebody."

"You did. We have company. Just for the night."

"Oh. Who?"

"Ramses Valjean. He didn't have anyplace else to go."

After a few seconds Cecily said, "That was good of you, Bobby." She sniffed his hair. "Cigar?"

"Uh-huh."

"Your breath. Not drunk are you?"

"I've been worse."

"You only drink hard liquor when something's really troubling you. Is it our money?"

"No. I'll get a game together down at the jail in a day or two."

"Bobby, do you ever lose at poker?"

"Try not to." He closed his eyes, getting comfortable next to her skin. "Has to do with Mally Shaw."

"Is there a problem about what happened to her?" Cecily said. She could be prescient lying with him late at night in that twilight of near-sleep where psychic nerve endings were adrift like jellyfish in a tame sea.

"Shaping up to be a big problem, and I don't know how to handle it."

Cecily breathed deeply and after a minute or so he thought she'd gone back to sleep snuggled against him, nightgown hiked above the ivory beauty of her little rump.

"How would Luther handle it if he was here?"

"Luther? He'd sit tight until the problem went away."

"Will it go away eventually, Bobby?"

"I think so."

"Then maybe that's all you need to do. Sit tight and wait."

EIGHT

Fresh Magic

A Vacant Man

Nighttime on the *Black Serpent Express*

Alex woke up *in a macrame hammock in the gazebo be-*
hind the two-story brick Colonial house when Francie Swift gave the
hammock a push. She was wearing jodhpurs and her second-best riding boots and a short-sleeved blue-and-white-check gingham shirt.
There was a riding helmet and leather crop under her left arm.

"Did you spend the night here?" she said, unsurprised, as if she
found half-wild children around the place all the time.

Alex yawned, then nodded. The sun had been up for half an
hour, hot spots on his face and long, tanned legs from light streaming
through the morning-glory-covered latticework.

"Why? Do you have a problem at home?"

Francie had an old dog with her, snow white muzzle and a low
growl in his throat when Alex sat up and put his bare feet on the
gazebo floor. He was semihard in his shorts. If Francie noticed, it
wasn't a novelty: She had three brothers. At fourteen her own sexual-
ity was awake but as still as a hiding rabbit.

Alex looked up at her with the agreeable heartshock of the
charmed. Francie had shoulder-length hair, summer-paled. Her oval
face was overlaid with tiny freckles, as if she had been cola-spritzed
through screenwire. He longed to tell her everything. But words that
had come effortlessly to his tongue only hours ago failed to show up.
Strangled sounds instead of speech; he had left the fresh magic of language behind him as well when he turned his back on Mally at Cole's
Crossing. He slumped in disappointment and bit his sore lip, a failure
again, unable to look at Francie now.

Francie reached down to silence her dog with a couple of taps of her forefinger on the bony muzzle.

"My folks are in Bowling Green. They won't be back until tomorrow afternoon late. You can use the shower in the tack room. I'll fix you some breakfast. You won't get so many skeeter bites if you sleep on the porch tonight. Unless you decide to go on home."

Alex shook his head.

"I'm schooling Tigertown this morning. If you want to watch. Probably it would be boring for you. Do you ride?"

No.

"We're shorthanded this week. So if you wanted to help there's stalls to muck out. Plenty pairs of boots around here; you ought to be able to find some that'll fit you."

He looked up again. Francie gave a toss of her head. She wore her hair in two blond wings from a center part as straight as if she'd drawn it with a ruler. Pale eyes swam with sun-motes. There was humor in her glance.

"Don't think I'm going to give you breakfast if you're allergic to work. Now get going, son. Wash up." She pretended she was going to stamp his toes with her boot. Alex shot up from the hammock and gave Francie his sidelong disdainful look while slipping into his moccasins. She pointed businesslike to the center of his chest with her riding crop. Both of them about to smile. Alex feigned alarm and ran across the gazebo and straight down, a six-foot drop, landed gracefully on all fours and took off in a sprint. Halfway to the barn he threw in a difficult running somersault in the air, added a cartwheel to amuse Francie. He figured she would still be watching.

R*amses Valjean was about to begin* brushing his teeth when the bathroom door opened and Bernice Clauson started in, sleep still fogging her eyes, the hem of her sheer blue nightgown swirling around her ankles. She was carrying a glass of water in her left hand.

With her other hand on the doorknob, Bernice drew up tautly at the sight of Ramses in his undershirt and trousers with red suspenders dangling, hunched over the basin. She might not have been as surprised to find a six-foot alligator there.

"Good morning," Ramses said. "You must be Mrs. Clauson."

Bernie dropped the tumbler, which had her upper plate in solution, on the tile floor. Her hand flew up to cover her open mouth in its gummy vacancy, muffling a cry of horror. She backpedaled into the hall, pulling the door shut.

Ramses looked at the pearly set of dentures in shattered glass on the blue floor. He put his toothbrush down, gripped the basin with both hands, and shook from suppressed laughter until his efforts provoked a coughing fit instead.

O*n the way to Mally Shaw's house* in his prowler, Bobby received a message from Dispatch.

"Bobby, Francie Swift called and said Alex spent the night at their place, but she didn't know until she got up this morning or she would have called sooner."

"He there now?"

"Francie said to tell you he's had breakfast, he's doing some work around the stables and he's fine, you shouldn't worry about him."

"Thanks, Deb."

Ramses was looking at him. Bobby said, "Alex is being a pain in the butt. Right now we're not seeing eye to eye about him going away to a school in Louisville where they could help him. He'll be fourteen in a couple of months, but he doesn't want to grow up. Probably I spoiled him. Our folks died in a fire, I mention that last night? Anyway he's too dependent on me, and I don't know how to handle it."

"I would be the last one to give advice about being a parent, or a surrogate parent. Mally always made it easy, forgiving me for the neglect I showed her. I wonder why?"

"She had a good heart. Maybe she always believed you'd be

around when she needed you most. You never hurt her on purpose, what you've told me."

"Willful absence can be the most hurtful thing of all. Emotional silence. Your brother is unable to speak, but he is wild to be understood. He writes very well, by the way. Does he keep a diary?"

"Wouldn't know. I don't poke around in his room. Sometimes he shows me stories. Shoot-'em-ups mostly. Maybe that's his way of getting some of the hurtful things out of his system."

"I hope to meet Alex, now that I've slept in his bed and experienced through his possessions and the imprint of his soul what it must be like to be a boy. I was born into hard labor on my father's farm, a slave as surely as if I'd been dragged off a ship in chains a century ago. Born with an old man's spite and iron will. My father was subversive in black society; he had earned his portion and his mules by being a white man's nigger. I was always ashamed of him."

The radio again. A Negro in his forties had been found dead in a ditch. Natural causes, apparently. Cocaine in his snuff box. His name was Lindell Jones.

"Natural causes?" Ramses said.

"Around here cocaine and 'shine go down as natural causes."

"Should it happen to be a man of color. Or a woman."

"The tonks are full of cocaine. Lots of it coming down from the north since the war. Not much we can do."

"Just another form of slavery." Ramses fell silent, looking out the window.

"Look, if there's money in it for Luther, I don't know about it or want to know."

Ramses looked at Bobby again.

"You don't care for law enforcement, do you?"

"What I care about is the law. That's what I bust my butt going to night school for."

At the boarded-up rib shack Bobby turned right off Route 19 and was greeted by the sight of Eddie Paradise Galphin lounging against his dusty red roadster.

"Goddamn it."

"I do have to admire his tenacity."

"You stepping out of the front seat of my prowler, Eddie'll think you've got a hoodoo on me."

"Behave as if I know my place. Count on me, Boss."

"You'll be gone from here in a couple of days."

"Although not as far as Eternity's Gates—"

"You can joke about the damnedest things."

"It's a matter of keeping some perspective on the unimaginable."

"I have to go on dealing with my people, and I can't afford to get a leery eye from any man."

"I fully understand, Boss."

"Why when you say 'Boss' does it sound sort of like 'shithead'?"

"Takes years of practice," Ramses acknowledged.

Ramses smiled and Bobby smiled too, slightly, then put on a different face getting out of the prowler to deal with Eddie Paradise Galphin.

"I'm wearing you like a bad suit, Eddie."

"Just wanting to be of some service in Dr. Valjean's time of tribulation," Eddie said with hand-wringing sincerity. "What happened to you last night, Doctor? I was waiting up 'til half past—"

Bobby walked up to within one foot of Eddie, causing him to scoot up straight against the side of his car.

"You still yearning to get to Chicago, Eddie?"

"Well, I—"

"I can arrange it for you. Overnight to Chicago, naked as the day you were born, in an Illinois Central reefer. Ever seen a man with eyeballs froze solid, Eddie?"

"No sir."

"Not to mention his dick."

"Oh-*oh*."

"Lindell Jones is lying dead in a ditch out by Lovett Plantation. There's a story for you. No story here."

"Yes sir."

When *Eddie Paradise Galphin's roadster* had disappeared on the highway Ramses said, "An interesting exercise in public relations."

"They have to believe you'll do exactly what you say you'll do. The more inventive I am thinking up punishment, the quicker it turns into folklore. I never have hit a colored man with a nightstick. Just doesn't make an impression. White man, nightstick's always best."

"And that impressive revolver you carry?"

"It's a .44. I'm plenty good on the range, but I've never shot a man and hope I never have to."

Inside the house they found that the electricity was off. Bobby traced the problem to its source on the highway and radioed for a utility truck.

When he returned to the house Ramses Valjean was standing by the windows in the front room where the light was good, reading a page from one of Alex's notebooks.

"What have you got there?" Bobby said, although it was a familiar type of notebook, and he had a hunch.

"A short story your brother wrote when he was in the fifth grade. I wonder how Mally happened to—"

"If it was here then Alex gave it to her."

Ramses closed the notebook. "They knew each other?"

Bobby shrugged. "Not long. Mally did him a good turn when he spilled off his bike around here. Cleaned him up, put some iodine on his cuts." Ramses didn't say anything. "Alex was in some trouble at the house that turned out not to be his doing. He might have come over looking for some sympathy from Mally. She was one hell of a fine woman, always nursing somebody I guess."

"Yes, she was like that. A sweetness in her nature that couldn't have come from either of us. But wildflowers stubbornly will appear, even on stony ground."

"I called for a lineman; power will be back on directly. I need to go to work."

"Of course."

"You're kind of isolated here. I didn't notice a phone line to the house. But Mallard's store is only a short walk going back toward town. There's a pay phone. You need a ride somewhere, call and I'll come myself or send a deputy for you."

"I only need to go by Godsong and Wundall's to make final arrangements for tomorrow."

"Staying here tonight?"

"I'm sure I can make myself comfortable. While I bring myself up to date on Mally's affairs. I suppose I could find this out myself, but you might be able to tell me. Did she have a lover?"

"I wouldn't know."

"Before you leave, why don't you have a look in the bedroom?"

Bobby walked down the hall to Mally's bedroom, stood in the doorway for a few moments, then went inside and raised the window shade all the way to get a better look at the condition of her bed. He returned to the living room.

"Somebody played rough with her. Or there could've been—"

"No. I don't think it was more than one man. Judging from the condition of the soft tissues of her vulva and vagina, there can be only one conclusion: Mally was forced, perhaps repeatedly. There also were small hemorrhages of blood vessels of the inner thighs: fingertip bruises, as if he held her thighs well apart while he raped her. He has large hands, by the way. The rape, or rapes, occurred well before the dogs got hold of her."

"You examined Mally's—"

Ramses said harshly, "I examined a dead woman's remains for the truth she was beyond telling us."

"So she was raped here, then taken somewhere else, where she died. Then she was moved again."

Ramses held out his right fist and slowly opened it. He was holding crumpled cellophane.

"I found one on the floor by the sofa, two more in the bedroom. The same wrappers that were left in Mally's Dodge. He likes hard candy."

"Or Mally had a sweet tooth."

"So far I haven't found any candy in the house. Nor was there any in her purse or car."

Bobby let out a slow breath. "Better let me have those wrappers. I'll put them with the other . . . evidence that's coming over from the mortuary this morning."

"Where in town would you be likely to find Brach's hard candies?"

"Reaves Rexall and probably the five and dime. I'll check those first, but a lot of people—"

"Buy candy. Of course. But you're looking for a white man, blond, six feet one or two inches tall, who wears a size-ten boot and has probably purchased his candy within the last three days."

"How in the hell—"

"The front seat of the Dodge was pushed nearly all the way back. Mally was a small person; I doubt that she could have operated her car with the seat in that position. I'll assume that whoever drove the car to Little Grove had enough sense not to leave his fingerprints all over it."

"Blond?"

"During intercourse he left a few of his pubic hairs behind: three to be exact, stuck with blood or semen to Mally's pudendum and her own pubic hair, which is quite coarse compared to the Nordic—"

"Why don't I just hand over my badge to you, Ramses, and you finish up what I didn't do much of a job of in the first place!"

"No need to feel insulted or slighted, Bobby. I've had years of experience working with the Nashville police department on some of their difficult cases of homicide. Here I have only made a necessary beginning. The real detective work is up to you. Find him, Bobby. Or do you know who I'm talking about already?"

Bobby couldn't answer him. His throat was tight as a fist.

Ramses said quietly, "Is he untouchable, Bobby?"

"Nobody . . . is untouchable, a thing like this."

"I've only given you information. What you don't have is proof."

"I know that."

"Then you have so much at risk. If you're going to pursue this. *Will* you pursue it, Bobby?"

"For God's sake, what do you expect me to say?"

Ramses nodded, then looked around the front room of Mally's house, his scan halting at the picture wall behind the sofa. Arrested by an image of himself and a young Mally holding his hand and smiling up at him. His beardless face in this photo was stern, as if he found himself an unwilling accomplice to something.

"I already know myself to be a vacant man," Ramses said at length. "Looking at *'L'horreur d'une profonde nuit.'* The horror of a deep night, as Racine put it. But what you must face is the rest of your life." He smiled. "Try it on right now, Bobby, have a look in the mirror of your soul. How do you like the fit? Comfortable? Or will you ever-after be wearing your life, as you said to Eddie, like a bad suit?"

Leland Howard's man Jim Giles ate his lunch at the Hob-Nob Cafe on Courthouse Square: Monday's Special, which was overdone roast beef with mashed potatoes and gravy and a side dish of stewed tomatoes and okra, eighty-five cents. He had two more cups of black coffee, which he had been drinking steadily for the last thirty-six hours while catching only a couple of hours' sleep on the road. All the caffeine had his brain abuzz like wearing-out neon, his heart jarring to the beat. Still, he didn't mind being off the campaign trail for a while. Politics amused Giles, but dourly: all of those candidates with shotgun mouths, loaded with double-aught bullshit.

After lunch he went outside into full noon glare, a kitchen match in one tight corner of his mouth. He stood beneath a rusted tin canopy over the sidewalk shielding his eyes with a saluting hand as if there was something to single out that made this courthouse square much different from so many others in Dixie, but the only difference may have been in the quality of upkeep, desultory civic pride. Everything needed to be swept or hosed. Some begonias and zinnias were suffocating in dust in a couple of filled-in horse troughs that fronted the squat yellow brick courthouse. There were cracked store windows here and there that the merchants lacked funds to replace. He saw kids with ice cream—they looked well-scrubbed, at any rate—including a lanky blond boy pushing his blue-and-white Schwinn bike along with one hand, keeping pace with a girl blonder than he was on an idling, new-looking Cushman motor scooter. He didn't know who they were—didn't know a soul in Evening Shade—but the bicycle was familiar. He had seen one like it on Mally Shaw's porch during the rainstorm Saturday night. With a piece of the red reflector on the back fender missing.

Giles took the match out of his mouth, walked down three steps to street level, where he spat, waited on a panel delivery truck to pass him, then strolled across the wide concrete pavement with its Medusa-like snakes of asphalt patching going every which way and fell in behind the oblivious teenagers. She appeared to be doing all of the talking. Then, as if she had talked herself dry, she stopped to get a drink from the granite fountain in the shaded border of park around the courthouse—the trees growing here, true to the nondescript, down-in-the-mouth look of the town, were trash mimosas and scabby sycamores instead of oaks deeply rooted in century-old grandeur.

Giles had a good look at the reflector on the Schwinn. Same piece missing, all right. That's when the boy turned casually and saw him from thirty feet away and couldn't conceal the surprise, or dismay, that flashed into his face. Giles didn't change expression; the boy looked immediately at his scuffed moccasins where a tie had come loose, then at the girl fetchingly bent over the water fountain in her sleeveless blouse and Bermudas. But she didn't hold Giles' attention for long, and he resumed studying the boy. Turned abruptly away when the girl finished getting her drink. Giles walked across the square to where he had parked the Pontiac Eight. He had seen enough to realize Leland Howard's problems in Evening Shade had begun to multiply.

In his office in the courthouse basement Bobby Gambier turned the pages of another notebook, smelling of vomit, that he had previously locked in a drawer of his desk. The door to the office was closed, shutting off circulation of air between his open windows and the large fans outside in the hall. He sweated profusely while he reread Alex's account of Mally Shaw's rape, which had led to something unspeakable later on in the night, where there might not have been an eyewitness. He didn't know yet.

Bobby had served at the end of a war in a defeated nation, rat-rubble cities, the chewed, littered countryside still criss-crossed by tank treads and reeking of shellfire, country into which lesser members of the SS Death's Head formations and death-camp administrators tried to slip away. Lacking the resources of some of their superiors to escape across borders. Bobby had seen the faces of those rounded up and shipped to Heidelberg in chains. Stolid unrepentant faces, eyes that had seen everything inhuman and hearts that felt nothing. No more guilt in the SS guards than there had been in the shepherd dogs trained to dismember prisoners on command. Sometimes for sport.

He didn't know Leland Howard, but Bobby couldn't imagine him standing by while dogs (his dogs?) destroyed Mally. But if there was an explanation for the manner of her death, he might be the only man who could give it.

When he'd finished reading, Bobby tore the pages from Alex's notebook and struck a match. The pages curled like dark phantoms in the bottom of his metal wastebasket, drifted into ash that he stirred with the end of another match. Then he sat back in his chair with his hands laced behind his head, looking at the slow flutter of a moth inside a chamberpot light fixture.

At least Alex was protected now.

O*n the platform at Cole's Crossing* after the nightly run of the *Dixie Traveler,* Mally said to Alex, "So you've got a girlfriend? What's her name?"

"Francie. She's not exactly my girlfriend. She said I could stay over there again tonight if I want. When her folks get home, different story."

"But she likes you."

"I don't think it makes any difference to Francie that I can't talk to her the way I'm talking to you—in this place."

Alex's head jerked, and he gave a startled look at something or someone that was gone before his brain could assimilate what his eyes had picked up. Mally looked momentarily troubled by his apprehension, then smiled.

"Bet she's a pretty one."

"Francie? Uh-huh. Anyway—Francie says she likes to do the talking because most people don't have much on their minds, although she sees in my eyes I have a serious nature"—Alex's cheeks reddened a little—"and it's a relief, she says, to be with somebody who pays attention to her and isn't always telling her, Francie, zip it." Alex shied as if he'd brushed against something invisible but tactile in the air and took a side step closer to the depot wall, his image flashing in a broken piece of pane in a window frame. "You know, she can be real funny. She got peed off at her horse, Tigertown, today. Said he has only three gaits—walk, stumble, and fall. Stuff like that; I never laughed so much."

"By the way," Mally said, admiring her evening's finery, a sleeveless dark blue shantung dress and a gold bangle-bracelet on her right wrist, "thanks for the dress and the jewelry. But I didn't really need *this.*" She held up her left arm. She was wearing a gold strap watch that looked like Bernice Clauson's. "Never could afford anything this choice, that's for sure."

Alex glanced at Mally's bare feet.

"Oh-oh."

"Never mind. I'm not likely to pick up splinters."

"Uh, how about a pair of riding boots like Francie—"

"Not with this outfit, thank you very much."

"I still don't get what, I mean how I—"

"You dress me up in your mind before I—come. Otherwise, who knows what I'd look like?"

"You mean dead?"

Alex bit his sore underlip, looking away from Mally because he didn't like to see that she wasn't breathing. Made it difficult for him to draw breath himself.

"Reckon so, Alex. Dead and getting deader all the time."

He could see Mally perfectly, as if she created her own serene light, shining through her skin and not on it, a paper-lantern sort of light; otherwise there was a depth of blackness at the Crossing like nothing he'd known before. It was like being at the absolute silent faceless edge of the universe.

There was an apparitional stir within the depot that he felt rather than saw. He looked in there through thick mesh wire covering one of the jagged windows, looked quickly away. He could dress up Mally, but not the other souls crowded inside, wanting to get a look at him.

"Train's on the way," Mally said.

"Another of those spook trains?" Alex said with an unnerved grin.

Mally gave him a dire look. "There are white folks waitin' to board too, Alex."

"I know, I"—his lip was bleeding, never would heal if he didn't leave it alone—"see them. Long as you're with me, I don't have anything to worry about, do I?"

"Oh, Alex. Maybe it's not such a good thing, you being so close to a Crossing." She looked east and up the tracks. "Don't care for the looks of this one. Step back, Alex, against the depot wall. You don't want to get sucked in."

He did as he was told, heart seizing up, although he saw nothing, east- or westbound, on the track. But he could feel, again, pressure against his body. Suddenly there it was, like a silent explosion, sparks flying from the grinding of huge driver wheels on steel rails. A headlamp cold as a reptile's eye. Then he heard low wailing, but not from human throats.

Mally was in front of him, shielding him with her mildly luminous body, although he had no sense of that body, her skin on his. He only felt *protected*.

"Close your eyes and stop your ears. Do it now!"

There was an outpouring of souls from inside the depot. He felt as if the mild temperature on the platform had dropped to zero. The wailing, although he held his ears tightly, had the pitch of cataclysm. He felt such bottomless despair that he burst into tears and dropped slowly to his knees. When they touched the rough planks of the platform, all sound and phantom motion ceased.

Mally had stepped away from him. He looked up to see the last coaches of a train that was part black steel and, oh God!, part armored serpent slipping round the bend at Half Mile and into a red wound of the sky as terrible as a torn heart. It lasted for two blinks of his dazzled eyes.

"Are they going to hell?" he sobbed.

"There's no heaven or hell, which is what I always suspected 'spite of Sunday school and the Old Testament and those preachers who use hellfire for a fund-raiser. There's only other worlds to go to, some a lot nicer than . . . the one I just left, and others that are—well, I can't say for sure. It's like on your side some folks get Palm Beach and others get Pittsburgh. But in the grand scheme of things, Alex, no matter how bad you mess up in one try at life, you get to do it again, like if you failed fourth grade. Difference is, next time around your fourth-grade teacher is going to be a lot stricter, and the new school won't have that nice playground, and there's no free lunch. Fail twice, it only gets tougher each time to make up your work."

Mally looked west, where the sky was no longer fulminating. All black again.

"Those folks ridin' westbound now are just some of your stubborn diehard failures, those who loafed and la-di-da'd through life or
did real harm to others. Where they wind up, fourth grade is gonna
be a lot like gladiator school." She looked at Alex from that character-
istic side slant of her head, those calm, smart, brown eyes, her expression wry and piquant. That wise crease of a smile. "Maybe you ought
not come here anymore. I'm real concerned that you may have too
much—what's the word?—*affinity* for the Crossing and what goes on
here. Like you said, something has been drawing you here nearly all
of your young life, and there are . . . forces that will try to take advantage. No, don't ask me to explain. I'm just beginning to have a
sense of things on this side. You could have been killed here twice already that I know about. Now, Alex. Whatever time it's got to be, that
cute girl of yours must be waitin' and maybe worried that you
haven't showed up."

"Telling me you won't be here anymore if I do come?" Alex said,
getting to his feet.

"No. I'm not saying that. Because it's probably not up to me. The
arrangement, or attraction we seem to have for each other, the power
of it is strongest on your part."

"I *need* to see you, Mally. Because there's nobody else I can talk to!"

"Baby, language isn't just words. Which you may have latched
onto already today, and you know what I'm saying."

"She'll change," Alex said dourly. "Sooner or later Francie will
dump on me like everybody else does."

"Whoa now. Don't be bringin' that attitude around here, or
maybe I'll just hop aboard the next train out, wherever it's bound."

Alex's eyes were streaming again. "You can't, Mally! You have to
help me put Leland Howard in jail, because Bobby doesn't have the
guts to do it!"

"Told you before—"

"But that must be it, Mally! Why I'm here and *you're* still here, because, like it or not, you can't rest until that yellabelly gets what he has
coming!"

Mally folded her arms pensively. She had begun to appear insubstantial to him, yellow caution light from the signal bridge by the trestle shining where her heart ought to be. His power to attract and hold Mally was subject to a dynamism he understood no better than his own emotional peaks and falls.

"If you're right," she said, "I could be in for a long stay here. 'Cause that man may never get all he deserves—over there on your side."

"Can't you help me?"

"Show up in a courtroom like Banquo's ghost at a feast? Point an accusing finger at the man who raped me? You already know I can't . . ." Mally fell silent even as she slipped a little further away from his perception. "Huh. I'm forgettin' something. Alex, on his deathbed Priest Howard raised up to call Mr. Leland 'thief.'"

"What about it?"

"Mr. Leland worked in town at the bank for a good many years 'til he quit to politic. Was in charge of the Trust Department."

"What's that?"

"Managed accounts for bank customers, those who had a good bit of money put by. Evening Shade is a poor county, but there's always those farmers and business people who save and save and don't spend much and invest in stocks and bonds or let a Trust Officer at the bank do it for them. A clever man like Mr. Leland could have done something tricky with a few of those accounts that would put money in his own pocket, and if he was patient and not greedy, his thieving might not be found out for a long time."

"But Old Man Howard could've got on to him?"

"Well, it was his bank."

"Mally, I'm not seeing you so good anymore! Don't leave yet."

"Not up to me. Just keep studyin' how I was, as if you were looking at an old snapshot. While I think on this. Mr. Howard gave me something a few days before he passed. Now what—?"

"Which train did he catch?"

"Not the prettiest, but far from the worst. Alex, you got to keep heart and mind focused on me now, I'm trying to—"

194

"He gave you something. A letter or—"

"No. It was a key. One that Mr. Howard said would unlock secrets that it was time to tell."

"So where—what did you do with—"

"I don't know."

"He gave you a key he said was important, and you don't know what you *did* with it?"

"We don't carry a lot of memories beyond the Crossing. Because our reckoning is done the second we all die, and there's no need to think anymore about how we acted or what we were like in our past life. That's only like a long dream we had. How much do you recollect from your dreams, not when you first wake up but a day or two later?"

"I don't know. You've got to tell me where that key is!"

"Was maybe two inches long. Steel, not brass. Umhmm. And it's buried now—or did I bury it?" He slammed a fist against the depot wall in exasperation. "Alex, I'm trying."

"I can hardly see you!"

"Just hold on. Think about me. Was I pretty to you, Alex? Did you maybe have a little crush on me like you do on Francie? *Remember.* Bring me back."

"Mal-LY!"

"Oh. It was canning day, with Verona. So hot. I was melting."

"Melting what?"

"The paraffin, of course."

"What was it you were putting up?"

"Tomatoes," Mally said.

Or had she said "potatoes"? He wasn't sure, and like that she had escaped his last tenuous hold on her, starlight where Mally had been, a bleak angle of the old depot's roof. The night at Cole's Crossing had resumed in full tranquility, the sky calm as the surface of a mirror reflecting a portion of the universe's blaze of wonders and benign night, quiet except for peeper frogs along the steeping banks of the moon-chased Yella Dog River.

"Oh shit," he said, tried to get it out. But with Mally's disappearance, his fluency was gone, voicebox corroded like an old tin lock. Alex felt something brush his cheek, a light touch, whisk of gossamer, a remembrance kiss. Nothing more, although he stayed on the rotting platform by the shut depot used now only by ghosts spirited and dispirited, until the next train showed up, this one a rumbling earthbound freight with cattle, hopper, and flat cars that carried new harvesting machinery west, ammonium nitrate tanks sliding silver in the moonlight. A bindle stiff smoked in the partly open doorway of a Rock Island boxcar, nothing supernatural about him. All of it rolling by at a sedate forty-five miles an hour.

Alex retrieved his bike and pedaled down the road past Little Grove Holiness Church, past a parked stake-sided pickup truck with a whiff of pigs about it that he hadn't seen an hour earlier when he arrived for his nightly visit to Cole's Crossing, a truck with an accordian fender and empty cab; paid little attention as he side-slipped past. Maybe a young couple, blanket on the ground somewhere in leafy shadows having at it, no time for spying them out to lay low and enjoy a bare-ass show, and if he ever got the chance with Francie Swift, oh boy, slipping her panties down knees ankles burying his nose in them smelling *it* Jesus wonderful but that was a midnight fancy with the moonlight through his bedroom windows falling on his naked groin, one hand twisting the fat Schwinn handgrip and pedaling faster, flinging gravel, not seeing the red tip of a cigarette across the road in the shelter and shadow of a modest two-story lancet portico framing church doors. And faster, because he was excited and not only about his nascent sex life—young Alex.

Paraffin. Tomatoes.

He knew what Mally must have done with the key entrusted to her.

NINE

Cocktails
Runaways
False Sanctuary

Will he be *coming back here tonight?"* *Bernice Clauson* said. "There is so much talk in town already, you would not believe the gossip."

"I wonder who started it?" Cecily said, sitting in the kitchen with her blouse unbuttoned and Brendan drowsy at one breast but still suckling.

"Things just become *known* in a small town like Evening Shade, especially unsavory things. I was aware at the market today of a certain— well, hostility, to give it a name. The Gambiers have a nigra living at their house—"

"A Negro doctor who was educated at the Sorbonne."

"—as an invited *guest.*" Bernie peered down through half glasses at the game of solitaire she was amusing herself with until Brendan went off to bed and she and Cecily could play hearts. But the boy would not part with her nipple just yet. "Even Rhoda thinks Bobby has taken leave of his senses."

"This is not like you, Mom. Come on, Brendy, you've had enough; let go you little tiger, time for beddy-byes."

"Hem. I am from Wisconsin, a vastly more civilized state than this one, but as fate and an unfortunate marriage would have it, I've spent the better part of my last fifteen years in Evening Shade. I consider myself superior to bigoted attitudes, but really, dear, one must be sensitive to the mores of one's adopted place. What I am saying is, it was not seemly to have invited that man here in spite of his tragic circumstances, and of course I had *no warning*. At least couldn't Bobby have had the good judgment to offer Dr. Valjean your perfectly adequate accommodations in the basement instead of plopping him down in the room next to mine? It almost seemed to me like malice aforethought."

Cecily used her fingers to get Brendan off her nipple, which caused a sleepy fuss. "It's stifling in the basement in the summertime."

"Let him sweat then."

"He'll be going back to Nashville tomorrow or Wednesday. Meantime, I told you, just use our bathroom, and this topic is getting *old,* Mother. I'm taking Brendan upstairs now."

"Some of the talk that was reported back to me has been. Hem. Downright ugly."

"I'm not afraid of talk. Bobby is sheriff of Evening Shade, at least until Luther gets back from his wedding trip. Then the talk will just stop; people will find something else that outrages them. Mother, where did that red queen come from?"

"Winning is so much more fun than losing."

Cecily was halfway up the front stairs with Brendan on her shoulder when the cars came by fast on West Hatchie, no mufflers on a couple of them, and she heard the jeering voices just before something splattered the porch and screen door. She turned and walked back down the stairs and met her mother in the front hall. Bernice had a hand over her mouth, the whites of her eyes like small full moons.

"My *Lord*! Did you hear them? Were they screaming 'Nigger lovers?' And what is that *smell?*"

"It's shit, Mother. The little idiots emptied their bowels somewhere and then they threw their shit all over our porch. Take the baby."

Cecily was shaking as she handed Brendan off to Bernice.

"Oh, I'm going to become hysterical!" Bernie wailed.

"Like hell you are," Cecily snapped.

Bernice backed away in total confusion. Cecily talking to her in that forbidding voice.

"But—what will we do if they come again?"

"I'll call Dispatch right now to have a dep outside until Bobby gets home from night school. Then I'm going to scrub my porch and screen door with Lysol."

"Shouldn't Bobby see what they—"

Cecily swept tears off her cheeks with her fingertips.

"I don't want Dr. Valjean to see the porch dirty. Or to know it ever happened, if that's possible. Because he's a guest in *my* house. Anyone in this community who doesn't like it can shove a posthole digger straight up his ass."

Fifteen *exquisite ampules of morphine* arranged like miniature candelabra on the oval table with its embossed cigarette burn in the front room of Mally's house. Cunning glass ornaments and their steely contents of surcease. *Like colorless hard candies,* he thinks, choosing another and holding it up to the light of the lamp with its painted metal shade, turning the ampule between dark thumb and forefinger. The syringe is in his other hand. Bulge of vein like an engorged worm below the elbow of his tied-off arm. A couple of beads of blood on his glistening flesh. It is warm and close in the room, but his sweat is cold. Three of his hoard of ampules already broken open, drained. Fourteen to go after the next injection; but he won't make it all the way through his pretty candelabrum: Permanent slumber free of pain and regret will take hold first. He is a doctor. He knows the limits of the organism's tolerance for the potent morphine. His will shut down half an hour ago; now there is creeping numbness near his heart. But the human heart is a powerful rebel. Always the last hold-out in this scheme of things, dutifully conveying the refreshment of a narcotic turned poison in excess to that part of the brain that rules the heart.

His forearm is propped up on the arm of the bamboo sofa. The needle of the syringe wavers above the plump vein. The rest of Mally's house is unlighted, but he has heard that noise again. Curi-ous. Can't place it. A popping sound. Like a lid coming off an airtight jar of preserved goods. Earlier he thought he heard the squeak of floorboards. In the kitchen? Looking for food? Furtiveness murks the atmosphere of this house like cobweb, like stealthy mice. But the prowler, should there be one, apparently has no more interest in Ramses Valjean than Ramses has in him. He will not rise to his feet again. The matter needs no investigation, and anyway his death is well advanced.

Raising his eyes once more (how many times already tonight?) to the picture wall and the camera's portrait of eight-year-old Mally in frock and bows obliviously smiling up at the unresponsive face of her father, unknowing at her innocent age that a man can be haunted by his future as well as his past. He murmurs, yet again, *Forgive me,* but what would be the point in waiting? Just to see her closed coffin committed to the grave? The only point worth considering now is the dulled point of the syringe with which he seeks to pierce the sacrificial vein.

The first Molotov cocktail, a Royal Crown bottle filled with gasoline and stuffed at the neck with burning cotton garage waste, bursts through one of the half-open windows of the front room, instantly setting a frilly curtain afire, leaving a siegelike fire trail on the pine plank floor as it rolls close to the bamboo sofa, also setting the sofa aflame very near Ramses' sprawled and nearly inert body.

His foot lashes out reflexively at the fulminating bottle, spinning it away but lavishing more flame on anything that can burn: the fringed skirt of another table, a few magazines saved in a coal scuttle. The effort of kicking the bottle causes Ramses to slide off the sofa to the floor. He loses the syringe but pulls himself to his knees in the swarm of heat and smoke to grasp a handful of the morphine ampules from the table, which he stuffs into a coat pocket.

Another cocktail is hurled onto the front porch through the opened screen door and this one explodes against the cast-iron drum of Mally's washing machine; instantly the entire porch and front wall of the house are engulfed. Inside, Ramses, on all fours and with his head lolling like a sick dog's, backs away in spite of his earlier resolve not to live another day. The threat of runaway fire almost in his face has shut down all brain activity except for the most primitive of responses to peril: Life must be preserved, nature's imperative in spite of what tragic melancholy may have dispossessed the soul.

He can't run. He can barely stand upright. Wobbling numbly this way and that, hands splayed in a doorframe, his knees about to buckle. Sensing rather than seeing behind him the orange flash of another cocktail, this one heaved into the hall from the back porch. Rolling smoke and crackling flames, old wood all but exploding as it burns in searing heat.

The boy grabs him from behind. Drags him backward into the kitchen across uneven linoleum. Drops Ramses while he tugs and wrenches at a section of linoleum and peels it up from the floor in front of the sink. Then he seizes an ax and chops into the boards, fury in his face, ducking low as more fire sails in through a window. All of the house ablaze now, a twisty tail of burning debris rising above the erupted roof midhouse, white-hot tracers sizzling through the pale boughs of surrounding trees. The boy slinging the ax blade down and down, chips flying as he averts his face. He drops the ax and kicks a hole in the chopped floor that he can shove Ramses into, worming down then on top of him in the crawl space and taking hold of a lapel of Ramses' coat, dragging him like a swimmer through loose dirt and a hot cloud of smoke out from under the house, there lifting and carrying Ramses with more strength than Ramses would have thought the boy's slender body possessed. Dropping him down with a heavy, exhausted cough in the safety of the pole bean and cabbage garden, remaining doubled over, hands clutching his filthy knees, retching, while behind them the house shimmers like a fiery mirage.

*Y*ou *must be Alex,*" Ramses said when he could speak.

The boy looked at him with streaming eyes, holding his throat with one hand, still choking as he tried to breathe.

"Why, Alex? I really wasn't worth saving."

Alex stared down at Ramses in disbelief.

"What were you doing in Mally's house? What were you looking for?"

Alex looked around at the house, so much of it briskly consumed that at first light there would be only shoals of ash left around blackened islands of stove, washing machine, kitchen sink. He shook his head despondently, wiped a smeary cheek with the heel of one hand. His other hand, Ramses saw, was burned.

"You're hurt."

Alex grimaced, shaking his head again. No matter.

"I don't suppose you know . . . who is responsible."

No reply. But Alex took a quick look around, as if for suspects. Cars had stopped on the highway. People were getting out. Burning houses were an unbeatable crowd-pleaser.

"I apologize for my lack of gratitude. You risked your life for mine. Let me help you with that burn." Ramses made it up on one elbow, the arm that was still bound with rubber tubing. "But I can't. My medical bag was there in the house."

Voices from the road. *I don't know. Believe it were some nigger woman lived there.*

"Alex, if I had one of those bean poles to lean on, I think I could stand up now."

Alex wrenched a pole from the ground and offered his unburned hand to pull Ramses to his feet.

"I was going to kill myself," Ramses said, loosening the knotted tube above his elbow and discarding it like a pale noose. He looked at Alex, who had turned his back on him to kneel and run water from an irrigation pipe over his burns. "I have assumed another obligation. Unasked for, to be sure. Nevertheless an obligation. I may never redeem Mally's faith in me, but it's possible I can do something for you, Alex. Perhaps that would please her, if she knew."

Alex showed his face. Ramses was intrigued by the play of expression in the boy's eyes at the mention of Mally's name. Ramses touched his own throat with two fingers.

Alex shook his head sullenly, held it under the spigot for a few seconds, rinsed his parched mouth, spat, looked at Ramses again distrustfully.

"I will need to look at your medical history, of course, before I can make a recommendation."

Alex licked the back of his burned hand, shrugged, drew a forefinger across his own throat, a slashing gesture of finality, *Take your sense of obligation and shove it.* He got up from one knee and walked downhill toward the bicycle he had left in the yard. Ramses followed, leaning on his crooked bean pole, perplexed but feeling a perverse sense of happiness for one who so recently had renounced the remaining months of his life.

"There have been men grievously wounded in great battles, Alex, who survived worse injury than has been done to you! I devoted myself to many of them during the Great War. Turning your back on me settles nothing. I know about spiteful, runaway boys, Alex. I have been one all of my life, and I know better than to let you get away. You *will* fight that battle you've been avoiding!" Nearly out of breath, awkward, Ramses stumbled and almost fell. Alex pulled his bike off the ground and made a running mount, pedaling recklessly out to the highway. Ramses watched him go. His lips shaped his final words, but he barely heard himself.

"You'll fight it for both of us, Alex."

T*hat house you were interested in?* Thought I'd let you know it done burned to the ground tonight."

Past midnight and Leland Howard was alone in downtown Knoxville looking out at a rainy street, hunched feverishly over a telephone in semidarkness at a back-wall desk, getting the news from Jim Giles, a low point in his fortunes while his other persona, whom he was temporarily out of touch with, the exuberant vote-getter in an ice-cream suit, skin electric from storms of applause he'd generated at five different rallies during the day come rain or shine, *that* Leland

Howard smilingly occupied all four walls of tacked-up election posters in his regional campaign headquarters.

Leland the jumpy fugitive (in his mind) was cleaning between his teeth with his gold toothpick, responding in grunts and extremely sensitive to what was being said long-distance, bored telephone operators at this time of night, and although his name had not been mentioned, he was wary of eavesdroppers. Anywhere, everywhere.

"Now that boy I'm sure was in the house by himself, don't know if he perished in the far."

"Huh. Possibility he got out before it commenced to burning good?"

"When I drove by earlier on, his bicycle was a-lyin' in the yard. Next time I chanced to pass, the house was gone up in smoke. Bicycle wasn't there. Crowd of people just rubbernecking while the volunteer far department put out what still burned. Now, anybody could've picked up that good-looking bike and made off with it."

"How long before the, you know, investigators can tell for sure if—"

"There is a body, it will turn up oncet things cool off enough to have a look-see."

Leland poked the underside of his tongue with the toothpick and winced.

"So reckon I need to know," Jim Giles said, "are you still studyin' on my proposal?"

"I am. Now, if the . . . property we've been interested in is no longer in saleable condition, you might as well go on up to Nashville, wait for me there. But if he, I mean something, does come along that bears directly on my interests—"

"Get in touch?"

Leland stifled a sneeze—caught out in the open at the Jefferson County Fair in a sudden downpour—and tasted blood on the tip of his tongue. "No need for that. Handle it in your own fashion. You know as how I place a lot of confidence in your good judgment."

"I mighty do 'preciate it. Well, good night, sir."

Leland put down the receiver of the telephone, teeth clenched on the immobile toothpick. Cellophane candy wrappers littered the desk in front of him. His throat was raw, and he trembled. Chills. The dizzy pace of the last two campaign days in a mountainous area of Tennessee had him feeling nauseated much of the time. Aspirin was all he could take for the headache that had stayed with him since Mally Shaw knocked him cold with the fireplace poker; late in the day he'd been chewing an aspirin every twenty minutes along with a piece of hard candy. His gums and tongue burned, but nothing like the burn in his stomach. He wasn't keeping meals down. Somebody had left a half-eaten hamburger, heavy on the pickles and ketchup, in a wastebasket nearby. The smell fueled his nausea. There were flies.

Why couldn't it be over yet? Had Jim Giles managed to take care of the kid who had seen them with Mally Shaw? No matter how hard he tried to push Mally's death aside in his mind so he could concentrate on winning an election, something loomed up to distract him, distort his perception of the success he had worked so hard to achieve. A burning boy in a burning house. Where was it going to end when Mally was finally in the ground? He needed, deserved, to be at peace.

A fly brushed his perspiring forehead. There was a low tone of thunder over downtown Knoxville. His hotel was three blocks away. Right now, at a quarter past midnight according to his watch, he didn't have the strength to walk there. And it was raining.

He put his face in his hands for a few moments, then crossed his arms on the desk and laid his head down.

A few minutes later, as he was passing from a heavy doze into fevered sleep, the telephone rang. He reached for it without opening his eyes, fumbled the receiver to his ear.

"What? What is it you want now? Don't tell me anymore, I don't want to know! Just do your job."

No one answered him. The only sound he heard was the faraway tolling of a church bell. *The* church bell, the one that had begun to ring as he fled the graveyard at Little Grove in Jim Giles's pickup truck with the crumpled left fender. *Squirrels,* Giles said, with a hint of amusement at Leland's terrified expression. *Squirrels nesting in belfrys can do that, get a bell to going thataway.*

But it wasn't a squirrel outside on the street in the rain shaking the doorknob of the locked-up campaign headquarters trying to get in. Leland didn't know what, or who, he was looking at. Someone half-obscured by a large, glistening, black umbrella.

Leland hung up the phone and rubbed his swarmy eyes. When he rose from the swivel chair nausea resumed in his stomach like a cold, uplifting wave. He gripped the edge of the desk with both hands while the rattling of the doorknob continued. Whoever it was didn't bother to knock. As if no one was expected to be inside at this hour. Rain spritzed the glass in the door. Beside the door on his left there was a storefront window with a pleated shade drawn down.

A cruising fly nuzzled his ear; Leland batted it away. His nose was stuffy and he had to breathe through his mouth. Those heavy indrawn breaths fanned a spark of panic. He picked up a paper spike and walked slowly around the desk. The puffy side of his head throbbed. The injury Mally had done him didn't show beneath his wavy hair. He had smiled the livelong day and his voice was all but gone. He craved to rest, because tomorrow would be another endurance test, another spin of the political whirligig sending him on his way to the United States Senate. Eyedrops to get the red out, then keep the chin up and go on smiling like a man possessed by the mad glamour of his quest—but Goddamn it, *she* was determined not to let him get his rest!

Leland advanced through the long shadowy room with its haphazard arrangement of desks and other telephones, all of which seemed to be ringing now; the figure at the door kept working the knob, meantime concealing herself behind the umbrella. The spike protruded from between the middle and the index fingers of his fist. Ten feet from the door. *Let us have an end to it now.* Raw anger balancing on the hindbrain seesaw opposite paralytic dread. Five feet. *Rattle, rattle.* He reached with his other hand and clicked back the lock, grasped the knob, and snatched the door open.

The umbrella came at him, filling the doorspace as she stumbled across the threshold. The point of it like a foil in a duel. Leland struck back with the paper spike and ripped fabric, wrenched the umbrella from her hand. She backed fearfully into the wall behind the door.

She was a middle-aged Appalachian woman, frayed as an old broom but with some service left in her.

"Preserve me, Jesus!"

"Who are you?" Leland asked fuzzily. It was not the face or form he had prepared himself to see.

"The man there at the ho-tel said I was to come clean up this yere place when I done got off working in the laundry? He give to me three dollar. Said as how the door would be unlocked and nobody here. Are you fixing to stob me with that thing? The *Lord* is my shepherd! My name is Leona Tuggle, mister. And I'm a-needin' the three dollar right bad."

"Oh, no, I-I wasn't—" Leland dropped the paper spike on the floor. "It was—I thought you were somebody—" He cleared his throat. "It's all right. I'm sorry."

She looked from his congested face to the posters on the walls.

"I *know* you."

"Yes. It's me, all right." Found out, he hunched his shoulders, curiously abashed by her up-country foreignness.

"Well. Right pleased I am to make your acquaintance. 'Pears you tore my umberella; you see where it's tore right here?"

Ignorant, to be sure, he thought. But with that fervent shine of a preternatural keenness, of native wit, in her lime green eyes.

"It doesn't look too bad. Tell you what, Leona, let me give you a dollar for it."

"A dollar?" She rubbed her forehead in a calculating manner. "And I'll be a-keeping the other three dollar oncet my work is done here?"

"That was the deal, wasn't it?" Leland checked his pockets and came up with enough change, maybe a dime over, which he passed into Leona's hesitantly outstretched hand.

As soon as he did so, fingers making contact with her palm, she trembled and her thin lips parted in dismay. Teeth gone, others askew. She pressed back against the wall again. Her eyes seemed paler still, almost transparent, as if they had lost their seeing of this world. Her expression gave him skin crawls.

"What's wrong? Why are you looking at me like that?"

The coins fell from Leona's limp hand, rolled on the floor.

"No. No! Don't be a-touchin' me again!"

"Are you crazy? I wasn't trying to buy your skinny ass."

Leona's head fell back. Something, a slow shock, crawled through her body.

"She *waits*. She waits at the Crossing for you to come. I don't have the get of it. But there be pity in her for what you have done. The destruction ye will visit upon yourself!"

"Heyyy snap out of it, woman."

"I *see* the reckoning."

He wanted to grab, to shake her, but he was afraid of the way she was winding herself against the wall, head flipping one side to the other. He squinted hard at her, as if there was blood in his eyes.

"I haven't done anything. It wasn't me, do you understand—you old hoodoo bitch!"

Leland broke suddenly. With a low whine in his throat he dug out his wallet, snatched bills from it. Leona, released by the powerful current that had snugged her against the wall, slumped to the floor, eyes open and unblinking.

"From the throne of Jesus ye will tumble into the everlasting fiery pit."

"Here take it take more money it's all I've got on me *take* it and go back to the hills you came from! Never open your mouth about this. Never speak my name to anyone. It just happened! Nobody's fault. You hear me? She didn't have to run. You can't hold me responsible. I will not take the blame!"

He stepped over her and ran out into the street and looked around wildly. Saw the rooftop neon of his hotel mistily uphill. Inside

Leland Howard for U.S. Senate headquarters, Leona Tuggle was on her hands and knees picking up the money he had flung at her. Not acting in haste. A dollar for her silence; if she betrayed him, another dollar to see her dead. She would know. Her posture, except for nakedness, was exactly the one he had forced Mally to assume in his farmhouse the third and final time he mounted her. Damn it, nigra women were the white man's prerogative, always had been. Mally knew that. They all knew it.

In his hotel room at last he recalled a superstition handed down to him by a half-crazed great aunt also thought to be in touch with spirits. Thus he could not lie down until he had used a jackknife to slice up a pair of silk undershorts. With these pieces of fabric he plugged up the drains and spigots in the bathroom sink and tub so that nothing of an unearthly nature could visit him through these popular means of entry into the living's false sanctuary.

All lights ablaze in the room, Leland fell asleep at last on his side with knees drawn up, grasping his limp penis in one hand like a baby holds a rattle.

He's here," Francie Swift said a moment after opening the front door to Bobby Gambier. A moment after that she added, defensive on Alex's behalf, "Is he in trouble? He wouldn't tell me a blessed thing." She was fresh from her bath, slight frame in a cotton kimono, tortoiseshell hairbrush in one tanned hand.

"I don't know yet, Francie. Your mom or daddy at home?"

"No. They're horse-dealing in Kentucky. Hank's upstairs in his room and I don't know where Cotton's got to tonight, probably parked somewhere with Miss Watermelon Festival. Please come in. I think Alex fell asleep. He's using the hammock on the side porch."

He followed her through the living room of the Colonial house with its French furniture and gold-framed antique horse paintings to the all-weather porch. Painted concrete floor, stone hearth, a pool table, and a poker table with six captain's chairs around it. Alex was sprawled asleep in a hammock in one corner, bandaged right hand dangling near the floor.

"You fix him up?" Bobby asked Francie.

"Wasn't the worst burn I've seen. His eyebrows were singed pretty good, though. His clothes, phoo. I dumped everything, including his moccasins, in the trash. Doesn't he wear undershorts in the summertime? Those shorts and the shirt he's got on now belong to Fuller, but he won't miss 'em: He's lifeguarding at the underprivileged camp at Reelfoot 'til school starts up again. Do you know what happened to Alex?"

"House fire where he didn't have any business being at."

Francie's eyes got bigger. "Oh no."

"Wasn't Alex that burned it down, according to a reliable eyewitness."

Hearing voices caused Alex to twitch in his sleep. He didn't open his eyes.

"Sheriff, could I fetch you something cold to drink?"

"No uh thank you much, Francie. Sorry for keeping you up this late."

"That's okay." She cast a long look at the boy in the hammock. "Are you taking him home now?"

"Well I uh—"

"He's fine here! Really. We don't mind. I mean, it's just for tonight."

"Then if you're sure he's no bother. We've had a lot of upset at our house past couple of days. You know Alex."

"Been knowing him since kiddie Sunday School," Francie said quietly. "Whatever toy I had, he wanted to play with it. Didn't dream he'd turn out to be such a big old boy. From the size of his hands and feet he's got two-three more inches to grow don't you think?"

"Wouldn't doubt it."

"Want me to go somewhere else so you can talk to him?" Francie said, looking Bobby in the eye but crossing her arms to resist the request. "How do you do that, mind my asking?"

"Would you bring me that scorepad and pencil there on the poker table?"

Bobby pulled a wicker-basket chair to the hammock and turned on a brass standing lamp, illuminating Alex. He'd had a shower and didn't stink of smoke. Francie gave Bobby the writing tools and stayed behind the chair, slowly skimming down her blond hair that wafted, glistening, like spider's silk in a woodland sunrise.

Bobby gave his brother a shake. "Hey, pardner. Need to have some words with you."

Alex tensed and peeped at him.

"Did you get a look at who was chucking those firebombs to-night?"

He could see reflected in the louvered glass of the outside door Francie's hand with the brush suspended a couple of inches from her head, the tortoiseshell oval like a floating third eye of inquiry.

Alex made a slight negative gesture with his bandaged hand.

"Take you by surprise then?"

Nod.

"Ramses Valjean told me you were in Mally Shaw's kitchen look-ing for something when the house went up. What was it, and how did you come to know about it?"

Alex closed his eyes as if determined to go back to sleep. Bobby rocked the hammock. Alex gathered himself with a scowl and sat up, licking sore lips. Francie had provided him with Vaseline. He put his feet on the floor one at a time and looked for her. Then he sighed and took the pad with his left hand. He scrawled awkwardly with the pencil in his bandaged hand, showed Bobby the page.

"Mally told you? Told you what?"

Alex wrote one word. *Key.*

"What key? When did she tell you to look for it?"

Alex studied the porch beams overhead and shrugged.

"Where was this key supposed to be?"

Another word. *Kitchen.*

"Mally had a key that meant something, and she wanted somebody else to know about it just in case? That meant—what? She was afraid—but she didn't say a word to you, what the key was for? Padlock? Lockbox? Bus-station locker?"

Alex shook his head unhappily.

"What do you *think* it was for? Come on, Alex."

This time Alex printed two letters, then handed the pad facedown to Bobby so Francie couldn't catch a glimpse of them. Then Alex made a gesture of dismissal, a curt *that's all* motion with his hands.

Bobby knew the letters on the pad were probably initials. He tore the sheet of paper off, folded it, and put it in his shirt pocket. Alex glanced up and met Francie's eyes again. Smiled in a troubled way. He stretched out again in the hammock with his back to Bobby.

"Okay, pardner. I understand. See you tomorrow at the funeral. Better come by the house first thing and get a suit of clothes to wear."

Francie walked with Bobby to the front door. Not taking her eyes off him.

"Is this something real bad, Sheriff?"

"I believe it is, Francie."

"Will Alex be all right?"

"Yes."

"But you can't be sure."

"I've always taken the best care of him I know how, Francie."

"You just look so worried."

She went outside with him to the flagstone veranda. Bobby pausing to look over the hilltop property. Mostly open pasture with white fencing, isolated lightning-scarred old trees. But no trees near the house. He wondered if anyone had followed his brother here after the fire. There was a colored family in the caretaker's house well out back, but at fourteen Francie was the oldest at home in the main house. He decided to put a dep in a prowler at the Swifts' gate for the rest of the night, not saying anything to Francie about the arrangement.

"There are things going on, it's a matter of the law, I can't tell you about."

She nodded. "Maybe you could set me straight about something?"

"What's that, darlin'?"

"Alex's voice. A lot of the kids say he doesn't talk because he wants everybody to feel sorry."

"It was diptheria, Francie."

"Oh."

"With a lot of effort, maybe he could get out a few words. Maybe you'd halfway understand him. But we don't know for certain, and no doctor has been able to tell us."

"I just hate to think—"

"It's part of his life now. Not getting over it, but getting on in spite of bad odds. What we all need to do to ever amount to anything." He started down the steps to the gravel drive and his station wagon, then turned. "Francie?"

"Yes, sir?"

"Alex saved a man's life tonight. That house was an inferno before either of them had a hope of getting out. This was told to me by Dr. Valjean, Mally Shaw's father, who was in the house sorting her effects. Alex needed to chop a hole in the kitchen floor and pull Dr. Valjean out of there before the roof fell in. I wanted you to know that."

"Thank you. I'm glad you told me. He probably wouldn't have let me know." Francie regarded him gravely, eyes blue punctuation in the open book of her youth. "I'm going to sit up with Alex a little while longer. In case he needs anything. His hand really pains him, but he won't admit it. You know, he's strong in his own way. Even if nobody but us sees it yet."

Before calling it quits for the night, Bobby drove to the remains of Mally Shaw's house, his second visit in two hours. About an acre of brush and small trees had burned around the concrete-block foundation. A layer of smoke hovered in the windless night. One fire truck remained handy while the last pieces of blackened, smouldering wood were axed and doused.

He didn't get out of the Packard but slid the seat back and relaxed, smoked a cigarette and listened to the last half hour of Dewey Phillips on WHBQ Memphis. *Red, Hot and Blue.* "Tomorrow's forecast is for high winds, followed by high skirts, followed by Phillips." What a character. And the music was good rhythm and blues. When Phillips went off the air, Bobby dialed aimlessly around the clear channel stations. New Orleans, Del Rio, Texas. A radio evangelist worked his unseen flock like a pickpocket works a carnival lot. Bobby thinking about the possibile significance of the key Alex had tried hard to find. According to Ramses, Alex was unscrewing lids from Ball jars of preserved beans or tomatoes in the kitchen when a person or persons unknown—get back to that later. Bobby pictured a small key pressed into a half-inch round of warm paraffin before Mally had sealed one of those jars. Safe there. Vital to Mally that the key be safeguarded. Maybe she had managed to put by a small fortune in money somehow, or possessed a valuable heirloom. Bobby didn't think so, given the circumstances that had immediately followed Priest Howard's death and burial.

Priest Howard, Bobby thought with a jolt of lawman's intuition that felt exactly right to him. Who had that old man been able to trust in his dying days except his lawyer, and him not overly much; and Mally Shaw, who spent nearly every day at his bedside with the deft hands, the centeredness, that conviction of calling the best caregivers had; man could fall in love with a woman like that, never mind his age or the insufficiencies of the flesh. Suppose Priest had a secret to deal with, a secret that might lay waste the future of the unloved son? A secret under lock and key but also slyly on his tongue at an unguarded moment with a woman kinder to him than any of his wives had been.

And Leland knew, or suspected, his pitiless father's intentions. On the night Priest Howard was barely settled into his newly refurbished mausoleum, Leland came calling on Mally Shaw. Could have been a coincidence, and sexual favor was all he had on his mind. Sex with certain safety; what could Mally do?

Had his fun, but then . . . he took Mally away after. If he knew about the existence of the key and what it might bring to light, obviously it was causing him great anxiety. What if Mally already knew exactly what was in the hand his father had dealt him before dying? If she hadn't given the key to Leland, he required time to work on her. No call to damage other than her spirit. Best accomplish a breakdown in her resolve by handing her over to a couple of good old boys for a week of sport in the backwoods, then pay her some money and show her to the westbound bus.

But something went wrong; Mally died, and Bobby knew where it had happened.

As for the possibility of a key . . .

Bobby looked through his dusty windshield at the black crust of a house still wisping smoke, thinking of jars exploding in the intense heat.

No rain forecast. But by morning it should be possible to start raking through the coals, sifting the ashes.

Unlikely a key would be found. If one did show up, probably couldn't be determined what lock the key was meant for.

The firebombing might have been designed for this purpose. Mally wouldn't reveal to him where she'd hidden the key, so burn her house down. She wouldn't be needing it any longer. And another plus for Leland Howard, who so far had survived his late father's animus, dodged a wrongful-death charge, and was up twelve points in the weekend polls. Bound for glory with a grin and a hi-yo wave of his hand.

But Alex Gambier could be a charred mummy in a rubber sheet right now, because Leland Howard couldn't get enough of covering his tracks.

There were those things you had to get on with, Bobby thought, not without a taste of fear on the back of his tongue. In spite of bad odds. He yearned to see the face of his wife on her pillow and his infant son by moonlight in his crib.

Also he could use a beer.

He put his station wagon in gear and drove home.

TEN

Dog-Eared Deuce
Ghosts Don't Dream
Robert Mitchum Did It

The funeral service *for Mally Shaw, eleven o'clock*

Tuesday morning at Little Grove Holiness Church, was well attended: friends and relatives of the deceased plus a few older souls who had barely known Mally but had time on their hands and always enjoyed a good funeral when one was in the neighborhood.

Various artistically minded parishioners, a few of whom had a little talent, had painted so many biblical scenes on the church windows that the sun barely penetrated the sanctuary. Mally's coffin was of necessity closed, banked on all sides by floral tributes. Bobby and Cecily Gambier sat with Ramses Valjean, who stoically endured a Bible reading, a hymn, a soprano solo by Ike and Zerah Thurmond's middle girl Jadie, and two eulogies, the last delivered so sorrowfully by Mally's erstwhile suitor, Mr. Poke Chop Burdett, while he strummed his banjo that almost no one could understand what he was saying; but his grief was powerfully eloquent, and tears were falling everywhere in the one hundred and twenty-seat church. Ramses remained dry-eyed, but he was tense, perspiring and coming up on time for his second morphine fix of the day.

Alex Gambier, to Bobby's thinking, was neglectfully absent from the funeral, although he allowed it was possible Alex preferred keeping his distance somewhere outside. Not contrary but protective of his own feelings. While Mally's coffin was carried to the prepared site at the foot of her husband William's greened-over resting place, Bobby looked around but couldn't spot Alex. *Contrary after all, but put it down to anger,* Bobby thought.

After a fast graveside ceremony, mesh curtains were lowered on all sides of the canopy, and there the coffin would remain until the shovelers came to put Mally under in the cool of the evening. On the road, Bobby beckoned to Eddie Paradise Galphin, who had kept some distance from the proceedings. Bobby, Eddie, and Ramses had a heads-together conversation. Eddie nodding and nodding and trying not to look as if he'd just been offered a journalistic nugget of pure gold.

Bobby went back to work, and Ramses returned to the house on West Hatchie to lie down for a while in a cocoon of morphine.

One-ten in the afternoon.

Jim Giles sat in his pickup truck with the windows down to benefit from a mild cross-breeze and read the funnies from Sunday's *Memphis Commercial Appeal* while he enjoyed a chew from a luxury plug of tobacco. He used a Hopalong Cassidy glass with a chipped rim he'd found in a trash basket for a spit container. Kept an eye on the courthouse square and the black-marble facade of Dunkel's Department Store. The boy whom he had spotted right here yesterday and who ought to have burned to death in Mally Shaw's house last night was in Dunkel's with his girlfriend. Except for a bandaged hand apparently none the worse for his experience.

The boy's reappearance had given Giles, a man with little imagination, a decidedly creepy feeling to complicate his slowly simmering sense of anger and dismay that nothing seemed to be going quite as it should. Leland Howard had forbade him to get rid of the Catahoula hounds when Giles's instinct demanded they should do just that. Leland had sounded mentally out of kilter, more than a little spooked during their most recent cryptic telephone conversation. Trying to explain something woefully prophetic he'd heard from a fortune-telling hillbilly woman. Giles's opinion was that Mr. Howard needed to stay the hell away from the women for at least a week. But he just had to have that pussy after a long, hard day on the stump getting all worked up by his own rhetoric. Keep up his present pace with all that was worrying him, the day after the primary he would need a strait-jacket and a cold hosing down to straighten him out.

Good or bad, Jim Giles dutifully reported the news as it happened. But it was up to him to make sure his next report would put all of Mr. Howard's worries to rest.

Matter of time and place, Giles reflected, putting down the funny papers to stare at a damned boat-tailed bird taking a shit on the hood of his truck. He was a careful but decisive man. A kid who escaped the firebombing of a tinderbox house was worthy of some respect. But another opportunity would present itself. Thereafter the boy would be dead, and there would be no way to trace his death back to Jim Giles, the Senator-elect's man.

He tapped his horn, but the insolent bird refused to fly away. Another little thing not going right today. In another, more private place he would have taken down the double-barreled shotgun from the rack behind him and blown the bird into a bloody wad of feathers.

Giles spat brown juice into the Hopalong Cassidy glass and felt his pulse rate picking up. He had little or no tolerance for things that made him angry.

After deciding on and charging a pair of dress-up white sandals in the women's department of Dunkel's, Francie Swift located Alex one aisle over wearing the new shirt and moccasins he'd bought and also charged, to Bobby's account. He was looking raptly at an embroidered peasant blouse and denim skirt ensemble on a store dummy.

Francie came up behind him and said kiddingly, "Oh, you remembered my birthday's in two weeks."

He looked around at her, flustered.

"Bet I'd look good in that, if they had my size."

Alex smiled, reddening, and shrugged.

"I'm not having a party this year, just the family and maybe . . . one other person I decide to invite. Maybe we'll do a sit-down dinner. How does that sound, Alex?"

He wasn't sure if he was the one being invited to dinner.

Francie handed him her shopping bag to carry and made her intentions clear about the birthday by slipping an arm inside his.

"I'm a size two," she said. "Want to have lunch? My treat today."

On the way to Leland Howard's farm in the northeast corner of the county, Bobby said to Ramses Valjean, "Was Mally much of a churchgoer?"

"She probably was. Through no influence of mine, of course."

"Being a nonbeliever yourself."

Ramses' face was tired and perspiring. The air coming in through partly rolled-down windows was hot enough to brew tea. Clouds on the horizon looked flat as chalk lines. Trees mobbed the curving road, fields beyond, cotton in bursting rows, the brilliant green of soybeans. A tractor with a bush hog attached was cleaning out an irrigation ditch. They passed a slow pulpwood truck, its radio blaring Hank Williams, ghostly in the waveband. *Long Gone Lonesome Blues.* They drove by barns with sides of faded paint, the icons of a countryman's homely needs: Prince Albert, Martha White, Aunt Jemima. Two radios in the Packard, for business, for amusement. Sun flickered across the divided windshield like a movie yet to be imagined.

"God's off the map, but you got to have something to hold onto."

"Well, that's right," Ramses said indifferently. His eyes had been closed most of the way.

"What do you believe in then?"

Ramses stirred as if he had been made uncomfortable, and Bobby thought he was annoyed; but then Ramses smiled.

"I believe in the sanctity of my profession. I believe in the careworn human heart, a lovely fate for the deserving, the vastness of the human soul, and long shots at Hialeah that pay twenty to one. I believe that brown eyes mean more trouble than blue, that love is a Frankenstein of stitched-together implausible parts. I believe in the perfection of the skies, the divinity of Mr. William Shakespeare, the pleasures of the ego, and long train journeys with Gypsy women who give me sponge baths and nip at my testicles like moths on a woolen sleeve."

Bobby said with a perplexed grin, "Collar on that work shirt I borrowed for you too tight around the neck, Ramses?"

"Naw suh marse Bobby. But these heah overalls sho' be snug in the crotch."

"Best I could do on short notice. Rhoda's husband is about four inches shy of your height. Remember to keep that old fedora pulled down on your head, in case anybody up here takes a second look at you. Harlem hair don't go with overalls."

"The art of blending in is part of my heritage," Ramses said in his normal voice. "Do we have much farther to go?"

"We're looking for Jacobs' Gin Road. Used to come up this way before the war with my daddy, shoot quail in Edgar Moody's pasture on those nice crisp days before Thanksgiving."

"Got along with him pretty well, did you?"

"Yeah."

"You asked *me* a question."

"Okay, your turn."

"What is the best thing your father ever taught you?"

"Make room in your life for the people who love you."

"Second-best?"

"If you screw up, own up."

"He sounds as if he was a good man. What kind of sheriff did he make?"

"Except he liked the bottle too much, he never screwed up."

"Neither will you."

"When Leland Howard comes back to Evening Shade, he'll have a sledgehammer with him."

"Knowing what to expect, that may be half the battle."

"I hope so."

"The other half is, you're willing to make the fight."

A *familiar red roadster* was parked at a tilt off Jacobs' Gin Road and the weedy, rutted farm road to Leland Howard's place. Eddie Paradise Galphin was leaning against a back fender of his car. In anticipation of enhanced status in his chosen profession, he had treated himself to a cigar. Bobby slowed before making the turn and flashed the fingers of his right hand three times at Eddie, who touched the brim of his raffish straw boater in acknowledgment. *Fifteen minutes.*

Leland Howard's tillable acreage was lease-farmed by an old boy named Claude T. Long with the help of his middle-aged halfwit son, nicknamed Bird Dog because his face was spotty with birthmarks ranging in size from a dime to a half dollar. Claude was a deadeye at turkey shoots, his major claim to local fame. Also he had a grandniece who was married to one half of the blackface comedy act Jamup and Honey, who were featured on the Grand Ole Opry; a touch of show-business royalty in the family.

Claude and Bird Dog were tinkering with the engine of an old John Deere cultivator in front of the barn. Claude looked around when Bobby and Ramses got out of the Packard wagon, said to his son, "Give that wrench 'nother half turn there and hold on 'til I say quit." He was a tall, emaciated man with one short leg who walked as if he were forever going sideways on a steep hill. "Lord God. Bobby Gambier." Claude took off a salt-streaky brown felt hat and waved at some flies that had tagged along after him. The truth was, he had an odor that would attract vultures if he stopped moving long enough. "Reckon ain't laid eyes on you since the Hulsey boys got into their shootin' match over that fly-by-night wife of Elroy's. Heard Fuzzy was let go couple months back?"

"Fuzz drives a big rig for P.I.E. out of Little Rock now."

"Better job than ol' Elroy's ever likely to git, nose shot off that-away. But he never were a handsome boy. Brings you up our way?"

"Well sir, come to look at those dogs of Mr. Leland Howard's I've heard about."

"Them Catahoolers?" Ramses already was drifting toward the kennel fenceline, where the hounds had gathered at the arrival of the station wagon. One was whining, the other two were silent but alert. Their eyes had a stunning baleful brilliance in the lengthening angular shadow from the barn behind them.

"Looking for a new dog of my own. Old Rusty finally lived up to his name, couldn't drag himself around anymore."

"Let's see now, your pap, always partial to retrievers, wasn't he?"

"We always had a couple around."

"Now if you're lookin' for a good all-purpose gun dog, Lovett Moody's German shorthair bitch just throwed a litter over to his place in Hapsworth. Get me wrong, Cathoolers is fine strong-lookin' animals if you don't mind the wolf-dog eyes. Come across one of them loose in the nighttime you'll crap your britches. But they ain't good for much except trackin' hogs. Look how they astandin' there watchin' us. That's the killer bred in 'em. Takes a special breed to go after hogs, if you liken the sport."

"Time to time I do."

"They ain't pets, no sir, like a sweet-natured gun dog can be when he ain't workin'. I don't go near them three 'cept to feed and water 'em. Better tell your nigger not to put his fingers 'tween the links of that fence war neither."

"Ramses, the man said not to get too close."

"Yassuh, I heerd."

"Otherwise," Claude said, "you go right ahead, look 'em over all you please, Bobby."

"Thanks, Claude. Didn't mean to take you away from your chores. Boy doing all right?"

"Well, he's comp'ny since the woman done gone home to Jesus. And he don't wonder 'bout things too hard. Pitches himself a little fit now and then 'cause he can't recall whur she is."

Bobby drifted up to Ramses as Claude limped back to the John Deere cultivator. Ramses was almost within arm's reach of the chain-link fence and the grouped watchful dogs, who seemed to be grinning at him. A peculiarity of the breed. Bobby had read up on Catahoulas in the library after Mally's funeral.

"What do you see so far?"

"The kennel run was hosed down recently. The dogs too, I think. But the middle one still has some matted tufts on her chest that could be blood. If these are the dogs, then there ought to be traces of blood remaining between their toes. You would want to anesthetize them to do a thorough examination."

"What else are we looking for?"

"Lower right canine tooth, broken off near the gum line."

"That would cinch it."

"Yes."

Bobby walked up to the fence and kicked it a couple of times. One of the Catahoulas backed off soundlessly, but the others looked at him with lordly disdain. Bobby shook his head.

"Okay, I'm going in there."

"What? These dogs are not friendly."

"I want to see some snarls. Get them to open their mouths so I can count teeth."

"All three may attack you without warning if you set foot in there."

"If they get a notion I'm afraid of them. I've been around dogs all my life; I know how to handle them."

"Bobby—"

"If I'm wrong, back me up with the cattle prod I gave you in the car before they can tear an arm off."

Bobby walked to the gate at the end of the sixty-foot kennel run. Two of the dogs looked at him; the other continued to watch Ramses. Bobby drew a breath and opened the gate, walked in. Now he had all of the hounds' attention. He whistled sharply. Over by the cultivator, Claude Long looked around. Bobby hunkered down, whistling more softly, two repetitive notes. The dogs came just as softly in his direction, and Ramses moved along the fence with them, a hand on the cattle prod in one deep pocket of his overalls. Bobby smiled, hands relaxed and visible between his knees.

One of the leopard dogs, darker than the others and with only one marbeled eye, took the lead but stayed six feet or so away from him, on the prowl, sniffing. Bobby stayed aware of her movements but didn't turn his head. Tall dogs, Bobby crouched, they were all about eye level with him. The bitch with mismatched eyes came to within a foot of his left shoulder, paused. The other dogs stopped too. They were grinning, but not enough for him to get a look at a full set of teeth.

The bitch on his left put her nose against his forearm, a brief touch, then circled him and rejoined her sisters.

Bobby still didn't move.

One by one the dogs lay down, tongues out in the heat, close enough so that Bobby could smell their breaths.

Then the bitch with one marbled eye yawned, and he saw the broken canine tooth.

Bobby got up slowly, moved back, found the gate, and eased himself outside. Over by the cultivator, Claude Long slapped a thigh with his felt hat, a salute of sorts, and went back to work.

"What now?" Ramses said.

"Dogs will be impounded. If Mally's blood is on any of them, we'll know in three days."

"Can you get a warrant to search the house?"

"I wouldn't even try. Waddy Winship will give me that look over the edges of his glasses and say, 'But Bobby, there's no probable *cause*. Suppose Leland did have a colored woman up there with him for a good time last Satiddy night? And even that you don't know for a *fact*. I can think of many reasons why Mally Shaw could've been around that neck of the woods and run afoul of his huntin' dogs. A tragic accident, to be sure, but where is there evidence of a *crime?*'"

"There's evidence that she was moved to cover up the fact his dogs killed her. That is a felony; you said so yourself."

"Candy wrappers and a boot print and pubic hair is what we've got to prove a connection between them. Try getting the grand jury to even consider an indictment. Ramses, it's *Leland Howard* we're talking about. He has powerful support, relationships, endorsements from the political party that owns the State of Tennessee, owns *my* job and my personal butt besides."

"I didn't think you were afraid anymore."

"Fear's got nothing to do with it. Politics is a deck of playing cards, Ramses. It's got aces and kings and it's got the deuces like me; we get a little dog-eared or unlucky and we're out of the deal. An hour after I show up in Waddy's court looking for a search warrant, the phone calls will have been made and I'll be suspended from my job."

"You're saying—"

"I am saying that some subtlety is required here if I am to be effective and allowed to continue to do what I'm good at."

They looked up the road at the arrival of Eddie Paradise Galphin's red roadster.

"So is that your idea of subtlety?" Ramses said with a slow smile.

"Maybe," Bobby said, now willing to smile himself.

T*he double door entrance to the depot* at Cole's Crossing was no longer boarded up as it had been for many years. Alex saw that as soon as he left the road and got off his bicycle, stood seriously winded between the rails until he could catch his breath. Then, holding the bike by one handlebar, he bumped it over the crossties toward one end of the long station platform. The steel-mesh grills were missing from the wide windows on either side of the entrance; dozens of shard panes had been replaced with sparkling new glass, not a trace of soot on them.

The depot sported a new paint job too, green apple shade with plentiful gray trim, all of it glistening as if the paint hadn't completely dried.

Yet there wasn't a light anywhere except for the red filters on the lantern that the stationmaster was swinging casually back and forth as he watched Alex approach with his bike. He was a lanky man with a stuck-out Adam's apple and a grin that looked to be all false teeth. He wore his short-billed cap well back on the domed crown of his head.

"Hello!" the stationmaster said. "Here to see Mally?"

Alex left his bike across the track because he knew from previous visits that he wouldn't be able to push it through, up two steps from track level. He could easily pass from moonlight and creature-sounds and the heady swelter of a country summer night to the strange firmament, essentially a void, across the track, but his bike couldn't go with him.

Alex chose not to go either, not just yet. He had never seen the stationmaster before. His being there wasn't necessarily a good thing.

"It's all right, come on up," the stationmaster urged him, glancing over his shoulder at the restored depot. "How do you like what we've done to the old place? A lot more cheerful, hey? Not such a dump anymore."

Alex made a job of clearing his dry throat. But as long as he remained where he was, on his side of the track, he knew he couldn't speak. On *their* side—he nodded guardedly as the stationmaster looked around at him again with that unvarying cheeky grin. The red light continued to scythe through inky darkness.

"Mally will be along. Meantime aren't you just a little curious? Don't you want to have a peek inside? Everything's how it was, the way you remember. I'll just throw a few lights on to help you find your way."

Alex shook his head. The stationmaster eyed him indulgently.

"Nothing to be afraid of, Alex. Only a few new friends waiting. Young people like yourself, eager to get to know you." He stepped to the platform's edge and swung the lantern out over the track like a lure. The light flushed Alex's face. "What do you say, bud? Join us."

Alex didn't like the light; it came at him like a headache ball. At its glowing periphery with each long swing he saw figures ill-defined, long faces sorrowful but also threatening. He looked away and closed his eyes, shutting out of his mind everything but Mally's benign image.

When he looked up again, the depot was dilapidated and as shack-ugly as ever. The stationmaster was gone. Mally stood in his place, wearing the peasant blouse and denim skirt he had picked out for her at Dunkel's Department Store that afternoon. She didn't have a lantern with her. Self-illumined as always by the faint light covering her revealed skin surfaces, a wet, birthing glow.

"Alex, I told you," she said glumly. "You need to stay away from here. They're beginning to come through to you."

He was so happy to see her that he jumped boldly across both rails without looking first. Never a good idea. There were trains all the time in this starless place of Mally's that didn't announce their presence until they were almost on you. Moving fast like the snap of a whip but without much sound; that is if they didn't intend stopping at Cole's Crossing to pick up. No one got off there, of course.

"But I wanted to see you," Alex said, bounding up the steps to platform level. "And they're always here anyway, inside. Looking out. Less than shadows. Not scary except for the eyes sometimes. They're eyes with nothing to tell you." Still happy, moving around her as she followed him with her own eyes, Alex wallowing in the luxury of language, slinging words about until he got her to smile at last.

"You have a lot to learn. What happened to your hand?"

"They burned your house down last night while I was there looking for the key."

She seemed perplexed by the knowledge that she had had a house once. "Who did?"

"Leland Howard it must have been, and the sidewinder who drives for him. They threw Molotov cocktails through the windows. Oh, and I saw *him* in town today."

"Leland Howard?"

"No, the other one who came to the house with Howard the night you were—don't you remember *anything* anymore, for Christ's sake?"

Mally shrugged. "It's all so . . . far away now, Alex. I'm sorry."

"Well, they nearly killed me and your father. I didn't know he was in the house too until—Mally, I didn't have time to find the key. I'll never find it now, so we have to come up with another way to . . . to skin that polecat," he finished, reaching into his memory stash again for the rich lingo from a thousand western-story pulp pages.

"What key?"

"Mally, stop doing that, you know what I'm talking about!"

"I told you, it's . . . too far away."

"But you've only been—your funeral was *today*! Down there," Alex said with an angry sideways chop of his arm toward the Little Grove churchyard.

"Oh, it was? Were you there, Alex?"

"No. I *hate* funerals. Anyway, I knew I'd see you tonight; I can see you anytime I want to, so you're not really dead, Mally! You never will be as far as I'm concerned."

"Shouldn't I have something to say about that?"

"What do you mean?"

"Alex, your power over me is growing, but it's not right, don't you see? This is not an evil place, but you can make it evil just with your thoughts. You're . . . holding me back for your own selfish reasons."

"I'm selfish? I'm trying to help *you* get even with the sumbitch who did this to you!"

"I don't mean to hurt your feelings. But I'm okay now, really. Takes a little time to get used to being dead. I don't hate Leland anymore. Pity him, maybe, but on this Side it's all bygones. I barely remember when I'm with you what was done to me, and when you're not here, well, ghosts don't dream, baby. Will you listen to me now? I said you are holding me back from where I need to go next, and when you do that you harm yourself. What's it costing you to pop Across night after night to chat with me? More than you can imagine, and I'm afraid for you."

He didn't understand her or want to make the effort. He felt wonderful being there. He turned his back on Mally and discovered a train had slipped in while they were talking. Streamlined splendor, wreathed in huffing white vapors, silver and blue on the outside, bewitchingly lighted within the parlor cars. Happiness on the faces of the few who were boarding at Cole's Crossing. Young or old, they all had made their grades.

The portly conductor looked around inquiringly at Alex, nodded toward the open doorway of a coach.

"Catching this one, son?"

For an instant, Alex imagined stepping up into the vestibule, entering the fabulous coach. And that would be all right; why not join them? What was so great about the life he'd be leaving behind? Bad fate and worse prospects. Then he felt Mally's dismay and disapproval; the silver train dissolved before his eyes like mist from chilled glass and he was looking down at the railroad grade and men walking with flashlights, his bike where he had left it, his scattered body in beams of light and gobbets of blood on gray ballast. He shied away from the scene and faced Mally, staggered, almost contrite.

"*Now* do you get my meaning, Alex Gambier? You almost *went*. Set foot on one of these trains, you are right away a dead boy on the other Side. This is not your time nor place here. Step wrong where you're not welcome yet, it will cost you extra lifetimes of hard work to catch up to yourself. I'm telling you: Go home now. Get out of here while you still can."

The negative pull she was exerting tightened the skin around his skull; he felt her desire to fade away. But tonight he wasn't letting Mally go so easily. As she had said he needed to do, he focused his mind and heart on her and was pleased by a surge of energy in his breast, a contained storm. She seethed before his eyes, then settled back into her shape and the ensemble from Dunkel's Womens' Wear Department with a stunned expression.

"Didn't have to yank so *hard,*" Mally complained. She looked down at her feet. "Painted my toenails blue while you were at it," she said, marveling.

Alex smiled, just a little smug. "I don't want to go home yet. I make big medicine, Mally Shaw."

"What else can I *say* to you? It's not for my sake, Alex, that you're wanting revenge."

"Why is it so wrong for me to care? Nobody else gives a damn. Least of all—"

"Uh-huh. Almost spilled out there, didn't it? Because evening up the score with Leland Howard is really all about you and your brother

Bobby. You bein' so angry because you think he's let you down again."

"What if it is?"

Mally walked away from him, crossed her arms, uncrossed them, held her head for a few moments, trying to control agitation or possibly squeeze out some inspiration.

"All right. Maybe we can strike a bargain, Alex."

"Yeah? About what?"

She faced him. "Let's say if I can help settle all those scores that are so important to you, make things better between you and your brother, will you promise to get back to the life you belong in, grow up to be the man I know you can be, and let me go once and for all? Because you're not needing me half as much as you've convinced yourself you do, Alex."

He was a long time replying.

"Fix Leland Howard?"

Mally nodded.

"You said your medicine wasn't that big."

"Let's just put our heads together and think about how. If we have ourselves a bargain, that is." Looking straight at him, challenging his doubts.

"Only if things work out like you're saying," he said reluctantly, hungry that whatever scheme they settled upon for Leland Howard's downfall would work out, agonized at the prospect of never seeing her again.

She took another walk. Deep in thought, nodding to herself. "Alex?"

"What?"

"Next time I see you, maybe it ought to be an occasion. I'd like a red dress. Fiery. Silk. Clinging."

"Okay."

"Pearls. Earrings too."

He smiled; she was enjoying herself. "Sure. Why?"

"Well, it's dim in my mind, understand, but I don't believe I was looking my best the last time I entertained Mr. Howard."

"The last—? I don't—*entertain*? What are you talking about?"

"Gettin' even, sugar. That's what we're both talking about, isn't it?"

A*fter following the boy* around Evening Shade for the better part of two days and observing his antics on the platform of the abandoned depot at Cole's Crossing, Jim Giles was convinced he had a mental deficiency. Walking up and down, crouching, springing up, waving his arms, crying; probably talking to himself in other people's voices although not a word or a shout reached Giles's ears. His half-brother Eugene was thataway before he lowered his common-law's eyebrows a good two inches with an iron fry pan and had to be committed. They said Eugene had multiple personalities. However many that was, Giles would have bet the kid at the Crossing probably wasn't far behind Eugene's entourage of spooky-doo's and insolent hangers-on.

So he came down here nights to rant and howl at the moon, which was nearly full, and get it or *them* out of his system if he could. Giles waited on the boy to cool out and wondered how to kill him tonight. Broke neck was a sure thing but obvious murder would mean a more intensive investigation. The past two nights other vehicles had driven by Little Grove, carrying niggers, kids, livestock; somebody curious might recall the old pickup parked directly across from the church two nights in a row. But nobody had seen Giles. He had broken the bulb in the gooseneck fixture above the doorway to wait in full dark, except for the tiny glow of the occasional cigarette he liked to smoke when he was tired of chew.

He already had left one body in the immediate vicinity, so it wasn't going to happen here. Giles would look from time to time at the double-barred grill protector on his '48 Chevy. A notion forming. The blue-and-white bicycle lying down at trackside. Giles didn't wear a watch, but he knew it was late. The boy had come down from the platform at last and was standing between the rails. There was a green signal up, his face and mussed hair tinted putrid greenish like something from a foul-water grave. He hadn't bothered to unbutton his shorts, just hiked up one side to reveal most of an untanned flank, holding his cock out on that side, long arc of piss in the moonlight. Okay. Giles took the nearly smoked cigarette from his mouth, dropped it on the concrete stoop, his hand going to his groin. It had been a long time since he had cornholed a boy. But this one was crazy. Didn't fit in with his plans nohow.

Giles let go of himself. He was thirsty from waiting. A beer would taste good afterward. Didn't drink alkyhall but liked an occasional beer. So come on, kid. Let's get this over with. He had been studying on the risk involved. Other vehicles on the road with them as the boy pedaled doggedly toward town. But at this hour traffic was bound to be sparse. He knew where to do it. No guardrail. Accelerate on the curve, ram the bike with that high bumper, take off a leg at least before the boy and bike went tumbling thirty feet into a snaggled moccasin-infested slough. If he didn't break his neck in the fall, he'd bleed to death fast. Days, even a week before anyone chanced to find him down there.

Giles yawned. The boy had picked up his bike, thumbed on the streaky beam of the fender-mounted light. Giles felt a keenness rising in his blood.

Okay.

Francie, this is Bobby Gambier. Sorry to be calling so late."

"That's all right, Sheriff. Mama and Daddy came back from Kentucky with just the prettiest two-year-old bay filly. Everybody else's out in the barn with a case of new-horse fever; I came in a minute ago to put coffee on. If you're wanting Alex, I don't know. He left here hours ago. Wanted to borrow my scooter, but I had to say no; Daddy would bust a blood vessel and I'd be grounded 'til school starts. He didn't make it home?"

"Not yet."

"Ohh, that worries me too."

"Give you some idea of what he wanted the borrow of your scooter for?"

"I think he was going someplace it's a chore to get to from here on his bike." She paused in thought. "Someplace he had to be at a special time, because he kept looking at the clock. Had him excited, because he didn't finish half his supper."

"Such as the movies? No, I didn't see his bike in the rack out front of the Gem. He's not shooting pool either."

"I wish I could help."

"You've been a good friend to both of us, Francie. He's just got this wandering streak in him, Lord knows. Has to be running off somewhere all the time."

Bobby put the receiver of his phone on the hook and looked at Ramses, who had been at his stash of morphine in the bathroom and was sitting now, slack and exhausted, in the only other chair in the office. Eyes closing, opening to focus woozily on a yellow chamberpot light, one of a pair overhead with dark residues of insects inside them.

"This dear friend of mine I was telling you about. Dr. Charles Martorell? He was also a medical officer during the Great War. Which is how we met, at the base hospital outside of Amiens in 1917. For more than thirty years he has specialized in repairing acute trauma done to the throats of soldiers damaged by gunshot or war gasses; also *pompieres* or workers in hazardous places who breathe invisible flame from explosions or flash fires. In the past few years he has performed successful surgeries on children muted by diseases such as pneumonia and diptheria. Charles has established an international reputation."

"That so? All the specialists who looked at Alex when he was younger said that his larynx was just shot to hell." Bobby was looking at a six-foot-square map of Evening Shade on the wall behind his desk, the yellowed celluloid sheet covering the map pinholed and marked up with a grease pencil. "My mother and my daddy had Alex up to St. Loo and down to New Orleans, trying to find him help. All

Alex got out of it was the train rides, but at least he always enjoyed those. His Lionel electric train set was destroyed in the house fire and I never did replace it, but most weekends after I came home from Germany we'd drive out to Cole's Crossing, sit for hours watching the freights and the big streamliners go by. The *Dixie Traveler,* there's a humdinger, every night at"—Bobby looked at the clock over the door to his office—"nine oh four sharp it would hit the Crossing, ten coaches long plus the dining and club cars. We talked, I mean I talked, about getting on sometime for the trip to Washington, D.C. but I've always been so busy—"

Something clicked behind Bobby's eyes.

"Think I'll drive down to the Crossing before I call it a night. Want to go along or lie down on the couch in Luther's office?"

"Some fresh air would be a good idea," Ramses said, sweating and looking as if his latest injection of morphine was not getting the job done fast enough.

There is something lonely about peddling a bicycle hard, getting up to twenty miles an hour on the good stretches on a little-used country road in the dark of a sultry summer's night with only a D-cell battery light and the yellow moon sometimes visible through high-banked trees to the left of the road for illumination, the asphalt lumpy or even gummy except where there are potholes or large washouts along the crumbling right shoulder (northbound) that Alex has nearly memorized in all of his excursions up and down that road; hit one at speed and take a nasty tumble. His light ignites the eyes of animals (possum, coon, armadillo, a skunk), and the moon puts a high shine on portions of the mucky slough downhill to his right that are not covered by a froglike skin. There are insects, of course; mosquitos can't keep up with him, but hardshell fliers aiming at the bouncy light sometimes veer off course to smack him in the face or tangle spikily in his coarse mop of hair. If he forgets and breathes momentarily through his mouth during a particularly tough stretch of road, he can catch an insect spang in his teeth. They all taste the same, bitter, takes a lot of spitting to get one off his tongue and his spit is scarce; he's always near to dehydration by the time he winds up back in town. Not uncommon for his calves to cramp and his quads burn unmercifully but he doesn't like to slow down and hates to stop. Expanding his endurance is one of his summer's goals. He expects a lot out of his growing body, lifts weights in the garage, does pull-ups on an iron pipe nailed between a couple of elm trees in the backyard of the house he is not sure he can call a home anymore.

The headlights of the car or small truck that has been about a hundred yards behind him almost since he left Cole's Crossing appear like smeared apparitions in the mirror on his left handlebar. He's stopped paying it any mind. Trying to decide now, with four miles to go until he hits the town square, where he'll spend the rest of the night. Francie's house is out; her folks are back from Bowling Green, and they think he's dirt. Maybe he ought just to go home, hose off in the driveway, curl up in Bobby's station wagon to sleep. Not bother *anybody,* he thinks grimly, a burning dismal anger in his breast. They didn't want him in the house anymore. So what? He'd get some breakfast out the back door, like a tramp passing through, from sympathetic Rhoda. Cut the grass for his grits and gravy. Owe them nothing. Then take off. He is almost fourteen. He can bum his way around the country. Robert Mitchum did it, and now he's a big movie star (Alex has learned this reading one of Francie's fan magazines). Robert Mitchum has done jail time as well and doesn't take shit from anybody. Just hop a freight, never look back . . .

That will have to come later. First he and Mally need to take care of Leland Howard. But Alex doesn't have a clue where to find that mangy owlhoot, and if he does find him, how to get his attention.

Coming now to the sixty-foot bridge spanning a ravine with a mostly dry creek at the bottom of it. Stagnant pools of water amid some big flat rocks. The bridge isn't paved. There are two lanes of planks laid over four-by-fours with space between them. Six-inch-high wooden curbs but no railing on either side. Strict load limit.

Most drivers obey the yellow warning signs posted well in advance and go across the bridge in low gear.

So Alex wonders why the driver who has been lagging behind him for miles is now speeding up.

Jim Giles in his assassin's mind gave the accelerator of his rackety pickup a goosing, and large reflectors nailed to posts on either side of the dangerous bridge strafed his own headlights back at him. The boy darted a look around at momentum sprung on him like a lion charging in a 3-D picture show and lost his cycling rhythm halfway across. The front tire of the bike slipped off the worn plank on the right side of the bridge and hit a space between four-by-fours. The boy lost his grip and left his seat in a soaring sprawl. As the upended bike jumped and pivoted in the air the truck ran into it and crunched it whole beneath the front wheels. Twisted metal dragged the undercarriage and loosened the oil pan. Giles blinked at the impact as he braked, too hard, and the pickup's back end swerved off the planks. He was busy trying to avoid dumping his truck into the ravine and lost sight of the boy.

When Giles had control again, he didn't see the boy anywhere.

He shifted to neutral, grabbed a flashlight, and got out. While he was dragging the wrecked bike out from under his pickup, he heard the pierced radiator hissing and smelled hot oil dripping. Well Goddamn. But he had to make sure this sorry business was over with and *right now.*

Giles walked slowly along the left side of the bridge where there was a wooden curb six inches high. He flashed his light down through some dead trees and saw the boy beside the rocky creek bed. Sitting up, not lying there unconscious. Holding the back of his neck. He didn't look up when Giles flashed the light on him. There was blood on his face.

"Hey, kid!"

He looked up slowly, dazed and maybe with a cracked skull, but

241

obviously he had a lot of luck going for him. Giles reckoned his brains ought to be coming out of his ears. A litter of dry branches sticking to his clothing suggested his fall had been broken somewhat. So that's how it was, still alive; but Giles wasn't going to wait around town for a third crack at him. It was going to be Murder One after all and the hell with it.

Giles returned to his pickup and reached inside to take his Remington shotgun down from the rack. Eighteen-inch barrels, customized by a gunsmith, but enough range to do the job from, say, a distance of thirty feet. Deer slugs. Giles cocked his shotgun and was on his way back to a good vantage point, flashlight beam lancing into the ravine, when somebody else showed up.

Headlights a quarter of a mile up the road toward town. A lone car, but still it was turning into a party. He was lit up by the truck's headlights behind him. Truck blocking the bridge, blowing steam from the radiator and leaking oil. Well Goddamn.

Giles ran back to the pickup, laid the shotgun on the seat beside him. He needed valuable seconds to ease the truck back onto the planks. By then the other car had reached the place where the road narrowed to one lane for the bridge crossing. He shifted into reverse and began backing up. Let them go on by, keep his face hidden. Then, when he had the bridge to himself again, drive back and finish the boy.

But he had momentarily forgotten about the tell-tale bike lying wrecked on the bridge. And his engine was overheating.

Torn up as it was, Bobby Gambier recognized Alex's Schwinn bicycle even as Ramses said, "Looks like there's been an accident."

"God, it's Alex," Bobby said with a thickening of fear in his throat. He stopped a few feet short of the bridge, staring at the pickup truck that was backing away from the scene. He heard gears grinding; the driver was having transmission problems. Apparently he couldn't move his smoking truck any direction but reverse.

"Flashlight's clamped under the dash," Bobby said to Ramses.

"See if you can find Alex. He must have gone off the bridge. I need to find out what that son of a bitch in the pickup had to do with this!"

Ramses got out of the Packard, moving fast for a man of his age and in a terminal condition. Bobby gunned the Packard across the rumbling bridge straight at the retreating truck. Now the other driver was pouring it on, zig-zagging backward at nearly forty miles an hour on narrow blacktop. Bobby flashed the Packard's high beams to try to get him to stop and increased his own speed. *Flash, flash.* He could make out the driver, head turned halfway around as he steered erratically. The smoke around his beat-up truck was blue-black. Burning oil; Bobby could smell it as he put his Packard almost nose to nose with the runaway Chevy truck.

The driver looked around at Bobby, his face grim in the headlights. Then he picked up what looked like a sawed-off shotgun from the seat beside him. Bobby panic-stopped. The pickup slewed around on the road in its own spilling oil and ran out of control up the embankment to one side of the road, stopping when it hung up on the half-rotted stump of an osage orange tree that had fallen years ago. The truck was tilted to one side at an angle of about fifteen degrees, left front wheel spinning aimlessly off the ground.

Bobby and the Chevy driver sat still for several seconds, eyeing each other through the dust and smoke settling out of the air. Bobby reached for the short-nosed .44 Bulldog he always had in the Packard and slipped out the door, crouching.

"Deputy sheriff! Climb out of there; you're under arrest! I want to see hands, see your hands!"

What he saw was the downhill slant of the shotgun barrels as the door on the driver's side creaked open. Half of a hatted man in silhouette. Bobby ducked lower as a slug from the shotgun blew out part of the Packard's windshield and ripped open the seat on the driver's side. Bobby darted out past the front fender and shot twice from his crouch, dumped the shotgun man on his back, sending him in a slide past his smoking truck on thick leaf mold and other woodsy detritus.

Bobby straightened slowly, revolver in a two-handed grip, ears ringing. Adrenaline was giving him a kick. The sky was flecked with birds chased from their high roosts by the gunplay.

"Christ, I'm shot!" the man hollered. "Don't shoot again, I'm done!"

"Get your hands in the air where I can see them."

"Christ no, I can't do it. Shoulder's smashed all to hell. Got me down low too. I can't move atall."

"You got one good hand on that shotgun. Slide it on down the slope away from you!"

Bobby heard him groan; then the shotgun slithered a couple of yards as the man weakly pushed it away from him.

"Is that it?"

"Yes sir that be all. Don't have 'nother piece on me."

"I'm coming, and you better not be a liar."

"No sir. You did me good. Can't feel my right arm nor nothing below my belt buckle."

Bobby picked up the shotgun and looked at the face of the man who had tried to kill him. Although he was going into shock, he still seemed like a tough guy. That frequent-offender look.

"What's your name?"

"Giles. Jim Giles."

"You wanted for anything, Giles?"

"No."

"Did you run over my brother on his bike back there at the bridge?"

Giles was breathing heavily. "Your brother?"

"What I said, partner."

"There was a boy. In my way. Didn't see him. It were purely accidental."

"Then why did you try to drive away, throw down on me with this twelve-gauge? I'm not buying it, Giles."

"Night's turned cold, hain't it?" His eyes acquired an electric sheen of terror as a notion of his mortality veered through his brain. "I'm cold all over."

"You're going to the hospital. Just hold on, Giles."

Bobby heard Ramses shout from the ravine beneath the bridge, his voice echoing. Bobby shouted back.

"I'm okay! Did you find Alex?"

"He's here! Concussion. But he's conscious."

Giles licked his lips again, and a momentary confused expression resolved into bleak amusement.

"That's a lucky boy. Yes sir. Uncommon lucky, I'd say."

While Bobby was cleaning up at three-thirty in the morning, the shower curtains around the tub parted a few inches in the middle and Cecily looked in, a little puffy under the eyes from sleep. She looked him up and down thoughtfully.

"The man of my dreams," she said. "Which is the only place I see much of you lately."

"I shot a man tonight," Bobby said.

"Oh?" Cecily said, holding the curtains tight around her face so that not much of her hair or nightgown would get wet. "Is he dead?"

"Smashed pelvis, broken shoulder. He was in surgery at the hospital the last I heard of him."

"What did he do?"

Bobby told her.

"Oh my God! How bad is Alex hurt?"

"Concussion, some stitches. X rays didn't show anything. He's sedated and in a semiprivate room until they decide to let him go. Thursday would be my guess. Giles, he'll go straight back to the joint when he can travel to finish a twenty-year term with another five or six tossed in for good measure. Soap my back? Don't see any pimples, do you?"

"I'll get all wet." She yawned.

"Put on a shower cap and climb in here with me."

"Why didn't I think of that?"

She closed the curtains. Through the mist Bobby could see

shadowy Cecily's profile as she shucked her nightgown and tucked her hair beneath the shower cap. He felt deliriously in love with her. As for her nude body, seeing it again was as wonderful as the first time. Matter of fact, that had been in the shower too, in a motor court outside of Jackson two months before the wedding.

Bobby pulled her against him as soon as she had her footing inside the tub.

"Do I need to wash that too?" she said, a fingertip on the head of his erect penis.

"No. You ready?"

"Not yet. I need a minute. I've never seen you like this, Bobby. You're just all snap, crackle, and pop. Is it from shooting that guy?" Looking up at him, beads of water on her long lashes, finding allure in this new aspect of his maleness.

"Partly, I guess. It was an experience, I can tell you. Did I say who he was?"

"Mr. Giles?"

"He's Leland Howard's man."

"And you think he deliberately ran over Alex? Why?"

"Between you and me," Bobby said, closing her lips gently with thumb and forefinger. "Alex was hanging out at Mally Shaw's the night Leland Howard raped her. Howard, or maybe it was Giles, must have seen him there."

"Leland Howard did *what*?"

"And Alex witnessed the rape."

"This is beginning to sound like big trouble," she said, fingers of one hand plucking at the hairs on his chest while with her other hand she worked his penis between her thighs as if it were a rolling pin. Her lips parted in a dreamy smile. Trouble could wait.

"Leland Howard will be in town later today. At my request."

"What can you do to him?"

"It's already taken care of. He won't go to jail; I don't have enough on him. And I want to keep Alex out of it. Even if Howard sidesteps an indictment, he'll be smelling so bad by week's end the party will have to dump his ass."

"Well then are you going to be in a jam with Luther?"

"No, honey. I'll get the riot act, but as long as I don't leave shit on his doorstep . . ."

Cecily put her lips against Bobby's ear.

"Thirty seconds," she said.

"I'll just step out and get a towel."

"Uh uh don't. I want you to screw me straight out of the shower, wet and naked in our bed."

"Why, Cecily Jeanine; who taught you that kind of shockin' talk?"

"You did. *Twenty* seconds, Booger, and I don't mean one second longer."

ELEVEN

Sledgehammer
A Bedful of Naked Miss Americas
Mally Says Hello

At eleven twenty-six *Wednesday morning, Leland* Howard landed in a small plane at the Jackson, Tennessee, airport, twenty-three miles east of Evening Shade. He was met by a motorcade escorted by state troopers. His rescue team, spread out in sedans and a limo, included the senior partner of the Memphis firm Speer Fain Culverhouse, Gipson Culverhouse, Jr.; two junior partners in the firm, Sinclair Judkins and Ray Villapando, both sharp young guys adroit at dealing with unfortunate circumstances while under pressure; and two legal secretaries. Also with them was Culverhouse's personal PR man and his pet political columnist from the Memphis *Commercial Appeal,* the state's most influential newspaper.

Leland Howard arrived moderately disheveled and bleary-eyed from lack of sleep: three miserable nights in a row. He and Gipson got into the limousine, where they were assured of maximum privacy. Culverhouse was a massive man, six-seven and three hundred pounds. Flowing white hair, a look of unimpeachable veracity and deep wisdom. He didn't just address jurors; he took them into his arms (figuratively) and cuddled them, gently solicitating fealty. The same with his clients.

The motorcade was stationary for twenty minutes while Leland spilled his guts to Culverhouse about the Mally Shaw mess, the mistakes he'd made. Broke down sobbing at the end of his recitation.

His lawyer said not a word, only stroked an interesting mole to one side of his lowermost chin as if he were petting a gerbil. In the twenty minutes with his client he rarely blinked even in disbelief or disapproval. Then he handed the blubbering Leland his pocket handkerchief. He opened the door on his side of the limo, and sunlight flooded them both.

"I brought you a fresh shirt, change of linen, and choice of suiting," Culverhouse said. "The occasion does not call for white today. I feel the dark blue double-breasted chalk-stripe suit is best for your appearance at the Evening Shade Sheriff's Office and subsequent press conference. There are eye drops, benzedrine, painkiller, and an electric shaver in the valise one of the girls will give to you. And brush your teeth, Leland. You're eating too much candy."

"Where are you going?" Leland cried.

"To dictate a confession, sir."

"Oh my *God!*"

"Nothing to fear," Gipson Culverhouse said. He seldom smiled but often he would twinkle. "This is an easy one. I thought you were in real straits. You will be back on the stump tomorrow morning, with no wear and tear on your reputation. Enjoy yourself in Washington, sir. Fabulous town. Don't get there often enough myself."

R*amses Valjean got off the creaky elevator* on the second floor of Evening Shade's community hospital carrying a duffel bag and a Christmas-decorated tin of cookies fresh-baked by Rhoda this morning. The hospital was old, underfunded, and looked it. A brick oven in summertime, a sieve to the north winds in winter. A Negro porter was mopping the pockmarked linoleum, amber from accumulated paste wax, in front of the nurses' station in an alcove opposite the elevator. There were wilted and dead flowers on a shelf of his cleaning cart. The wet mop looked virulently unclean.

The charge nurse, Mrs. India Breedlove, looked up at Ramses, not prepared to be hostile but steadfastly indifferent to his presence. A standing fan behind her riffled the paperwork on her clipboard. She did some writing with an old Waterman that had inked her fingers.

After a while she said, "Just put them there on the side of the desk," referring to the cookie tin. "Who did you say they were for?"

"I am not a delivery boy. My name is Dr. Ramses Valjean, and you have a young patient of mine on this floor."

India Breedlove was one of those doughty country women, heavyset but not fat, complexion like a speckled hen's egg, somewhat gone to seed in long service to the ill and suffering. Fallen arches an excellent bet, Ramses thought, and from the way she held herself, she had a bad sacroiliac. Thrombosed veins in her legs, of course. He had known so many like her.

"There's no colored up here," India said, sharp with him now. "Your people are in the temporary building out by the 'cinerator."

Ramses had seen the building when Cecily Gambier dropped him off. Temporary since the Spanish-American War.

"A hellhole, no doubt," he said mildly.

The old man mopping linoleum gave him a look. Mrs. India Breedlove crossed her beefy arms.

"Like it or not, that will be where you will find any patient of yours; that is, if you *are* a medical professional."

Ramses put down the duffel bag and handed India one of Bobby's embossed business cards. Sheriff's Department. Bobby had written on the back, *Please extend to Dr. Valjean of Paris, France, every courtesy.*

"Well," India said. "Paris France. You don't say. I hear tell they treat you people differently over there?"

Ramses smiled nostalgically. "How is Alex doing today, Nurse Breedlove?"

"Oh! Alex Gambier. Dr. Wheeliss saw him already this morning. Headache was his worst complaint. A little blood in his bedpan? But he kept his breakfast down and went back to sleep. You know where to find his chart. Room 217 . . . Doctor."

Ramses thanked her and went down the stifling hall with its bluish fluorescent illumination at half-past noon and opened the door to a semiprivate room occupied for now only by Alex. He was lying partly upright in the bed nearest the window. On the south side of the building the August sun wasn't a big problem. The opaque green shade was half-drawn, the window up. Small table fan pushing the swelter around, sharp flavor of recent bedpan feces, alcohol, medicinals.

Alex's eyes were closed. Some hair over his left ear had been shaved away to allow for six stitches. Other, unbandaged cuts on his face and neck had been daubed with orange Mercurochrome. He had salve on his abused lower lip. His hands were slack at his sides.

Ramses set the duffel bag on a chair and picked up the chart from the foot of Alex's bed, spent a few seconds scanning vital signs. When he looked up again, Alex's eyes, bloodshot, were open, staring at him.

Ramses smiled. "Looks as if you'll pull through okay. Another twenty-four hours in hospital should do it. How's the headache?"

Alex blinked and winced, looked at the pitcher of water on the bedside table. Ramses poured him some in a clean glass and held the glass for him while he drank.

"Mrs. Gambier dropped me off, but she'll be back to visit you in a little while. Brendan had an appointment with his pediatrician. She sent a change of clothes for you. Rhoda baked cookies."

Question in Alex's eyes. Several questions, rapid-fire as he blinked.

"You would like to know what happened. A man named James Giles, employed by Mr. Leland Howard—" Alex held up a hand. He knew all that. Ramses nodded. "Bobby and I came along shortly after Giles ran you down on your bicycle. You ended up in the ravine below that dangerous little bridge on the way to—you remember that as well?" Alex grimaced. "You were semiconscious when I climbed down there to check for signs of life. Bobby pursued Mr. Giles. It was necessary for Bobby to shoot the man in order to arrest him."

Whoa!

"He wounded Giles twice. A desperate character, it would seem, was our Mr. Giles. On parole, serving a long prison sentence. He's recuperating here following surgery to repair his pelvis. He also lost a considerable volume of blood. Oh, Bobby asked me to apologize for him because he's having a very busy day. He'll be by once he's had his talk with Mr. Leland Howard in his office this afternoon. Mr. Howard's political future appears to have acquired considerable tarnish. Bobby is ready to, as he put it this morning, 'tie the can to his tail.'"

That earned a smile from Alex.

"The sad part is, not enough evidence exists to put him behind bars unless Mr. Giles implicates him. Which he has little reason to do."

Alex's smile vanished.

"But we must accept what satisfaction we can get."

Alex raised his head from the pillow for a few seconds, moved it weakly side to side. He made writing motions with his hand.

Ramses fished a notebook from his coat pocket and offered it to Alex with his fountain pen. Alex scribbled furiously. Ramses moved closer to the right side of the bed and looked down at the pad where Alex had written *Mally will take care L.H.* And underlined the words twice.

"Well . . . whatever does lie beyond the grave, I'm afraid supernatural revenge is the stuff of the stories you enjoy. What was the name of the horse in your western tale? Silver Ghost? I very much enjoyed reading—"

Alex had torn the top page off the pad and was writing again.

She's here still here!

Ramses looked into Alex's hazy, bloodshot eyes as if for a sign of head trauma that he had overlooked a few hours ago.

"I don't know what you mean, Alex."

Mallys at Cole Cross. Depot. Saw her Sun. night. Mon. What day is this?

"It's Wednesday afternoon," Ramses said quietly. Alex's face had reddened from excitement or stress. He was writing again.

Still be there. Tonight. Waiting for L.H. Wants me to bring L.H. to her.

"Let me understand. You believe that you saw—" Ramses suddenly lost his ability to breathe. He pressed a hand hard against his midsection. The pain like a white-hot iron stuck clear through him. Alex didn't notice his distress.

Did see her! Underlining *did*.

Ramses gripped the windowsill with one hand behind him until he could breathe again. Less than two hours had passed, and already he needed more of his dwindling supply of morphine. For only the second time since he had diagnosed his own terminal disease, Ramses felt desperately afraid.

"Alex—you had a narrow escape last night. The fall you took easily might have killed you. Fortunately, you have a hard head. But the concussion you suffered may be responsible for—what you're imagining now."

No! Its true!

"Mally is dead, Alex. Now, you know that. We buried her yesterday at Little Grove."

Alex let the notepad fall from his hands, which were shaking. Ink dotted the yellowed sheet drawn over the lower half of his body. Tears leaked from one eye and ran down the outside of his nose.

Ramses wiped his own eyes. "You cared for Mally, and I appreciate that. But don't keep on with this fantasy, Alex. It could be very harmful to you. And now I—I must visit the 'colored' ward to see if I can find a doctor to write a prescription for me. I may lie down there for a while. But I'll come back to see you."

R*amses was leaving* by the main entrance when Leland Howard and his entourage, led by the Highway Patrol cruiser, pulled into the drive. Ramses paused on the brick walk beside a low boxwood hedge and watched as Leland and several other men, one of them huge but light on his feet, left a sedan and a limousine and walked quickly across the drive. A trooper joined them. Nobody but the trooper paid attention to Ramses; he gave Ramses the Look. *Step aside boy. We have important people here.* The walk was a good fifteen feet wide. Ramses might have just continued on his way, but he was hurting, and when he looked at Leland Howard's face he hurt even more.

Then Leland popped a piece of hard candy into his mouth and tossed a wad of cellophane away.

"Mr. Howard!"

They all looked toward him, no one breaking stride. The trooper angling toward Ramses with a thumb tucked inside his gun belt and the other hand on the baton in its holster, ready to draw it.

"I am Dr. Ramses Valjean. Mally Shaw was my daughter."

Leland, opposite Ramses now and six feet away, fell out of step with the others, consternation and, possibly, fear in his bright blue eyes.

"Oh, yes, I—I'm sorry for your loss."

The huge man with the florid face and plentiful white hair that stuck out like a scarecrow's fright wig from beneath the brim of his Mississippi planter's straw hat put a hand on Leland's elbow as if to get him back in step. Leland grimaced slightly, the piece of candy bulging in one cheek.

"Enjoy your candy, sir," Ramses said, raising his voice. "The next time you rape a woman, as you raped my daughter, you shouldn't leave the wrappers all over her house or in her car."

Ramses was satisfied with Leland's gaping reaction, although he had only a moment to enjoy it. He knew what was coming next and didn't try to protect himself. The trooper left his baton on his belt and instead used his elbow, hitting Ramses in the breastbone over the heart, driving him backward over the three-foot-high hedge.

By the time Ramses had recovered sufficiently to get to his knees in his grass-stained suit, Leland Howard and his lawyers had entered the hospital. The trooper who had knocked Ramses down had posted himself, arms folded, outside the entrance. He didn't give Ramses a glance. The rest of the entourage had left their sedans and were smoking on the oblong of lawn that contained three flagpoles. Old Glory, the Tennessee state flag, and the Stars and Bars. There were two women and two men, one of whom was a runt with a beaked nose. He wore a porkpie hat on the back of his head and looked around with a lively attitude. He was the only one who showed interest as Ramses picked himself up and limped off in the direction of the shabby, barracks-style Jim Crow infirmary on the far side of the parking lot.

On *Alex's first attempt* to get out of bed he was able to take four steps before semicollapsing against the wall next to the window. His head was killing him; he felt faint. He made it back to the bed and lay down across it on his stomach until his heart stopped palpitating. Then he tried walking again, gaining a few more shuffling steps this time before he began to see skyrockets behind his eyes. He rested, gritted his teeth, persisted. He wasn't going to stay in the hospital. He had shopping to do, for one thing. A red dress for Mally.

Alex was leaning buck-naked against the high bed going through the contents of the duffel bag when he heard a commotion on the floor, the voice of Mrs. India Breedlove in protest mode, two or three authoritative male voices. He pawed past a couple of his notebooks and pens, reading material—*Weird Tales, Doc Savage, Dime Western,* and the latest copy of *Boy's Life*—to select some clothing.

He skipped underwear, pulled on a knit sports shirt and a pair of shorts. Then he went barefoot to crack open the door another couple of inches. Looked outside, blinking to sharpen his vision. They were all near the opposite end of the hall. Mrs. Breedlove, another nurse, and some well-dressed men.

Even at that distance Alex easily recognized Leland Howard.

He didn't feel any great surge of surprise. It had seemed inevitable to Alex, going back to last night when he and Mally had talked it over, that their paths would soon cross. As if the growing power invested in him the last few nights at Cole's Crossing had ordained Howard's coming.

He's here, Mally. Now we can do it.

The *runt in the porkpie hat* looked into the small room Ramses was occupying, lying on a simple iron bed with a thin mattress, his fingers laced over his sore breastbone as he stared at a watermarked ceiling.

"How you doing?"

Ramses lowered his eyes to take him in, didn't speak.

"Floyd Smart, Memphis *Commercial Appeal*. I write a column. Could be you've heard of me."

"No."

"That's all right, my feelings aren't hurt. I respect your need for solitude in your time of grief. There's always been allegations where our boy Leland is concerned, but sounded to my old ears like you know more than you were given the opportunity to say. What kind of junk you on, Doc? You *did* say you were a doctor?"

"Yes. Be good enough to leave me alone."

"Sure. I can tell you don't feel so hot. I'll just leave my card. Home and work numbers. Reverse the charges if you like. That's if you'd appreciate a sympathetic ear later on. Something I can get in the paper, not more allegations. We're all up here to do a whitewash on the candidate, you understand. He'll leave Evening Shade tonight clean as a choirboy. Kinda like the guy, understand, but I dunno, rape? I like to believe I haven't lost all my juice should there be a good scoop around. Smart. Floyd Smart, in case you didn't catch my name the first time. So long, Doc."

Jim Giles lay on his own bed of pain and got the bleak news straight from the shoulder, as Gipson Culverhouse, Jr. put it. He was going back for the rest of his twenty-year stretch, no parole hearings this time, and a possible ten more years for ADW.

"Sorry, Jim, there's no authority under heaven can do a damn thing for you. But still, and you already know this: There's all manner of ways to do your time, and suitable arrangements can be made that will considerably lighten the load."

"I ain't going back there," Giles said, loaded with opiates and looking, as they say, at everyone in the room as if through the wrong end of a telescope.

"Or," Culverhouse said, his eyes narrowing, "it can become well-nigh intolerable. No man is made of iron."

Giles licked dry lips. His tongue and his left hand, which was pressed against his forehead, were about the only parts of his body that he could move.

"Goddamn that deputy," he muttered. "Six months in a God-damned body cast."

"Jim, I feel so terrible about this," Leland Howard said, looking over Culverhouse's shoulder. The big lawyer from Memphis was astride a sturdy wooden chair only a couple of feet from the side of the wounded felon's bed.

"What is it going to be, Jim?" Culverhouse said.

"I don't have no feeling in my right hand atall."

"We'll help you sign, Jim. All six copies." He looked sharply back at one of the young lawyers, who unbuckled his briefcase. Silence in the room except for the squeak of Leland Howard's shoes as he paced, sweating, sucking hard candy. Jim Giles breathed through his mouth.

"All right. Give me the fucken thing."

"You've made the right choice," Culverhouse assured him as he was handed the papers and a clipboard. He produced his own 18-carat-gold writing instrument for the occasion.

"But I ain't goin' back," Giles repeated. His voice had fallen low along with his eyelids, so either the other men in the room didn't hear him or chose to ignore what he was trying to tell them.

C<i>ecily Gambier drove to the hospital</i> in her Plymouth coupe, Rhoda beside her in the front seat holding Brendan on her shoulder; he was asleep after a cranky visit to his pediatrician in Jackson.

On the second floor of the hospital, Cecily encountered a cross Mrs. Breedlove, who was continuing to have a bad day. Cecily's youth and freshness further aggravated her. They had looked everywhere, she curtly explained. Alex was missing with his duffel bag. Nobody around the hospital admitted having the slightest. Mrs. Breedlove saw fit to lecture Cecily about this folly of Alex's. Head injuries were nothing to trifle with. Serious consequences could arise. Cecily replied that common sense was never Alex's strong point. To get away from Mrs. Breedlove, she walked down to the semiprivate room to see if Alex had left anything behind. Like a message scrawled in blood on one of the walls. While she was looking in from the doorway, the fluorescent fixtures along the hall began to flicker.

There was an elderly Negro porter at the far end. He looked up and around, leaning on his mop handle. Then he put the mop aside and ventured a few slow steps to the room occupied by Jim Giles. Cocked his head, listening, then pushed the door open. He was inside for several seconds while Cecily walked back to the nurses' station. Mrs. Breedlove was frowning as her desk lamp misbehaved.

Then the old porter came out of Jim Giles' room gesturing, pointing back and saying *Lawd Nuss Breedlove! Lawd God a'Mighty!*

There were extra chairs in Bobby's office. A pot of fresh coffee. A fan going. Bobby had changed his uniform blouse. He had Acting Chief Deputy J. B. Garretson with him and the departmental stenographer, Mary Wingfield, whom he had asked not to chew gum. He sat behind his desk with folded hands on the blotter. At two minutes past three by the clock over his door, he knew by the clamor of news people who had been gathering on the courthouse lawn for at least an hour that Leland Howard had arrived with his legal team.

"Reckon how did they all know he was a-comin'?" Garretson said. He was leaning with folded arms against the high sill of the window, peering up and out at street level, not able to see much.

Bobby shrugged. "He's news, that's all I know." But he wasn't happy. He felt something going wrong already, smelled it like old garbage, Leland Howard about to slip from his grasp. Those damn lawyers. Sledgehammers, and he was the peanut they'd come to crush.

Another deputy brought four men to Bobby's office. Three lawyers—or more like four and a half considering Gipson Culverhouse's reputation, a weighty man with a weighty name in Southern legal circles. The other lawyers were there to carry things and learn from the sage himself. Leland Howard wasn't wearing his trademark ice-cream suit, looking more like the banker he once was in dark blue and pinstripes, high collar in spite of the heat, and a fat necktie.

Introductions. Coffee, anyone? Sure. Three of his visitors took seats while Gipson Culverhouse remained standing behind Leland Howard's chair, which was squarely in front of Bobby's desk. He dominated the office, looking down on everyone.

Bobby got started.

"Mr. Howard, I greatly appreciate your taking time off from a busy campaign, sir, to be here today. I wanted to ask you a few questions relating to the death of Mally Shaw."

"Well, I'm certainly—"

Lawyer Culverhouse held up a hand to interrupt.

"Are we proceeding here with the understandin', Deputy Gambier"—Culverhouse had placed a faint but slighting emphasis on "deputy"—"that this will not be a formal interrogation?"

"That's right."

"Then with due apologies to your charmin' stenographer"—Culverhouse beamed at Mary Wingfield—"I see no reason for her continuing presence."

Bobby glanced at Mary. She packed up and left. Leland Howard stroked his upper lip with a forefinger and watched her go. Mary in polished cotton slacks was powerfully appealing.

"And now if I may read a brief statement of Mr. Howard's that will be given to the members of the press gathered outside the courthouse this afternoon, it might save us a good deal of time. And none of us have eaten lunch."

Bobby nodded. Culverhouse reached to his right without looking, and the typed one-paragraph statement was placed in his hand. He took his reading glasses from his shirt pocket and put them on.

"'I knew Mally Shaw as a dedicated and tireless professional nurse who provided care and comfort for my beloved father, Priest Howard, during his last days. I spoke to her only on one occasion, which was the afternoon that my father passed away. I was deeply shocked to hear of her untimely death. Mally will always have a special place in my heart for what she meant to all of our family.' "

Bobby held out a hand, and the statement was passed to him. He put it on his blotter, looked at Leland Howard for a few seconds, looked at Gipson Culverhouse, who was receiving another document.

"What I have here, Deputy Gambier, is a full, voluntary confession by Mr. James Giles of his involvement in Mally Shaw's death. Giles has acknowledged complete responsibility for the unfortunate circumstances that led to her being mauled by the Catahoula hounds owned by Mr. Howard, hounds which you have impounded."

"You must have done some good detective work," Leland commented. Culverhouse looked for a moment as if he wanted to swat his client on the back of the head.

J. B. Garretson, still by the window, cleared his throat with a fist against his mouth, watching Bobby, who was smiling in disbelief.

"When did you obtain this confession?"

"Half an hour ago, in his room at the hospital."

"If you please, sir."

Bobby was handed a copy of the confession, which he read through carefully. Jim Giles stated that on Saturday night, August the first, he acted on an impulse to have a little fun and called on Mally Shaw at her home. There he forced her to have sex with him. Subsequently, he drove Mally to Leland Howard's farm, where she jumped out of the car and ran from him. He was well liquored up and not thinking clearly when he turned the Catahoulas loose to track her down. Just having a little more fun. By the time he caught up to the dogs, he was too late to help Mally. It had never occurred to him that bitches in heat could be a danger to a panicked female human being on the run. Thinking a little more clearly by then, he sought to cover up what he'd done by moving her body from a field south of the farmhouse to the Little Grove cemetery. After that he turned a hose on the dogs to wash off most of the blood and changed his clothes. By seven o'clock Sunday morning, he was driving the unsuspecting Leland Howard to Knoxville, as he was paid to do.

Bobby put the two-page confession, duly signed by three witnesses and notarized, on top of Leland Howard's statement. As if he needed more time to think, he had a couple of sips of cooling coffee. He ignored Leland Howard and raised his eyes to Leland's lawyer, who was nodding almost imperceptibly with a look of savor and a twinkle in his eye.

"You'll be giving this to the press too, I imagine," Bobby said.

"Yes, they'll be eager to run it, along with those photos of the Catahoula hounds that somehow the *Tri-State Defender* got hold of early this morning. Quite a little scoop for them."

Bobby leaned back in his swivel chair. "Mr. Culverhouse, my father was high sheriff of Evening Shade for twenty-three years. I learned a lot from him. Learned more as a military policeman; and I have been a deputy in this department for almost five years. What I'm getting at, sir, I can smell a crock of shit when it's right under my nose."

Culverhouse's nodding became more pronounced; he smiled amiably. Leland did some twisting in his chair. J. B. Garretson cleared his throat again.

Bobby said to Leland Howard, "I suppose you'll have another statement about how terrible you feel, the way Giles betrayed your good faith and trust in his paroled ass."

Culverhouse pulled a round gold watch from the front pocket of his trousers and opened the initialed cover.

"If we have finished here—a good meal has long eluded us this day—"

"Not quite finished," Bobby interrupted. "I still need to hear from Mr. Howard, a few questions on my mind."

"As you wish." Culverhouse folded his arms over Leland's blond head, steadfast and stern as a personal god. Bobby smiled at the pose, softly cynical.

"Mr. Howard, can you account for your whereabouts Saturday last?"

"Yes. I was in Evening Shade, burying my father, sir."

"After that?"

"I didn't care to spend the night in my boyhood home, so I had Mr. Giles drive me to the farm."

"When was the last time you saw Mr. Giles on Saturday night?"

"He asked my permission to use the car. That was about nine o'clock."

"Was Mr. Giles drinking before he left the farm?"

"No."

"Before he took your car, did you warn him that if he dropped into a juke to hoist a few beers he would be in violation of his parole?"

"I never thought it was necessary. In the months he worked for me, James never gave reason for me to be concerned about his behavior."

"So on this particular Saturday night he goes off the deep end, rapes a woman—"

"I just can't account for it."

"Who he brought back to the farm with him, after which there was considerable commotion going on. Did you hear your hounds?"

"I was sound asleep. I'd read the papers, had a couple of whiskies—"

"A hunting man knows the voices of his dogs, Mr. Howard. They wake him from his deepest dreams. No matter how tired or drunk he is."

Culverhouse said sharply, "Mr. Howard was not drunk."

"Yet he claims to have slept through the night totally unaware of what, according to Giles's confession, must have been one hellacious uproar on his farm."

Leland said, "You have no idea how exhausted—"

"I lost both of my parents several years ago. A drawn-out death for my mother. It was an ordeal, and I certainly sympathize with you in your time of grief. But I don't believe your story. I don't believe this confession either. I do have reason to believe you went to Mally Shaw's house last Saturday night. Giles won't give you up, because what good does that do him? He's going back for a full stretch anyhow—"

Culverhouse stiffened and lit into Bobby with his eyes. That cooking-the-goose radiance he employed to finish off a flummoxed witness.

"Mr. Howard does not have to deal with any more of your questions or your allegations!"

"No, he doesn't. He's here voluntarily."

"Then if there is nothing else, we will be leaving, sir."

"Just one more thing, and thank y'all for your time," Bobby said. He looked thoughtfully at Howard. "You were at one time employed by your father's bank?"

Howard was half out of his chair. He sat down again, reluctantly.

"Yes. In the trust department."

"Uh-huh. Well, I was wondering if you could tell me"—Bobby rolled back in his chair far enough to pull open the middle desk drawer; he took out a manila key envelope, opened it, shook out a little fine ash along with a blackened steel key onto his desk blotter—"what this looks like to you, Mr. Howard."

No one but Bobby could see Leland's reaction. A puzzled moment, a flash of apprehension, a tightening of the bold blue eyes.

"It's a—yeah, could be a safe-deposit-box key."

"We found the key this morning while sifting through the remains of Mally Shaw's burned-out house. Burned out by some Molotov cocktails, according to Chief Sheffer." Bobby tapped a finger on the papers to one side of his blotter. "I wonder why that wasn't in Giles's confession too?"

"Sir, do I need to remind you—"

"Hold on, Mr. Culverhouse," Bobby said, not looking at him. All of his attention was on Leland. "Only one bank in town since Farmers and Merchants closed up shop. Then it's likely, don't you think, that this key is to a box at West State Bank? You can still make out the number on it if you care to have a closer look."

Leland shook his head slightly. He wiped at perspiration in the hollows beneath his eyes.

"I gave Joe Rollander at the bank a call about an hour ago," Bobby said. "Mally never had an account at West State, and she didn't have a safe-deposit box either. The same was true of her late husband, William. So if this is a key from your, I mean your *daddy's* bank, wonder how it happened to turn up where we found it? In the morning I'll obtain a court order—justified by the suspicious nature of the fire that destroyed Mally's home—and we'll find out who rented the box and have a look at the contents."

Leland nodded as if he'd been asked a question, but there was a tragic vacancy in his eyes for a few moments until Gipson Culverhouse gripped him by the shoulder from behind.

"We're finished here."

No one else spoke. Leland rose from his chair. J. B. Garretson coughed into his fist. Bobby, still watching Leland, put the key back into the envelope.

"Thank you, Mr. Howard. That is all I need from you. For now. Mr. Culverhouse, gentlemen—a pleasure."

Leland turned to look at his lawyer. He had the expression of someone trying to turn on the energy, rev up the manly confidence, the flair, that championship swagger. Reporters were waiting, and in tomorrow's press he would be absolved of any possible wrongdoing in Mally Shaw's death. But the smile he had for Gipson Culverhouse failed with a tremor, like the exhausted wings of a dying moth. Culverhouse's controlling hand slid down Leland's sleeve to his elbow. Before walking his client out of the office, he looked once more at Bobby with his own smile, lean and respectful, no more patronizing amiability for a hick deputy. He nodded. Bobby nodded back.

When they had all cleared out Garretson said to Bobby, "Your Daddy could do that."

"Do what?" Bobby said, bouncing the lightweight envelope and key in the palm of one hand, smiling abstractedly.

"Turn loose hell with your stare." Garretson took a sack of tobacco from his shirt pocket to roll one, ambled over to peer like an owl at the seat of the chair Leland Howard had occupied. "Like that cowboy actor he resembled, you know, Tim McCoy."

"What are you thinking about, J. B.?"

The deputy looked up from the chair seat. "Well, now, ol' Leland went out of here looking like Mr. Soft Cock in a bedful of naked Miss Americas. Thought he might have left his balls behind."

"He didn't have any when he walked in," Bobby said. "Something's eating him real bad, and I don't mean Mally Shaw. He's got moral termites. You can smell 'em before you see 'em."

Mary Wingfield's voice came over the intercom.

"Bobby, line two. It's the hospital."

A*lex Gambier didn't know* beans about women's clothes. The dress he eventually picked out for Mally to wear that night looked very nice to him. It wasn't silk; the department store on Courthouse Square didn't carry anything that expensive. But it was tomato red with hem- and neckline ruffles in a darker shade of red. And an extra helping of high style, as the shopgirl helpfully pointed out to Alex, were sparkly little mirrors of assorted sizes called pailettes. The shopgirl, Sylvia Blocker, a first cousin of Francie Swift's, said she wished they'd gotten in that dress in her size. She was a fourteen.

"Fall off your bike?" Sylvia asked Alex, looking again at the bandage over his ears and Mercurochromed scratches like warpaint on his face and neck.

Alex selected the dress in Cecily's size and charged it. He thought Mally and Cecily were about the same size. After Mally wore the dress tonight for her—what had she called it?—*rendezvous,* Bobby could give it to Cece later on as an anniversary present.

He watched Leland Howard's press conference on the courthouse walk through a front window of Dunkel's with a headache that was bad enough to occasionally blur his vision. He had used much of his low store of energy just hitching a ride into town. It felt like time to escape the heat, lie down, go to sleep. Yawn. For *hours.* The store manager's office would be vacant for the rest of the afternoon. No one at Dunkel's would mind if he stretched out on the deep red leather couch there.

But Mally wasn't having any of that. Her reflection right along-side his in Dunkel's window. Reminding him. He needed to write that all-important letter first.

You could bet she would nag him gently until he did.

Then it ought to be okay to get some rest before nightfall. Getting out to Cole's Crossing before the *Dixie Traveler* passed would be difficult without his bike.

A *reporter from the Chatanooga Times* asked Leland, "Are you planning on hiring any more ex-convicts to work for you?"

Leland didn't like his tone but gave the question grave consideration as he paused to brush perspiration from his eyelashes. Hell apparently had rented Evening Shade for the day.

One eyelid wouldn't stop its crazed twitching. He soothed it with a fingertip, looking up at the sky with its glare and wisps of clouds that held no promise of rain.

"In spite of the tragic and unforeseen events of the past few days, I think it is important for us all not to lose faith—in our system of justice and in our fellow man. Mr. Giles served eight years for the crime of manslaughter, and during that time he was considered to be a model prisoner. I had every reason to believe his rehabilitation was complete"—*Goddamn that fucking eye!*—"and therefore had no hesitation in providing him with a job as my chauffeur on the campaign trail, a first step toward regaining his dignity and usefulness as a member of society." Tears and perspiration crawling down his cheeks together with a couple of green flies sailing around his head as if he were a foundered horse gave Leland the heebie-jeebies. "To answer your question: Yes, I *would* hire another parolee from our state's excellent prison system. Let us nuh-never forget that acceptance of, and forgiveness for, another man's failings is—it's the heart and soul of a civilized community."

"That's all for today, gentlemen," Gipson Culverhouse said.

———

I *t had been a mistake* to order the fried-egg sandwich. After three bites Leland excused himself from the large booth at the rear of the Hob-Nob Cafe, went into the men's room with sweat all over him cold as mercury and the eye still twitching. He puked up his guts. It put a strain on his heart. Head down, he hung by his wide-spread hands in the stall crucifixion-style until Culverhouse sent Ray Villapando in to check on him.

"I'm not feeling so hot," Leland said. "Need to lie down. Have them cancel Murfreesboro tonight; I can't take another Goddamn county fair. And would you drive me up to my farm?"

They were walking through the nearly empty cafe, Leland in front, when he almost bumped into Bobby Gambier, who had just come in.

"You don't look so chipper, Mr. Howard."

"Yes, I know, it's the heat."

"Floyd Smart told me I'd probably find y'all in here. I have some news."

"Good or bad?" Leland attempted a smile. He just wanted Bobby to get out of his way.

"Depends on your point of view. James Giles killed himself this afternoon over to the community hospital."

Leland put a hand on the edge of the lunch counter. "What? How?"

"He managed to move himself enough in the bed to get his hand on the fan cord. Put it in his mouth and chewed until he electrocuted himself."

The others in the back of the cafe had their heads up. Listening.

"Good God. James. What a terrible end to—"

"If you could provide me with the name of his next of kin."

"There's a sister he mentioned. But I don't know anything about him really." The motion of overhead fan paddles repeated in a tinted mirror behind the counter matched the speed of Leland's heart.

"Well, we should be able to track somebody down might be willing to spring for the burial."

"That's all right. I mean I'll—take care of it. The expenses. Now if you'll excuse me—August, sweet Jesus. August won't let you breathe in these parts."

"For a fact." Bobby touched the brim of his hat and stepped aside. Followed by Villapando, Leland made it out to the sidewalk, where he looked around in confusion. Villapando took him the rest of the way to the limo, Leland popping a candy into his mouth. The limo was parked in the shade of a draggy-looking collection of river birches. They didn't like the heat either.

Bobby came out and stood beneath the sidewalk canopy watching the limo pull away, taking his hat off to let a breath of air and some light into his moody thoughts.

"That man is going to blow," he said to himself. "Question of when and where."

They had left the courthouse square behind, heading north, when Leland became aware of the pale blue envelope near him on the back seat. His name was on it. *Leland Howard.* Marked *Personal.* The handwriting neat, feminine.

He picked it up, turned it over. Put it in his lap and took out his gold toothpick, worked to dislodge bits of candy from his molars. His stomach still felt awful. A lava pit. He tasted blood on his tongue from his gums. Still he continued to poke away. He looked at the envelope again with the impulse to throw it out the window. He was always getting notes from women who wanted to fuck him. Frequently they enclosed photos. Lewd, most of the time. Women who took their own photos and, obviously, did their own developing. Those who hoped to tempt him with beaver shots.

He clenched his hands, which had been trembling, then used his toothpick to cut open the envelope. Slipped out the folded notepaper.

JOHN FARRIS

Hello, Leland
 It's time we saw each other
again, don't you think?
I have everything your
father gave to me. I don't
want it, but I want the
thousand dollars you
promised to give to me.
I expect you to keep that
promise, Leland.
 Meet me tonight by the
old depot at Cole's Crossing.
Nine-fifteen. Just after dark.
I've changed. But you'll
still know me when you
see me.
 Come alone. It isn't in
your best interests to
disappoint me.

Mally Shaw

TWELVE

The Red Dress

We missed you *at supper," Bobby said to Ramses Valjean.* "Not that it was all that special, but Rhoda's candied yams are pig-out famous at church suppers around Evening Shade."

Ramses sat on the edge of the low iron bed in the small room he had been given, a courtesy respectful of his status, in the Jim Crow ward of the community hospital. He had removed his dress shirt and tie and hung them over the back of a chair. His suspenders were down and he was barefoot. There was a tinge of yellow-gray to his complexion. A couple of raw cracks appeared at the corners of his mouth when he smiled.

"Candied yams. My mother made them too. I am, unfortunately, no longer digesting my food very well. There are other complications, so I have revised the timetable I mentioned to you a few days ago. My pancreas has nearly stopped producing insulin. I had a shot this afternoon from Dr. Crawford. Tomorrow—well, I'll have to see."

Bobby nodded. He didn't know what to say.

"But I could use a drink. If you have the time."

"I've got the time."

Leland Howard sat in the parlor of the house at his farm with a .38 revolver in his lap and sunset at the windows.

It isn't in your best interests to disappoint me.

The fifth of Maker's Mark on the table beside him was two-thirds empty. He poured another shot. So far he didn't feel a thing. His tongue a little numb at the edges, that was all. Otherwise he was sober.

The tremoring of his hands had nearly stopped. His mind was clear. But he was aware his limit wasn't too far away. There would come a point where one more shot—half a shot—would lay him out as limp as a two-dollar whore.

Someone was trying to make a fool of him. Best guess, a female relative of Mally Shaw's who also had been visiting Mally on Saturday night. Hid out when he arrived but overheard, maybe witnessed, everything that went on between him and Mally. Hadn't been a young white boy after all; Giles had been wrong about that, and it had cost him his life.

He heard a tractor outside, Claude Long yelling at his half-witted son to close the gate. They were going home to their own place adjacent to Leland's farm.

Jim Giles dead, a signed confession down at the sheriff's, and it wasn't enough, his father shriveling in his crypt but still one jump ahead of Leland . . . who pictured that aged head secretly alight in darkness with death's lolling grin. He felt a slippage of nerve, steeled himself. The damned key that the deputy had casually dropped on his desk blotter was, Leland had no doubt, to an extra safe-deposit box, perhaps under an assumed name, where his father had left the proof that would send Leland to prison. But the key was no longer a threat to him. The letter writer had made that clear. Mally, it would seem, had emptied the box before last Saturday.

I have everything your father gave to me.

Some greedy relation of Mally's now had the goods on Leland Howard.

Or thought she did. What was the point of pretending she was Mally? To scare him? As if he were simple, a lamebrain like Claude's speckled boy?

The thousand dollars you promised.

Leland felt insulted. It provided a keener edge to his anger. He raised the shot glass to his lips, reconsidered, and set the glass aside. He picked up the Colt from his lap and stood, opened the gate. The brass rounds of cartridges gleamed in the reddening light at the windows. So red the world might have been on fire.

No, this is what you get.

The tremor that had stilled in his hands was in his gut, an overture to massive fear that put him off balance.

But what if one killing wasn't enough? How many could there be—faceless, taunting conspirators, stepping out of shadows to make their own demands?

Leland closed the gate of the blue-steel revolver and put it in a boot, rolled down the cuff of his twill trousers to hide it.

He walked outside into the red shift of evening, wearing the day-long heat like a hair shirt. On the porch he looked past tinkly glass wind chimes at the empty kennel run. His dogs were being put to death. Something swung disastrously through his mind, a psychic weight like a wrecking ball. He almost lost his balance again but clung to a newel post.

. . . And the days of his childhood had run long and playful, the quick nights slept away while his heart held the heat and lure of the sun. Now his days were shorter, shadowed, intolerable; his heart, like the sun, was dying in his breast. There was no mercy in the hung prisms through which he backward viewed his fate. His life was dwindling, darkly, toward a climax of nightmarish calamity.

He had no run left in him. But his tormentors would keep coming. Wouldn't they.

Elegiac tears rolled down his cheeks.

If they made him kill them, who could say the fault was his?

B*obby said to Ramses Valjean,* "So the painters are almost finished at Bernie's house. She and Cece go over there this afternoon to check everything out, and can you believe it, Bernie's not happy. She's still gagging on the fumes although Cece says she can barely smell them herself, and to boot Bernie's second-guessing all of her color choices. Should have been peach in her bedroom, she decides, not apricot. Just have to do everything all over again. Also she's worried now that some paint may get on the upholstery of some of her heirloom furniture even though the boys use drop cloths everywhere. Asks Cece if she could move the stuff over to our house for now, seeing as how we're a little shy on furniture ourselves in a couple of rooms."

Ramses nodded. "The woman has wiles." They were at one of the picnic tables behind Pee-Wee's Good Eats with a paper-bagged pint provided by Pee-Wee, Ramses wearing his blind man's specs, facing a sunset like deep fire in a canyon of clouds. George Dickel in paper cups. At Bobby's urging, Ramses had eaten a couple of bites of a toasted cheese sandwich. Pee-Wee's was still open, but they were alone in the picnic area.

Bobby winked at Ramses. "Cecily just looked at her and said, 'Sure, Mom. We can take the furniture. But I almost forgot to tell you the good news. Bobby and I are pregnant again.'"

"Congratulations," Ramses said.

"Thanks. I don't feel all that pregnant yet. But anyhow, Cece says to her mom, 'So Bobby and I have decided to make over the guest room into Brendan's room. We'll do that while you're on your cruise.' And Bernie says, wish I could've been there to see the look on her face, '*What* cruise?' 'The cruise you and Aunt Edith have been talking about doing together for the past twenty years. Can't think of a more perfect time to go, while your house is getting fixed up, and I talked to Edith long-distance just last night. She is so excited, said she'd make all the arrangements, and I'll bet her bags are packed already.' So then here it comes. Bernie doesn't know if she feels well enough right now, Cece is going to need all the help she can get with Brendan during her new pregancy—and so on. But my wife just looked her in the eye and said, 'Mom, go. Have a good time. You deserve it.'" Bobby poured a little more of the Dickel into his cup. "Damn, I'm proud of her." He drank, smiling a little smugly. "I guess it did make an impression on Cece when I told her her mom's fingerprints were all over that Vaseline jar she tossed into Alex's wastebasket."

"How long does the cruise last?"

"Three months, I think Cecily told me. Want another?"

"Wouldn't mind." Bobby poured; Ramses tossed down the whiskey in a lump, finishing with a look of admiration and satisfaction. "I am going to miss this," he said.

"Plenty of time for a few more visits with ol' George D."

Ramses noted Bobby's discomfort and smiled to dismiss the spectre floating in and out of their awareness of every man's fate.

"I wanted to talk to you about Alex and his long-standing problem with his vocal cords. If there's a chance the damage can be repaired, I know the man for the job."

"Well, Ramses. Alex was disappointed so often I'd hate to—"

"This afternoon while waiting on the results of some tests, I had time to catch up on correspondence and attend to other, legal matters, the tidying-up that needs to be done." He took three envelopes from his coat pockets and laid them on the table. "I should drop these at the post office on my way back to the hospital. I seldom write letters. I suppose it's my reclusive nature. Dr. Charles Martorell, however, is someone I correspond with on a regular basis." He fingered the fattest envelope on the table. "In this letter I've provided him with an introduction to Alex's case along with photostats of the medical reports you gave to me. Of course he won't be able to make a decision regarding surgery until he's examined Alex personally. Next month, in Paris."

Bobby rubbed a mosquito bite under his chin and smiled skeptically. "Alex is going to Paris?"

"Yes. At no expense to you and Cecily. I've made the arrangements, rather sneakily I admit, but time may be of the essence." Ramses began to cough, and the wracking cough turned him into a shadow figure on the picnic bench, sideways and shuddering helplessly. Bobby's left hand was in his lap; he dug his fingernails into the palm while waiting out Ramses' ordeal. There was blood on the handkerchief Ramses whisked from his lips when the spasm ended, blood he didn't want Bobby to see. When he straightened again he was smiling, his face composed. "Thank you for your patience. How about another spot of the Dickel?"

"I uh feel like we ought to—"

Ramses looked around slowly. "No, not yet. It's so pleasant here. When the wind is right." He nodded toward Pee-Wee's ramshackle restaurant. Bobby laughed. There was no wind yet, and the odor of fry grease from Pee-Wee's was almost a visible smudge in the air. The sun a faded glory, nearby landscape taking on the first soft tones of summer night. Bobby passed the pint bottle to Ramses, who finished off the whiskey. "'Red sky at night, sailor's delight,'" he said. "And one long voyage is nearly over. I never imagined that I would find myself back where it began, in the heart of a boy behind a mule plowing fields while adrift in sailor dreams, so tired he could barely hold his head up but thinking, *Why can't I?*"

Bobby nodded solemnly. Words, he felt, would have been an intrusion just then.

Ramses sighed. "You shouldn't lose hope on Alex's behalf, Bobby."

"I never have intended to."

"Good. He's just beginning to wake up to life, whatever may be in store." Ramses smothered a cough before it could develop into something punishing. "I sold my home in Nashville when I was sure of my prognosis and put the proceeds from the sale aside for Mally, along with my savings." He made a small gesture of finality with his hand. "Alex's expenses and Charles's fee will be amply covered. Should Charles determine that Alex's condition is operable, then Alex will remain for some months as a guest in his house. He has twin grandchildren living with him and his wife, Alida, by the way, who are Alex's age. Both their parents were in the Resistance and were executed by the Gestapo."

"Ramses, have you had the chance to—"

"This afternoon I wanted to speak further to Alex about the surgery, but as we know, Alex decided to check himself out of the hospital." Now that the sun had set, Ramses removed his dark glasses and looked at Bobby. "Will you do this? It's for Alex, of course, but in a very important way it's for me as well."

"In this case I think—I want to do what Alex wants."

"Wonderful! Well, why don't we go and ask him right now?"

"You still think we'll find Alex hanging around the old depot at Cole's Crossing?"

"Yes, I'm sure we will. I'll explain while we're driving."

Alex *had hitched a ride* with an elderly farmer named Fred Edgar Moody and his wife, Eula, who was fresh from the dentist with a new set of choppers; she had a sack of peanut brittle to try them out on. There was room for Alex and his duffel bag in the truck bed along with a couple of cartons of baby chicks and some fifty-pound sacks of Purina chicken feed.

He got off at Cole's Crossing in the last full, red light of day, shedding a few chick feathers, his mouth sticky from peanut brittle. Not knowing precisely what time it was. But he had left the square at a few minutes past eight by the courthouse clock, and with Fred Edgar driving like a geriatric madman all the way, easily busting twenty-five miles an hour on the straight stretches of country road, Alex calculated that it was about eight-thirty now. That gave him a half hour or so to wait for the arrival of the *Dixie Traveler* out of Memphis, thereafter Leland Howard himself. Alex had no doubts that he would show.

After that it would be up to Mally. He didn't know what Mally was planning. She had only smiled secretively and said, *You'll see, Sugar.*

An emaciated dog was picking its way stiffly across the silver rails west of the leaning old water tank. The stray lifted his head but didn't pause during his limping progress toward Little Grove. Keeping the dog, or anything else, in focus was difficult for Alex, as if his eyes were cheap binoculars that couldn't be adequately adjusted. His headache was as bad as it had been all day. He felt weakened by the pain and stumbled as he walked down the center of the track with his duffel over one shoulder. He had always taken his reflexes and physical agility for granted. Now the parts of his body didn't seem to want to work together.

The gabled depot was stark against a rusty stain of sunset. Birds soared upward from the roof line. The Yella Dog River glinted like a scattered broken mirror beneath the long trestle. The air was still and thick where he walked, the earth no longer giving back the heat of day.

No sign of the stationmaster whom he'd seen on his last visit. But Alex couldn't complete the Crossing, of course, until the *Dixie Traveler* invested him with its power and Mally appeared. Then the old platform would swarm with bodies evanescent as locomotive smoke in the confused aftermath of their recent lives.

He climbed the steps from the roadbed and let his duffel drop on the platform, knelt to take out the crowbar he had purchased at Sy Carty's hardware store. He set about pulling off the boards that had been nailed over the depot's entrance. It was tough work that had him draining perspiration and feeling sparkly-faint before he was done.

Alex rested up, then put his shoulder to the door, forcing corroded hinges to give. The depot had been abandoned for years to birds and mice. Inside, the floor was cruddy with droppings. He'd been five years old the last time he stepped inside. The waiting room now seemed smaller. There were benches along two walls, a Franklin Stove in the corner between them. The stovepipe had collapsed across one bench and the floor. He heard the beat of wings above the rafters at his entry. A panic-shadow darted from the loft beneath the pitched roof and coursed around the walls, big as a kite in the still-bright reflection from the sky outside.

There was so much dust and crap on the floorboards, he left near-perfect footprints from the doorway. Alex had a sneezing fit that echoed like explosions at the back of his sore head. Weeping, he took a camp lantern, also from Carty's, out of his bag and set it on the scarred maple counter next to the pebbled-glass ticket window, which was miraculously intact. He lit the wick of the kerosene lamp and the expanding glow revealed mouse-scurry in a fallen stovepipe, more flutter of dark wings where the roof was pierced.

There were chalk traces from the depot's last day on the timetable beside the window. In spite of his vision problems and overflowing eyes, he saw *Hi, Alex!* appear, a big chalky scrawl in the middle of the blackboard. He smiled gratefully. Felt better already.

Jagged pieces of sooty glass in the trackside window frame took on a lurid glow as he walked with the lantern back to the entrance and closed the door. Then he chose a bench opposite the entrance on which to wait, the lamp beside him, the duffel between his feet, his head in his hands.

T*here had been a graveled parking lot* adjacent to the depot on the north side of the Southern's right-of-way, but it had gone to hip-high ragweed and milk thistle long ago. Leland Howard parked his Pontiac Eight at the edge of the overgrown lot, and after having a look around and seeing no one, he transferred the Colt revolver from his boot to his waistband. The ragweed pollen irritated his nose; he snuffled into a handkerchief. About a quarter of a mile on up the road, there was a small farmhouse, empty rockers on the porch. Disembodied voices of Negro children at play.

He heard the frying drone of cicadas and a tree frog tuning up for a night's romancing. There was no sense of weather, just bake-oven heat, although the sky had lost its flame, burned down to a sultry yellow streak in the west with a small green wafer on the dusky landscape, the signal block at Half Mile. All clear for the *Dixie Traveler.*

It was a few minutes before nine o'clock. Early for his appointment, or whatever it was.

The best way to get to the depot was to follow the track. Leland unwrapped a piece of candy, recalling that when he was a kid he could walk a single rail, light-boned, blithely balancing for half a mile or more. Tonight he plodded, one crosstie at a time, avoiding ballast, the crunch of footsteps, his nerves spinning out around him like spider's silk.

Halfway there, and he thought he saw a wink of light inside the depot.

Leland went slowly up the steps from track level and saw the litter of torn-away boards on the depot platform. Yes, and there was light inside, a modest flicker reflected from the jagged edges of glass in the window frame behind heavy wire mesh.

He looked in from the platform, a hand on the checkered walnut butt of his Colt.

Dust and silence. Footprints criss-crossing the floor.

Then his heart jumped. Someone was moving around in there. He saw the shadow on one wall, big, splayed out, shifting with her movements as she paced, as if she were impatient for him to come calling.

Leland moved a couple of steps himself to change his sight line through the wire mesh and caught a glimpse of swirling red in the part of the waiting room most distant from the pale flame of the camp lantern. The lantern had been placed on the floor beside a large duffel bag.

Red. She was wearing a red dress with something like sequins on it, he couldn't be sure. Flounces though, a party dress. Struttin' her stuff. He changed his angle of vision again, moved as far to his right as he could, and saw a bare arm, flash of skin tone, deep maple, quadroon probably. Like Mally herself. He grinned, but his heart was going like gangbusters.

From a long way down the line toward Memphis he heard the drawn-out howl of the eastbound *Dixie Traveler.*

Leland took three steps and kicked open the door to the depot's waiting room and stumbled off-balance inside. He drew his gun and took two more steps toward the woman in the red dress, who was turning to look at him in multiple flashes of little mirrors that stung Leland's eyes.

What a fancy dress.

But it wasn't a woman wearing it.

For God's sake!

It was a boy, a deeply tanned blond boy with a bandaged, scratched-up head and dopey-looking eyes. He was way too big for the size of the dress he had put on. The dress had split almost all the way down one side, and the ruffled hem was well above his bare knees. He wore khaki shorts underneath that skimpy dress.

"What the hell are you supposed to be?" Leland said, barely able to believe what he was looking at.

The boy's lips parted. He didn't seem particularly flustered. He put a hand to his throat, chin tilting up, and squeezed lightly.

"Hello, Leland. Don't you know me? It's Mally."

Leland flinched at this accurate but creepy impersonation of Mally Shaw's voice. He felt a sizzling charge the length of his backbone, exploding in the hindbrain and nearly lifting off the top of his skull. He had been in a war, but nothing that happened in the Pacific had ever scared him like this.

"Shut up! Don't you do that again, you little cocksucker!"

The boy's eyes still looked flawed, tranced, withdrawn; but he said in Mally's voice again, and with her slightly sad, cynical smile, "Bet you didn't bring that thousand dollars with you. Did you, Mist' Leland?"

For an instant he thought he saw her face too, looking at him the way she'd looked up from flat on her back on the bed in her house with him between her legs, that anguished, humiliated expression. Accepting what had to come, belittling him somehow even as he drilled her brains out.

Who the hell did she think she was?

"I brought you this!" Leland shouted, and shot the boy in a trigger-pulling frenzy five times up and down his body, missing once maybe but driving him back against the wall, where he slumped then sprawled in a downfall of splashy little mirrors, not making another sound.

Frozen. *Deafened.* A sharp twinge in his breast, the fascination giving way to horror like that following a viper's bite. His shadow thrown to the rafters above the heap of the boy lying up against the wall. Gun sagging in his hand. His mind half-cocked. Trying to make sense of it all. But he doesn't feel badly about what he has done. God-damned fairy kid! Then urgency gooses him out of his momentary shutdown. He hears the wail of the approaching train at Half Mile. Less than a minute until it reaches Cole's Crossing. *Move.*

Leland looks around at the duffel on the floor by the lantern. Time to fetch what he has come for. Then clear out.

They heard the gunshots that came from inside the depot as they were getting out of Bobby's station wagon, which he had parked in front of Leland Howard's Pontiac on the north side of the track. Immediately after that they heard the old bell, long thought to be useless, tolling in the belfry of Little Grove Holiness Church.

Bobby looked at Ramses and drew his own piece, then ran to the track (the going would be too slow any other way) and scrambled toward the depot. The headlamp beam of the *Dixie Traveler* was full in his face, twin four-thousand horsepower diesel-electric engines and a dozen luxury coaches, diners, and Pullmans. He felt the train's enormous pulse through the soles of his boots, felt it streaming upward through his veins, his bones electric.

From his calculations as he ran he thought it could be a dead heat at the near end of the two hundred-foot-long platform. He could play it safe, jump aside now and wait for the *Traveler* to thunder by, but he didn't know what was going on there in the depot, and he was afraid for his brother.

Leland Howard yanked everything out of the duffel, items of clothing and cheap magazines and a couple of notebooks that had mostly blank pages. He didn't find what he was looking for; but what that might have been was vague in his mind. Evidence of a criminal act on his part. He would recognize it when he—

The *Dixie Traveler* filled his conscious mind with a certain terror, seventy-plus miles an hour and bearing down on him. Its dynamic like a surge of water into a small cave, lifting Leland to his feet.

Behind the pebbled glass of the glowing ticket window he saw

another human form, unmistakably female, a rippling, shadowy movement right to left.

So there were two of them!

He brought the Colt across his body and flung a last shot at the
figure behind the window. She vanished with the cascade of thick,
sharded glass.

In two strides Leland reached the door to the stationmaster's office
and wrenched it open.

Mally Shaw was in there, five days dead and looking it. Only her
eyes were alive in her disfigured face. Their expression was as lively as
her pleased smile as she let slip the leashes of three Catahoula hounds.
They were just as dead and unearthly as Mally herself, but all violence
in trembling light and shadow.

He had a moment to regret that he couldn't think of their names
to call them off.

Bobby Gambier did a headlong leap to the end of the platform
and sprawled there as the *Dixie Traveler's* lead engine rocketed past
him. He pulled in a lungful of diesel-saturated air and made another
dash for the depot doorway.

He ran into Leland Howard, who was on his way out.

Leland was making an eerie sound, high-pitched, a kind of
whistling scream. It was the worst thing Bobby had heard from a human throat. There was blood on Leland's face from emptied eye sock-
ets. He had a maniac's strength. With one gory hand he flung Bobby
nearly ten feet.

Still making that unbearable keening sound, Leland wheeled
around directionless on the platform, tripped himself up and fell back
against the depot wall. His right hand opened on an egglike something. Bobby moved cautiously toward him. By the flashes of lighted
train windows flying past them, Bobby realized that what dangled
from Leland's fingers like an unlucky charm was one of his own blue
eyes.

So Leland sat there screaming like a second Doppler effect of the diesel engine's air horn, his body twitching out of control. His hand clamped shut on the eye, Bobby making an effort not to vomit with the back of his neck cold from horror. He didn't think Leland would be going anywhere. He walked around him and into the depot waiting room.

By lantern light he saw a blue-steel .38 Colt on the floor and nearby Leland's other eye, bloody roots and all. Alex was lying much too still against the far wall.

The club car of the *Traveler* cleared the depot with a last wink of its crimson running lights, and the sudden quiet was unnerving. He didn't hear Leland Howard anymore; not much sound except for his own panicked breath as he knelt beside his brother and tried to find a pulse. There was a steady flow of blood through the carotid artery; Alex's pulse was strong, and Bobby momentarily was light-headed from relief.

All Alex had on was a pair of shorts. He was lying on his red shirt, or so Bobby thought, but when he rolled the boy over saw it was a dress, fancy, tiny mirrors sewn to the bodice.

There were livid bruises on Alex's chest and stomach. When Bobby picked him up he was still holding fast to the dress. Four copper-jacketed .38 slugs fell out of the folds and rolled on the floor.

Now, what the hell?

"Is he shot?" Ramses asked as he came into the waiting room.

"Shot—yeah—I think—these bruises—but none of the slugs penetrated—I don't know what happened here! Alex is alive, that's all I care about. You better have a look at Leland Howard, he was screaming and screaming, I can't stand—"

"Mr. Howard is dead, Bobby."

"What?"

"Shock trauma, I would guess. His face is badly clawed. From the condition of his fingernails, I'm sure he did it to himself."

"Jesus! Why?"

"I think only Mally could answer that," Ramses said. He lifted one of Alex's eyelids, then the other, looking at Alex's pupils. "But she's not here anymore."

"Never was."

"Oh yes," Ramses said. "Mally was here, all right. I saw her. Why don't I tell you about that while you're driving? This boy is going back to the hospital as quickly as we can get him there."

Ramses hadn't been able to keep up with Bobby, and he waited until the *Dixie Traveler* was across the trestle before he trudged over the rails in front of the depot. A short run had used up another day of life and passion. His body now an adversarial creature of predestined design flaws. Testing his mettle with every breath and step he took beneath hotbeds of stars. He had a bloodbath fever.

As he was bending to the lifeless body on the platform (one fly already on the lower lip of Leland's silently shouting mouth), Ramses, in spite of fever, felt a chill like an arrow of ice in the humid, tarry night, as if another train were slowing down on the track behind him. The air he breathed turning storm-heavy, hovering, a weight on his chest.

Yes, another train—stopping at this crossing, ready for boarding now. Or was it the foment of his fever prompting this perception of the uncanny?

A tug like a child's hand caused him to turn his head. Fascinated, too old and debilitated to have fear.

So there was Mally, that sweet, pensive face. She wore a red dress with a scoop neckline and stars in their places: folderol but stylish, a holiday dress for celestial sight-seeing.

He saw his daughter elevated in stately drift, like an icon on a pallet in a religious procession. Certainly not altogether real to his eyes, yet she couldn't be called spirit.

The train (but one couldn't name it exactly that, just as "Silver Ghost" in Alex Gambier's fifth-grade story was something more than mere horseflesh). Supernatural, to be sure. Mally was aboard already, maybe the only soul traveling from here this night. An overdue soul;

when she turned her eyes on him for the last time, he felt pity over-whelmed by a surge of exaltation.

A *red dress?" Bobby said.* "With little mirrors on it? Like the one Alex had a grip on, bullets fell out of it when I lifted him off the floor of the depot?"

"I don't remember seeing it," Ramses said. He was in the back of the station wagon, holding Alex's head immobile while Bobby raced them to the hospital.

C*ecily Gambier found Bobby asleep* in a porch swing when she came outside with Brendan to take advantage of what coolness would be available to them that day in Evening Shade. Seven in the morning and the neighbors waking up and Bobby slumped over with an empty beer bottle in one hand. She gently took the bottle away, and he re-acted with a startled jump, then smiled sheepishly at his wife.

"Why didn't you come to bed last night?"

"Last night?" Bobby shrugged and looked around at a calm August morning on West Hatchie Road, the folded paper on the porch, bumblebees browsing through their roses. "I just drove home a little while ago." He yawned. "No point in going to sleep, it's bound to be a hell of a busy day. Brendan's on formula now?"

"I told you he was. We started last night. He had a tantrum. But Dr. Yost said it was already past time to wean him."

"Yeah. Did you ever notice that sometimes when you were breast-feeding him he'd get a hard-on?"

"Bobby! Don't be telling me things like *that.*"

"Well, he seems to be guzzling the stuff now."

"That's good, because Mom needs a break before the next kid shows up. Want to finish giving Brendan his bottle?"

"Sure." Bobby sat back on the swing and took Brendan from her. Brendan opened his eyes and looked up at his daddy, that look of purity and complete trust only seen in the youngest eyes. "Your mom okay?" Bobby asked.

"No, she's in a snit. Sure was a lot of fun around here last night. Bobby, how's Alex?"

"He may have some bleeding into the brain. But he was semi-conscious and responsive around five a.m. Ramses got a colleague who is supposed to be the best in the south, a neurosurgeon, to drive down here in the middle of the night."

"A Negro doctor?"

"No. But what difference would that make as long as he was good?"

Cecily gave him an appreciative look and said softly, "Why, Bobby."

Bobby looked at her, perplexed, then smiled. Brendan pushed the nipple of the nearly empty bottle out of his mouth and wriggled.

"I didn't understand half of what you were trying to tell me on the phone from the hospital," Cecily said, sitting on the top step of the porch. "What happened to Leland Howard?"

Bobby was a long time answering her. He stood Brendan up on the porch, holding him by one hand. Brendan looked at him. Bobby said, "You're gonna take your first steps any day now. I don't want to miss that. So why don't you just walk over there to your mom right now? You need changing anyway." And he let go of the boy's hand.

Rhoda was getting out of her husband's car at their front gate.

"Wait a minute!" she called. "Let me fetch the camera."

"It's on the refrigerator, Rhoda," Cecily said, and held out her hands to Brendan. He hadn't moved yet, but he looked steady on his feet. Knew very well that he was the center of attention and that big things were expected of him right now.

"Cecily, I have to write my investigative report this morning. I plan to keep it simple. But all any of us can do is speculate. So officially what happened was, Leland Howard was out for a drive by himself, suffered chest pains, pulled over at Cole's Crossing, and made his way to the depot there, maybe thinking he'd find a phone to call for help. Got into a panic trying to pull some boards away from the depot door so he could get inside. Injured himself doing it and brought on a fatal heart attack."

"What sort of injury?"

"Messed up his eyes pretty bad. I understand they can fix that at Hicks and Baggett before his funeral. You don't bury anyone with their eyes open anyhow."

"Of course not. What else will be in your report?"

"That's about all. I happened to be driving Ramses to visit a cousin of his, and we came across the Pontiac sitting empty on the road near the Southern's main line. I'm paid to be curious about such things, so that's how we found him."

Rhoda appeared with their Brownie camera just as Brendan took four full steps across the porch and fell laughing into his mother's arms.

"Did you get that, Rhoda?" Bobby said.

"Yes, sir! I got the pictures."

"Wish we had a movie camera," Cecily said.

"Someday." Bobby blinked and ducked his head. Tears.

"What about Alex though? Where did you find Alex last night? Bobby, he wasn't with Leland Howard, was he? I mean—it wasn't one of those things going on?"

"Hell, no."

"But there was *something* going on with Alex. Bobby, I had a call from Dunkel's late yesterday afternoon. Our charge account is over the limit because Alex has been going there and buying a lot of things. Including a red dress that cost ninety-eight dollars!"

"A red dress. What do you know?"

"Well, did he tell you anything about—"

"It was a gift for Mally Shaw," Bobby said, leaning back and clasping his hands behind his head, looking at the ceiling of the porch.

"Mally Shaw!"

"You don't like ghost stories, do you, Cecily?"

"*No.* They scare me to—" She looked sharply at him. Bobby was smiling. "Is this something that's not going into your report?"

"We'll just pay the charge at Dunkel's," Bobby said. "It was worth every penny."

Alex Gambier *was out of danger* and awake when Ramses paid his last visit of the day, shortly after four p.m. that Friday afternoon.

"I'm driving back to Nashville with Dr. Wallace this evening. I'll be in touch with the floor nurses here until you're discharged." Ramses sat on the edge of the bed. "Now, I'm not saying good-bye, you understand. But if it should happen that we don't see each other again . . ."

Alex frowned.

Ramses fished some coins from a pocket of his jacket and put them into Alex's hand, lying open at his side.

"*Quatre francs,*" he said. "Enough to buy two glasses of Bordeaux at a *boîte* that has long been a favorite of mine. On Rue de Bièvre near Place Maubert. A small street, an alley anywhere else. Some of the more interesting streets of Paris are those you have to make an effort to find. Couderc's isn't far from where you'll be living while in Paris. I'll write it down, but all of the Left Bank will be familiar to you in no time. As will the language. You'll learn it quickly because you want to write fiction, and every writer of fiction should know intimately the great French novelists."

Alex looked at the coins in his hand. He passed his other hand across his throat, a question.

"I have every confidence," Ramses said. "The wine, you see, will be in the nature of a celebration. A glass for each of us. Please remember me to Madame Couderc when you stop by. Tell her how sorry I am not to be there on this splendid occasion."

The muscles in Alex's throat tensed. He turned his face aside on the pillow. He closed his eyes, and after a little time passed he felt Ramses get up slowly from the bed. When he opened his eyes again, tears fell. He could barely make out Ramses in the doorway. Looking back. He seemed to be smiling.

A lifted hand, farewell; he was gone.

EPILOGUE

Hi Francie

The good news today is Dr Martorell says the vocal cord grafts he did are both "near 100 percent." The bad news (maybe) is I found out that the "donor" was a 23 year old Algerian woman (Yvie says she was murdered by a jelous lover but that is the kind of story shes always coming up with). So wonder what I will sound like if I ever do get to say anything. Haha.

For now I am not allowed to make a sound and theyre worried I could catch a cold (everybody in Paris has a cold this time of the year) and screwup the works. But in a week Im supposed to begin "exercises" with a vocal coach who works with famous stars of the Paris Opera. Maybe before I leave here I will be singing the ten r part from "Manon." (Haha again)

The last couple of letters I wanted to tell you something really strange that happened but every time I try it turns into a ghost story. Another ghost story. But you liked the first one and so Im counting on you not to blab this one either which would make me look like an idiot.

Schools over for the day (I actually understood most of a lecture I heard this morning) the wether's drery and Im sitting here in my usual haunt (there I go again) by the window of the cafe on Quai Monte-bello I already told you all about (easy to locate on the map I sent— across the Seine from Notre Dame cathedrel and on the Ile St Louis I can see the building where Im staying with the Martorells and Yvie-the-Brat—I dont understand how twins can be so different because

Max is a great guy and I dont beleve Yvie has a crush on me which is your ~~thery~~ theory. As you can see Im trying to improve my speling haha. I spell better when I type believe it or not. Anyway the twins will be here in a few minutes. Max has foils after classes on Tues. and I could care less what Yvies up to. Meanwhile let me try again.

Remember I told you Dr Valjean died the first week in Oct.? Before then he wrote me suggesting some places I ought to visit that were old favorites of his such as "Shakespeare and Company" a bookstore a few streets from here where all the famous writers like Hemingway used to go (hope you have read A Farewell to Arms by now). And the last thing Ramses put in his letter was "Dont forget to stop in at Coudercs."

Well I guess I forgot all right. In fact I didnt know what he was talking about. What was "Coudercs?" I wrote it down for Max who wasnt sure either but thought it might be a bistro he had gone past a couple of times. He said it might be in that maze of narrow streets between the quais and Saint-Germain.

I think it must have been a week later that I had a dream about Coudercs. I saw the place as if I was actually standing outside about thirty years ago. Thats what the clothes everybody had on looked like, around World War One. All the men were real "dandies." And Ramses Valjean was with them. Wearing a high collar and a derby. I saw the name above the door, Coudercs, and also the address.

Dr Martorell did his first surgery a few days after I had the dream so I couldn't go outside for a week after that. Which I hated because I love to walk in Paris. Then we had some beautiful days at the end of October and it was okay for me to go back to school.

Usually I walk home after classes with Max and a couple of his friends who are a little on the snobby side like they put down anything if it isn't French but you just have to ignore that here. Although the afternoon Im telling you about I was by myself so I thought I would see if Coudercs bistro was where it had been in my dream.

It was. And just the same, the sign over the door with a lantern on each side, half shutters in the window, two small metal tables and wire-back chairs and a polished brass horse hitch on the banquette. That's sidewalk in French.

The door stood open, but they werent doing any business in the midle of the afternoon.

I didnt think about going in. I had my school books with me (but Ive grown another inch and Yvie says I look like I could be studying at the Sorbonne instead of the Ecole St. Peres. The crucial fact was, I didnt have any money. Even though I was thinking I could really go for a glass of vin rouge.

While I was thinking that my hand was going through my coat pockets as if it didnt get the message how broke I was. And I found some coins in a torn place of the lining. Four francs to be exact!

So I went as far as the thresh hold and looked inside. Empty, like I said. Six tables and one booth in a back corner where there was a small brick hearth. Neat and clean and a fire was going. Bottles gleamed on the backbar. But not a soul.

I was about to leave when I saw an old woman coming down some stairs behind the bar. There was a partition or it might have been a folding screen so I didnt actually see the stairs, just her from the shoulders up, her hair pure white and done up in what French women call a chignon. She was looking at me in the doorway as if— I don't know. From the expresion on her face she had been expecting to see me with four francs in my hand. She was at least eighty. Not a tooth showing in her smile. But smiling big all the same. And she motioned for me to come in.

It was chilly in the bistro, a morning kind of chill before the fire gets going. Not a gloomy place even though it was on a side street where they didnt see much of the sun except for an hour or two each day. But the best seats in the bistro were those in the carved wood booth, the sides curving up and over to make a little roof. Next to the fireplace. That had been Ramses favorite spot, I knew that before she gestured for me to sit down there.

I put my four francs on the table and looked at her. Because I cant talk usually when I go into a place I point to something behind the counter or on the menu or, like here where they know me they just bring coffee without asking.

I knew she must be the Madame Couderc that Ramses told me about when I was in the hospital in Evening Shade and really groggy the last time I saw him.

She nodded when she looked at the coins but left them on the table. Then she shuffled behind the bar and took her time looking for a bottle she might have put away years ago but couldnt remember where. Muttering to herself like real old people do. Then she found the bottle and brought it with a corkscrew and two glasses back to the booth.

Like she knew she was supposed to, that I was expecting him. But she probably couldnt have known that Ramses died.

Her hands were knarled up, in bad shape and a little shaky besides when she showed me the label on the bottle. I took it from her like it was a treasure and she nodded then looked at where Ramses was going to sit she thought and I nodded too and then I opened the bottle. It was a Bordeaux but I dont know much yet about vintages. Special I suppose.

She stood there watching while I poured a glass and tasted it the way you are supposed to. Then she looked again at the other glass and kept nodding and smiling so I poured that glass half full too.

And thats it. Nothing else happened while I was there. I sipped my wine and had another glass besides and the wine I poured for Ramses just sat there on the table, was still there with firelight shining through it when I left. By then Madame Couderc was on a high stool behind the bar with a feather duster in her lap and nodding like she was half asleep. She didnt look up or say "Au revoir come again."

And now I bet your nodding half asleep and saying to yourself Geezo Pete, Alex, that was no ghost story. But wait.

At dinner that night when it was my turn to "join the conversation" I wrote in my book that I had been in Couderc's that afternoon. Alida (Dr Martorell's wife who has lived on or near Rive Gauche most of her life) said oh have they reopened? "Where?" I didnt remember the street name I only knew that I had been curious to find the little bistro and my feet had taken me there. (I didnt write anything about my dream). But I wrote that I had had a glass of wine from a bottle I was sure Madame Couderc had been saving for Ramses return to Paris.

Alida just looked out the dining room windows at the back side of Notre Dame and said no Alex, Mssr. Couderc was killed in the war and Madame passed away was it four years ago? There is a curio shop where Couderc's used to be. You must be thinking of another bistro. There are so many within a short distance of Place Maubert.

What could I do, Francie? I just shrugged because by then Yvie was giving it to me and I was embarassed. But I knew I couldn't be wrong.

That was about five weeks ago. Every chance I get since then I go down to Boul' Saint Germain and work my way north towards the river through that maze of narrow streets. Carrying a map with me. Marking off each adress on every street. There are bistros, all right. Plenty. But the Bistro Couderc's not one of them. It was there on that afternoon in October but its gone now. Vanished along with the white haired old woman and the glass of Bordeaux I left on the table in the booth for Ramses.

Did that wake you up? Do you feel a little shuder down your backbone?

I still do.

Either Im a total nutcase, or else—

Theres something about me that <u>they</u> like. You know what I mean, Francie.

Mally told me once on the depot platform that I had an "afinity" for the Crossing. Or something like that.

Whatever it is, its better than being crazy, dont you think?

Your friend forever (I hope)

Alex